THE ORION LINE

NICHOLAS

LUARD

THE ORION LINE

HARCOURT
BRACE
JOVANOVICH

NEW YORK
AND LONDON

Printed in the United States of America

Library of Congress Cataloging in Publication Data

Luard, Nicholas.
The Orion line.

I. Title.
PZ4.L9256Or3 [PR6062.U12]   823'.9'14   76–12456
ISBN 0–15–170158–X

B C D E

FOR TONY GODWIN

THE ORION LINE

The boy moved like the foxes.

He'd learned by watching them for hours at dusk and dawn. The cautious waits, nostrils flared to the wind, after they appeared through the mist on the edge of some field; the bursts of speed across the open grass with their bellies flattened low to the ground; the silent fastidious stepping through the undergrowth of the woods and coverts.

He was six when he started. Five years later—a raggedy pale-faced child of eleven—he knew the Flanders landscape almost as well as the small wild predators that hunted it.

It was his one secret, a private nighttime world he inhabited alone with the animals. He'd eat his evening meal, study for a while by the fire, then go up to his room—an attic under the rafters of his parents' cottage in the northern Belgian mining village. Later, when darkness came, he'd climb through the open window, drop from the low roof and set off.

The border with Holland was only a mile away. Often he'd cross it and roam deep into the Dutch countryside. The frontier itself—a line of barbed-wire fencing, customs' posts and the occasional police patrol—had long since meant nothing to him. Traveling the hidden lanes and corridors the foxes used, he could slip through it unnoticed at will.

It was in Holland one October night that he found the cache.

He'd been exploring the outbuildings of a farm when a dog scented him and started barking. A moment later a bedroom light went on and a man's voice called down. The boy turned and ran back through the woods towards the point where he'd crossed from Belgium. There was a harvest moon that night and the level space of turf between the end of the trees and the border fence was brilliantly lit. Since he'd wriggled under the wire a pair of guards had set up a checkpoint on the other side; he could hear the murmur of voices and see the glow of their cigarettes.

The boy hesitated. Then he glanced up. Although the moon was still high, it was already curving down towards the west. In two hours it would disappear and the turf would be in darkness. Until then, when he could return in safety, he'd have to find somewhere to wait.

He worked his way along the edge of the wood, scrambled down into an overgrown gulley and saw the ruined walls of a cottage. It had belonged to a charcoal burner—the flat charred-earth circles of the fires were still visible under the brambles. The boy stepped inside. The roof had caved in and everything seemed to have been stripped from the interior, but just as he was about to leave he noticed something gleam at the back. He picked his way carefully over the fallen tiles to investigate.

The gleam had come from the mouth of a beehive-shaped bread oven whose brick roof, unlike the cottage's, was still intact. The boy reached in and pulled out a bulky package wrapped in half-rotted oilskin. Inside the package were two British army revolvers and a dismantled Sten gun. He put the guns down, crept into the oven's entrance and began to search further.

Ten minutes later, touseled and blackened by the ancient soot, he was standing on the cottage's floor with the entire trove spread out around his feet. Apart from the guns there were eleven boxes of ammunition, a mildewed parachute smock, a carton of raw gelignite, a map case, a prismatic compass, a leather wrist-bandolier of detonators and, incongruously, a rusted card-index box—containing a stack of pale pink cards.

The boy examined his find for a time. Then he tucked the oilskin package under one arm, put everything else in the parachute smock, heaved the bundle onto his shoulder and set off back for the bank at the edge of the trees. There he tore the smock into squares, wrapped each of the items individually and buried them under a shallow layer of sand. Finally, with the moon down now, he crawled across the turf, slid under the wire and went home.

The "treasure" gave a new dimension to his night excursions and for three months he crossed the border every few weeks to inspect 'it. Each time, he'd dig up the little packets and study them in the moonlight, wondering where they'd come from, who'd left them in the oven, what use he could put them to, before he reburied them in the sand. Then, at Christmas, winter set in. A hard bitter winter of chilling ground frost followed by snow. With first the frost and then the snowdrifts lying thick on the earth the boy couldn't cross the border any longer; even using the fox-runs his footprints still showed sharp and clear on the whiteness. Instead he ranged the woods around the village, waiting impatiently for the spring.

Spring came suddenly, at the end of February, with storms and rain. The rain was torrential, the heaviest in memory. It slashed across the Flanders plain, flooding streams, beating down the early wheat, gouging and washing away the light topsoil from culverts, dikes and banks. Then, equally suddenly at the start of March, the weather changed and the first sun of the new year came out.

The day the rain stopped a high wind was blowing. Pausing to look through the border wire in the morning sunlight, a Belgian frontier guard noticed what appeared to be a paper-chain of remnants of late autumn leaves being tugged and whirled towards him across the dead grass. As one of them fluttered against his feet he saw it wasn't a leaf at all; it was a card—pink, water-stained and covered in blurred handwriting.

A second followed it, a third, then more, until the wire was patchworked with sodden scraps of pink. Puzzled, he switched on his pocket transmitter, contacted his Dutch counterpart and obtained permission to cross into Holland.

Then he unlocked a gate in the fence and walked forward to the sandy bank from which the cards were still being plucked up into the bright and gusty March air.

1

"Remarkable man, don't you think?" Mathieson said.

"I've heard he's very good, sir," Owen answered.

"Oh, quite outstanding. Whole career's been extraordinary from the start—"

Mathieson hunched himself over his pipe, holding it cupped tight in his hand as if it were some small animal trying to escape. Owen watched as he juggled with a battered metal lighter and a sudden lance of flame played over the bowl.

It was chill and damp on the landing of the Foreign Office annex. Outside stirrup irons jangled distantly and a voice shouted orders as the Household Cavalry guard in

Whitehall was changed. Behind them the door of the conference room was still open. The long table gleamed in the gray April light and the security shredder, trundled around behind the empty chairs by the duty clerk, grunted hungrily as it swallowed down the discarded heaps of notepaper.

"Won a DFC and two bars in a single month, know that?"

Mathieson straightened up, puffing out a cloud of smoke that mingled with the steam from Owen's breath.

"No, sir."

Owen stepped back. Like many tall men—at his full height he towered eight inches above Owen—Mathieson had a disconcerting habit of standing very close to anyone he was talking to.

"Well, he did. Astonishing achievement. Only time in the war it happened."

Mathieson dropped the lighter back in his pocket and shook his head reflectively.

Apart from the two of them there'd been six other people at the meeting. The permanent undersecretary of state in the chair, heavy lidded and sardonic as a merchant banker with all his margins covered. To his left, the deputy director of Mil 5 facing his opposite number from "over the water" (the designation had stuck stubbornly to the SIS ever since they'd moved south of the Thames). Finally, grouped at the end of the table, the three heads of the armed services intelligence agencies.

Mathieson was talking about the Air Force representative. He'd caught him at the door after the meeting, introduced Owen and talked casually for a few minutes as Owen listened. Air Marshal Bouverie. About fifty-five,

Owen guessed, the same age as Mathieson. Trim and neat and small, a bird-boned little man (he'd cocked his head to one side like a sparrow as Mathieson loomed over him) with striking different-colored eyes, one slate gray, the other hazel, a dry voice and a smile—it showed briefly when he shook hands—of totally unexpected charm.

There'd been three rows of medal ribbons on his tunic and his small black boots had glistened against the dull pile of the ministry carpet.

"Going a long way." Mathieson added, "Well, good heavens, he's gone far enough already. But the word is it'll be NATO next, our chunk of the nuclear umbrella, and after that God knows where, maybe even the joint chiefs. Anyway, good idea for you to meet him. Friends at court really—"

He glanced at his watch and headed for the marble staircase.

"We should be getting back. What are the chances of a cab?"

"We could try the Mall, sir."

It was raining outside, a thin gritty drizzle that darkened the morning air.

Mathieson, hatless, coatless, impervious to the weather, loped ahead with a long swift stride that made Owen hurry to keep up. Both their reflections flickered across the pools of water on the pavement. Mathieson's tall, erect, corncob pipe jutting from his mouth, dark jacket flared out like a cloak by the wind. Owen's short, heavy-shouldered, stocky, face flashing white on the ripples, body tilting awkwardly at each step as the limp—and the pain—came back with the wetness.

"Valley weather, Owen, right?" Mathieson looked back

as they reached the Mall. "Full of hwyl and straight from the Arm's Park."

"Yes, sir."

Owen managed a grin in return, not least because a taxi was just discharging someone opposite the Ministry of Defence annex. Mathieson saw it too, shouted vigorously at the driver and set off across the road.

"Soldier, scholar, horseman he and all he did—done with an eye to the next annual estimates."

The parody of Yeats had been chalked above a staff washbasin by a cynical clerk in accounts. Substitute fisherman for horseman—his lapel was invariably flecked with trout flies—and it summarized Mathieson perfectly. Part Wavell (he'd served under the poet-general in the western desert) and part Patton—with the pipe replacing the ivory-handled revolvers. And interweaving both a Machiavellian mind in constant, unremitting battle with the mandarins of the Treasury.

"Bloody great waste of time, aren't they?"

"I suppose as a means of coordinating policy they serve some purpose—"

They were in the taxi, Mathieson casually sprawled out in the back, Owen opposite him on the jump seat—his hip hurt less if he sat upright.

"Don't serve anything," Mathieson said. "Fancy little bazaar, that's all. Everyone troops in, lays out his wares on the table, waits while our lord and master inspects them, then files out offering up prayers for a larger share of the market next time around."

Smoke billowed across the cab as the lance of flame spurted again. Outside, through the misted glass, springtime London was shabby, furtive, moist, a twilight city peopled with huddled shapes under dripping canopies.

10

"That's why we need them, friends at court, I mean—"

Mathieson waved in the direction of Whitehall. They'd passed St. James's Palace and were swinging up towards Piccadilly. Boodle's was on their right.

Five years ago—the month after Owen had been brought back—Mathieson had asked him there for a drink, as he invited everyone who was called in from the field. Owen arrived early. He was waiting in the hall when a club member came through from the bar—a swollen-bellied man with a veined nose and cheeks flushed from several martinis.

The porter had disappeared and the man mistook Owen for a temporary club servant. He gave him a letter and told him to "hop out" and post it. Owen was still holding the envelope when Mathieson came through the door. The next day he put away the old raincoat he'd been wearing and bought himself something in hound's-tooth check from Austin Reed.

"Real trouble is, what with all their satellite gadgets and so on, they don't quite know what to make of us now. They *think* they need us, but they're not absolutely sure. It's that, plus their perennial obsession about 'embarrassment,' which explains why they keep chipping away. The only answer's to be on one's guard constantly."

Mathieson lapsed into silence as they cut across Park Lane. Owen leaned forward and opened the window to let out the smoke. Then he sat back stiffly, listening to the hiss of the tires on the wet roadway.

Five minutes later they turned into Baker Street behind a No. 30 bus.

"Baker Street." The department had never been known as anything else from the moment it was created at the start of the war, although the four Georgian houses weren't in fact on the street itself—they were in a small side alley just behind. To Owen, walking through the paneled doors, it was, as always, like coming home.

Partly it was the warmth. Baker Street's central heating was legendary—massive iron grilles against the Adams plaster that gave off the gurgling heat of an ocean liner's engine room. The first time he went there Owen had noticed his hip seemed less painful as soon as he stepped into the hall.

Yet more than the warmth, there was the rock-hard unchanging permanence of the place. The mahogany slab of the entrance desk with Wilson, the sour-mouthed balding doorguard (a former marine sergeant and five times inter-services middleweight champion) propped implacably on a stool behind. The worn brass letter racks. The elephant's-foot umbrella stand, relic of some long-forgotten empire posting. The curving stairrail and the nineteenth-century copy of Stubbs' *Diomed* above—the great black racehorse in gallop against a turquoise evening sky.

Even the smells were unvarying, comfortable, familiar. Coffee from the glory-hole canteen on the right. (No plastic vending machines for Mathieson; he insisted the coffee be freshly ground every day and he even stipulated the brand, Blue Mountain beans from Jamaica.) Coffee and furniture wax, dust from the passage that led to archives, the "oriental magic" scent of the lotion Wilson rubbed on the gray bristles above his ears, whiskey fumes seeping out of the in-house bar along the corridor.

Owen took off his coat. Baker Street was safety. The place you started in, the place you remembered out in the field, the place—if you were good enough and lucky enough—they brought you back to. Now, like the others who'd come in, he'd stay there for as long as he remained with the department.

"Is that all, sir?"

Mathieson had been strangely indecisive since the street door closed. He'd nodded at Wilson, peered into his own letter rack, examined the bulletin board and wandered vaguely around the hall. Now he was standing at the foot of the stairs frowning.

"Ah." He glanced up as Owen spoke. "Well, as a matter of fact I was just thinking—can you spare another couple of moments?"

"Yes, of course."

"Come up to my room and have a chat, would you?"

Owen breathed out slowly. Then he tossed his coat onto the umbrella stand and followed Mathieson upstairs.

From the moment the message had come down for him to accompany Mathieson to the conference, he'd known something had happened. Middle-echelon staff didn't attend joint intelligence meetings—not even the routine monthly one as that morning's had been. Typically, Mathieson hadn't so much as hinted at the real reason. Even now, walking behind him along the top landing, Owen hadn't the slightest idea what it involved.

He stepped into Mathieson's office, a cluttered ramshackle room with a cracked ceiling that looked out towards Regent's Park, and saw there was a file on the desk. A green file with the letters PR—for "Personnel Record"—stenciled in scarlet across the front.

In the private idiom of the department PR files meant postings, promotion—or problems.

"Hullo, James—"

Mathieson's greeting was addressed to Wintour, propped on the radiator by the window.

"Morning, sir."

Wintour half-stood, dropped some ash on the carpet, then heaved himself back on the grille—squatting there with his shoulders hunched and his knees drawn up like some malevolent organ grinder's monkey.

Nominally Wintour was in charge of administration. In practice he worked exclusively with Mathieson, was virtually an extension of him, the two of them—the "unholy alliance" as they were known on the floors below—a single organic unit. Physically and in every other way the pairing was improbable. Mathieson imposing, articulate, silver-headed, almost debonair. Wintour seedy and husky-voiced —a crumpled ill-made bundle of a man who shuffled sideways like a crab and whose yellow-gray hair was stained with the nicotine that colored his fingers.

Mathieson's world was country houses by Hawksmoor, port after dinner and a leather-bound first edition of Le Gallienne's *European Flora*. Wintour came from a Tuesday afternoon line of middle-aged men standing in the rain on a Soho pavement to buy tickets for the next "private" showing of *She Was a Virgin—Until*.

Together they were reputed to be the most effective combination the department had ever had.

"Asked Owen up for a talk." Mathieson cleared some paper from the center of his desk. "That business we had a word about yesterday. Oh, I'm sorry, Owen, sit down, do sit down—"

He waved at the single leather armchair.

"Exactly five years, isn't it?"

Mathieson had picked up the file and was pretending to study it.

"Yes," Owen nodded—aware that Mathieson knew as well as he did himself.

"And you're enjoying the French side?"

"It's extremely interesting."

"Of course, Laval's first-class, isn't he?"

"Yes, sir, it makes a great difference."

Jean-Louis Laval, the Paris resident, was very good. After the ten years he'd spent as a field control himself, Owen knew how lucky he'd been. Laval ran a broad-based network, he had excellent penetration and his intelligence came back in a consistently well-organized form.

It made Owen's task of analysis and evaluation far easier than it would have been at most of the other European desks.

"Wish to God they all came like that—"

Mathieson clutched the bowl of the pipe again, a small black mouse between his fingers, and tapped it into submission with his thumb.

"You know what I think we really do—?"

Mathieson rocked back as the smoke funneled upwards. Owen said nothing. The question had been rhetorical. Mathieson would answer it himself. He did.

"We look after the past, a sort of trusteeship in human archaeology. The rest of them—"

The gesture with the pipe implicitly indicated the others who'd been gathered around the undersecretary in the chill of Whitehall.

"Their concerns are with the now and the future. Not us. We dig, excavate, burrow around in the rubble of what's been. Give us a childhood grudge, a few impetuous letters and a discarded mistress—and we can tell them more about Israel's nuclear capability than they'll learn from a year's satellite photographs. Bloody nuisance it's so hard to get them to understand it, right, James?"

Wintour nodded—a slight movement of his head against the window, with the gray sky behind—but didn't speak.

"Ever heard of the Orion line, Owen?"

The question came abruptly after a short silence. Instantly the atmosphere in the room changed.

Owen frowned. The Orion line. Somewhere, stored away in some remote part of his brain, the phrase touched a nerve of memory. Stubbornly, irritatingly, the cell which held it stayed locked. He shook his head.

"I can't place it for the moment."

"Understandable, totally understandable—"

Briefly Mathieson's voice was contented, almost congratulatory.

"Apart from anything else it was long before your time. And in a way a good thing too. Fresh mind, uncluttered with preconceptions, see things much clearer. Just what's needed, James, isn't that so?"

Wintour, a conscience, a touchstone of judgment, flaked some more ash on the floor and nodded again.

"Owen." Mathieson leaned forward. "I'd be most grateful if you'd have a look at the Orion line. James can fill you in on the background, give you the contacts and so on. It's another archaeological job really; talk to a few people, see what they remember, size it up, form your own views. A couple of days should be enough, although take your time, of course. But let me know what you think when you've finished. You see—"

Until then Mathieson had been looking at Owen's face. Now he glanced down, sucked at the pipe and fiddled abstractedly with the cord on the file.

"Well, let me put it like this. The Orion line was rolled up thirty years ago. A lot of people got killed in the process, but that should have been the end of it. The trouble is, it doesn't seem to be the case. And if that's so, then I'm afraid that to find out why—"

Another silence. Wintour coughed, a hoarse grating sound against the rustle of the April rain, and swayed slowly on the radiator.

"I suppose it could mean going out again for a while."

Owen sat very still in his chair. He'd forgotten the ache in his hip. Instead, for the first time since he'd known Baker Street, he felt cold.

2

Owen stood in the darkness looking west, up the valley towards Nantynth Cwm and the saddle-backed hills beyond.

Behind him they were singing in the pub. Saturday night men's voices, high and clear in the old language against the rattle of the mugs. The rain had stopped and the stars were bright, April stars with an April moon rising and a scent in the night wind of the coming summer. The old colliery—his father had worked there for almost forty years—was on his left. Beyond it, hidden in the fall of the land, was the new one; two of his cousins went down it now, a third was about to join them.

He turned right and walked slowly along the ridge towards the station hotel.

He'd come there that morning, taking the early train from Paddington so he arrived in time for lunch—"dinner" they called it in the village—just as he'd done every weekend for five years. Meg had been waiting for him at the door with the children—she could hear the train's whistle as it rounded the Cwm.

"Well, always waiting, haven't I been, then? Only not any more, not for things as I don't know when they're going to come. Just the ones I'm sure of and them I'll choose."

She'd said it slowly, simply, defiantly in Welsh when she'd left. Left London, taken the children and gone back to the valley. Five years ago—it seemed much longer—and only a few months before Mathieson brought him back. "They had had a flat in Bayswater at the time. ("They" because with Owen running Algiers field control, she'd been there on her own for eleven months out of every twelve.)

Meg had hated it. London, the language, the grime and noise and concrete. Most of all the loneliness. One telephone call every Friday night (the most accounts allowed) —and then only if the Spanish-Algerian circuits were open. In the end she'd simply rebelled; she'd said no and she'd gone home.

People outgrow each other, Owen had decided at the time. That was the explanation. They change and develop in different ways and at different times. If the gap, in the process of change, of development, becomes too great, then they come apart. It had happened to them. Meg the girl who belonged to the valley, who neither knew nor wanted any other world; he the *bachgen dawnus* who'd nowhere to go but forward and in doing so had inevitably left her behind.

Owen smiled. *Bachgen dawnus*. In English, "boy wonder." In either language the phrase meant the same. They'd used it about him ever since he could remember; his father, grinning when he won the scholarship; the local paper, when he was chosen to captain the Welsh schoolboys; the miners in the pub, when he'd been bought his first drink —and tonight the same.

"How's it going then, bach? Making them sit up and think, are you, then? Hey, Dai—"

Menyth Williams, big, hang-jawed, white-headed, the father of the local chapel, shouting for the landlord after Owen had walked in.

"Come on, where's the glass then for Nantynth's *bachgen dawnus?*"

Laughter, pride, affection—all of them mingling in the voice. Gareth Owen. Nantynth's own boy wonder. Once in a generation every village produced one and he was theirs. The gift for mathematics and the languages, the place at Cardiff Grammar School, the running fly-half—a stocky pale-faced boy who, they said, could walk on mud like Christ on water—that even Llanelli had tried to bribe away.

Well, Llanelli had got him. Not in the way they'd hoped for but as ruthlessly, finally, effectively as if they'd never wanted anything else. Other days he might forget, that one never. Sheeting December rain with the field sodden underfoot, the gaunt black shapes of the pitheads rearing against the clouds, voices shouting on every side.

They came at him midway through the second half. Two of them, rangy scar-faced flankers of the sort Llanelli bred, breaking fast from an untidy ruck and scissoring him, one from each side, as the ball came back. He felt the ligaments go the instant they hit, a wrenching tearing pain. Then he rolled away, they carried him off and that was that; he'd never played competitively again.

Afterwards he realized they'd been out to get him from the opening whistle. It was part of the price you paid.

But even if there was no more rugby, there was still the scholarship and Cambridge, and for Nantynth that was enough, more than enough. The gift that had turned into a first in French and German, and taken him to Baker Street. He'd met the man a couple of months before he sat for his finals. His tutor had arranged it, calling Owen into his rooms one day as he walked across the court.

"Haven't made any decisions yet, have you, Gareth?"

Owen shook his head.

"Well, there's someone coming down next week, old friend of mine attached to the Foreign Office. Might be interesting for you to meet him. Drop by for a glass of sherry on Wednesday."

He turned out to be called Winstanley, an affable tweedy figure with a pipe and a military tie like a scaled-down version of Mathieson. They had a drink, Winstanley suggested dinner, then a week after his exams Owen had gone for a longer, more formal interview in London. It was his first view of the four linked Georgian houses.

They were vague, almost offhand, about the work at the start.

"Political and economic intelligence," Winstanley had called it. "Travel a lot, mainly Europe in your case, not exactly diplomatic status but the embassies can be very helpful. Why not start in September, give it a try for six months and let's see how we go from there."

Owen had returned to Nantynth with his degree. He and Meg were married that summer. Then in the autumn they moved to London.

The first five years attached to Baker Street itself; cypher courses, agent-recruitment procedures, communications and unarmed combat (he'd excelled at that) in the isolated house near Bath, the whole complex preparation for field control. Then the long spell abroad when he'd put it all to use. Marseilles, Berlin, Casablanca, finally Algiers.

The working life of a good field control was normally estimated to be about fifteen years. Owen had lasted ten. Not because he wasn't good, but because of something that had happened one night in a small hotel on the outskirts of the Algerian capital. Sayd Rifai, his liaison in the Algerian police, had found him there the next morning when he failed to keep the fall-back contact. Rifai had managed to get an ambulance and Owen spent the next month in the American hospital being treated for injuries from a "car accident."

He'd never even told Meg about that night. She'd gone back by then and she still thought he limped, as he'd done before, because of his knee. Mathieson of course knew the truth. He'd brought Owen in, assigned him first to satellite-traffic monitoring, then eighteen months ago had given him the French desk.

And now Mathieson wanted him to go out again.

Owen stopped on the crest of the ridge. The village lights glittered below and the voices—they were into "Sospan Fach" and there was laughter between the choruses—floated distantly upwards on the wind. It was colder here and late snow was still lying like cloud on the flanks of the Cwm.

There was a convention in the department, unwritten but inflexible, which as far as he knew had never been broken: once you came in you were never sent out again. It was that above all which made Baker Street safe, the lifeline you held on to outside, the final reward for everything you did in the field—and the things that were done to you. The one tacit promise that was always kept.

Except by Mathieson.

"Not going to force you of course, Owen, wouldn't dream of it. As I say take your time, size up the background first, then make up your own mind—"

Mathieson, coiled in smoke, still preoccupied, still plucking vaguely at the file.

"But if you reach the same conclusion James and I have come to, then I think you'll probably agree there's no other way of tackling it."

An hour after he'd sat down in Mathieson's office. By then Wintour, coughing, never moving from his perch on the radiator, talking in the shifty, wheedling voice of a Port Said Arab peddling dirty postcards, had given Owen the briefing.

The Orion line. The most famous of the wartime escape routes across Nazi-occupied Europe. (Owen knew why he'd half-recognized the name the moment Wintour started—a book about it had been one of the classics of background reading when he joined the department.) A maquis network with a chain of safe-houses that ran from Brussels to the Pyrenees.

In the three years between 1941 and 1944 over two hundred Allied pilots had been funneled down the line to safety. Then, a week before the Normandy landings, the Gestapo had uncovered the network and rolled it up. As

Mathieson said, that should have been the end. It was all so long ago now—a thirty-year-old footnote in the official histories of European resistance.

Yet if Mathieson was right it wasn't the end. Afterwards, long afterwards, there'd been the killings. Somewhere, in one of the chambers along the ancient, musty rabbit warren that had been burrowed across Europe all those years before, a smell still lingered—a smell so nasty that two senior members of the department had died because someone believed they'd caught the scent of it.

If Mathieson was right.

"I'll be quite frank, Owen, we simply don't know. Perfectly possible, of course, that those two unfortunate incidents weren't remotely connected with the line. On the other hand they just might be. Either way I think it's worth taking a look, don't you?"

Owen hadn't answered. Soon afterwards he'd left Mathieson's office with a sheet of paper—and a conviction. The paper, which Wintour gave to him before he went out, listed four names and telephone numbers. The conviction was private, intuitive, supported only by an obdurate certainty that he was right.

Mathieson had said he was being "quite frank" and had looked Owen straight in the eyes as he spoke. To Owen total frankness and a steady gaze were unmistakable signals that someone—in this case Mathieson—was lying.

After thirty years something had happened which had brought the Orion line to life again. Not the two murders, the "unfortunate incidents" as Mathieson called them; the first was almost ancient history now, the second had taken place three years ago and the file was closed. It was something else. Something Mathieson and Wintour knew and weren't prepared to tell him until he'd gone back into the past and formed his own opinion.

And if it was the same as theirs, he'd have to go out again to learn why.

Owen swore and shivered in the rising wind. Then he turned and walked back down the ridge towards the house. He still stayed there every Saturday night although he slept alone in the attic above Meg's room. "Keeping the name good," as she put it, "and not just for me, not just for the children, Gareth, but for you too."

He would have to tell her and she would be furious. Meg saw things very simply. A bargain was a bargain. You made it and you kept it. She to hold the house, to keep the name good; he to play his part by visiting her and the children scrupulously every weekend. In five years he hadn't missed a single Saturday. Only now—

He reached the colliery and his feet struck sparks on the rusting tracks of the old coal-dumper line. One of his first memories was a gray pit pony pulling a cart along it from the head of the seam. On his sixteenth birthday his father had given him a pair of steel-tipped mountain boots, the sort the hill farmers wore. To get him out on the Cwm, his father had said, and strengthen his legs for the game. In fact, as Owen realized later, the gift was an unconscious confirmation that he'd be the first in four generations not to follow the ponies from the pithead.

He still changed into the boots every weekend when he returned to the valley. They were fine for playing football with young Gareth in the field by the school.

Meg he could deal with—he was passing the chapel. Granite. Barred, bolted and shuttered, a bleak and vengeful shadow across his childhood. Meg and everything else, like the arrangements to hand over the French desk to his deputy while he was away. Yet he wasn't thinking of any of that now—not even the two days grace or the four names on the sheet of paper in his wallet.

Owen was remembering the door opening in the hotel bedroom outside Algiers.

He found the gate, pushed it back, fumbled with the lock above the steps, climbed in darkness to his room and lay down on his bed. Normally he slept well wherever he was—and best of all in the valley.

That night he lay awake until dawn.

3

The house was on the south side of Eaton Square, one of the immense Edwardian private residences that had long since been converted into luxury apartments.

Owen stood on the doorstep. Monday evening. It was raining again in London, not the damp drizzle of Friday but a steady, remorseless downpour. The water had curled under the porch and blurred the brass panel of nameplates. He rubbed the panel with his sleeve, found the name he was looking for, pressed the bell beside it and waited.

"Yes?"

A thin electronic crackle and an accented voice coming out of the intercom. Owen leaned forward against the microphone.

"My name's Owen. I have an appointment with the Comte de Sourraines."

The Comte de Sourraines. The first of the four names on the list Wintour had given him. "In a way—" Mathieson had smiled—"I suppose you could call him the original— if not the only—begetter of the Orion line."

"Come up, please."

A buzz as the latch clicked open. Inside an envelope was lying on the floor, presumably dropped through the letter box a few minutes earlier. Automatically Owen picked it up and put it on the marble-topped table. There was an engraved coronet on the back and the name was followed by a row of letters; in addition to de Sourraines five of the occupants on the brass panel had titles.

He got into the elevator and went up to the top floor.

"Mr. Owen?"

An elderly manservant in a black coat and striped trousers. The same accented voice he'd heard through the intercom. Owen nodded and stepped through the gates.

"Monsieur le Comte is waiting for you in the salon."

The man pointed at a door at the end of the hall. Owen began to walk towards it.

"Perhaps you'd like to leave your coat, sir."

"Oh, yes."

Embarrassed, Owen stopped, took off his raincoat—he'd gone back to it a few months after the incident in Boodle's —and handed it to him. The manservant hung it in a closet and led Owen down the corridor.

"Mr. Owen, monsieur."

Owen stepped forward. It was a huge room with a plate-glass window occupying the entire outer wall. The curtains were only half-drawn and the tops of the trees in the square, glistening with water and studded with flecks of green, brushed like surf outside. To his right a Gobelin tapestry shimmered with silver thread. In front an immense Empire desk, lit by a green globe lamp, was piled with invitations, hunting magazines and maps. Around it on the deep golden carpet small tables were cluttered with framed photographs, *objets d'art*, terra-cotta figures, jeweled boxes.

Luxury, that was the overwhelming impression, the effortless unstudied elegance of the very rich—and even then only of those who'd been rich as a natural way of living, as a law of the universe, for generations.

For a moment he couldn't see the Count. Then he spotted him at the far end of the room, by the fire. A tiny wizened figure in a red velvet dinner jacket—framed in the wings of an armchair like a child waiting for bed. He was reading the *Evening Standard* and for a minute at least he didn't look up. Then he suddenly tossed the paper aside and glanced at the door.

"Well, what can I do for you?"

The voice was strong, the English accent faultless, the eyes examining Owen ringed with green and brown.

"I was asked—"

Owen stopped. The question was abrupt and disconcerting. He wasn't sure how to answer it.

"I know damn well who asked you to come and what for. Get yourself a drink—"

He pointed at a medieval cabinet beside the desk.

"Get me one too. Armagnac. It's in the decanter at

the back. But don't you touch it. That's mine, can't get the bloody stuff anymore. Selfish enough to keep what's left for myself."

Owen went over, poured a whiskey for himself, then a measure of the pale, dry liquid into an engraved glass and carried both the drinks to the fire.

"My God, I thought they'd finished—"

He swirled the brandy around, studying it intently against the light without drinking.

"Even the books, they're all written now. You must have read them, haven't you?"

"I spent today in the library—"

"And you think you'll get something new from me? Well, you're wrong, you won't. Not a damn chance. Everything I know I've said."

He shook his head vigorously. Then he looked at the window.

"Open those damn curtains further, will you? It's Philippe, blast him, tell him every night but he still closes them like a tart's boudoir. Can't stand it. Like air, space, being able to breathe."

Owen pulled back the curtains. The rain was still falling thick and hard and a post-office van, braking at the Belgrave Street lights, had skidded up onto the pavement.

He went back to the fire. Something about de Sourraines had been familiar, some image from the past plucking at his memory from the instant he noticed him in the chair. Now he realized what it was. A newspaper photograph of Churchill and Beaverbrook sitting together on a sofa after the old man's eightieth birthday dinner. The two of them wasted by years, slack-mouthed, dreaming, alive only because of a common indomitable will to survive.

De Sourraines belonged on that sofa. The difference lay in his eyes. Theirs had been bleary and slumbering. His were sharp, clear, irritable.

"God Almighty, sit down, man, won't you?"

"I'd prefer to stand."

"That limp of yours, that the reason?"

He hadn't appeared to have looked up from his glass, but he must have noticed Owen walking back from the window.

"Yes."

"Got hurt, I suppose. Well, it happens, God knows it happens. Plenty of people got hurt much worse than that along the Orion line."

He stopped and drank for the first time, finishing half the glass at a mouthful. Then he started to talk.

Brussels in 1940. The brave honorable defiance, the gallant little Belgium of legend, that crumbled so pathetically before the iron tide of the panzer waves. Almost overnight the country had been swamped, occupied, annexed as a contemptible fief of the new European empire.

"They talked then, they still do, of German correctness —civility and punctiliousness. Rubbish! Pigs, that's what they were, privates to generals—pigs to a man."

Anger in the voice, real anger. Not the anger of outrage at his nation's violation, not even the anger of an aristocrat about the conduct of the sans-culottes. Rather, a simple objective rage at standards of human behavior that were unacceptable at any time under any conditions.

"Never forget the very first day they came into the city. Spring it was and the garden magnificent, best roses we'd had in ten years. They sent a staff car around to the house, some young swine of a captain. Told us what to do, the new regulations and so on. Then, on the way out, he saw the roses. Said could he take some for the mess. Yes, I said—well, wasn't much point in saying anything else. So this captain told his driver to pick some and the man started pulling up the bushes by the roots—"

He shook his head, the incredulity of it still defying belief after almost forty years.

"I suggested he might cut the flowers instead. Fellow just gaped at me as if I were a bloody lunatic."

It began by accident a few months later. Across the channel the Battle of Britain was raging in the air; Dowding's Spitfires and Hurricanes taking on—and hurling back—Goering's vaunted Luftwaffe. One day an English pilot, chasing out in some dogfight over the sea, overran the Belgian coast and was caught by the German antiaircraft batteries.

"Late afternoon it was. We watched the whole performance from the back terrace. They got him a couple of miles from the house. You could see the shells exploding in the air—a damn great spark, then smoke, then the sound afterwards. All around the plane until they hit. Pilot bailed out—saw the parachute open—and we thought that was that."

It wasn't. The de Sourraines estate was on the outskirts of the city, a thousand acres of park, farm, lake and wood. The pilot landed, somehow he evaded the German patrols sent out to catch him and he set off across country. Just before midnight he arrived at the house and knocked at the back door.

"I was in the study with Marie, my daughter. Philippe knocked and came in, the same Philippe—"

He waved at the corridor.

"Said there was someone downstairs. Thought at first he meant another of those swine so I told him to say we'd gone to bed and they could leave their card—if they knew what a bloody card was."

Owen could see it very clearly. The old man and his daughter by the fire, the manservant—in the same uniform —knocking, the imperious instruction.

"No, I'd got it wrong. It was this pilot. I said bring him up—didn't have the slightest idea what we'd do, but thought it only civil to give him a drink. Philippe said the man had been hit, so Marie and I went down."

He'd fainted by the time they reached the hall, lying on the floor with a shell fragment in his shoulder. They put him to bed in one of the guest rooms and nursed him until he was well enough to move again.

"And that was where Marie took over—"

With Belgium, Holland and most of northern Europe occupied, the problems of getting him back to Britain seemed insurmountable. Yet, eight hundred miles south, the Spanish border was still penetrable and Spain's neutrality remained tenuous, unenforceable by the Spanish authorities after the chaos of the civil war. In Spain, too, there were British consulates at Bilbao and Santander with British cargo boats docking regularly.

Alone, Marie set off to see whether she could open a route south. As a de Sourraines, all else apart, she had one great advantage. The family was among the oldest and most influential in Belgium. At a time when the Axis powers were trying to engage local support, it meant that for Marie passes were no problem; unlike the rest of the population she could travel at will throughout Europe.

"Away about a month that first time, I suppose. I kept

33

this fellow, Thompson he was called, up in the nursery wing. Nice chap, he was, played a useful game of chess too—"

The old man looked at the flames. Owen finished his whiskey. Pawn to king four with the sirens echoing from the city and the bombers overhead.

"Anyway, Marie came back and she'd got it set up, at least well enough to try, if this Thompson fellow was game —which he was. Train to Mons, papers to see him over, a night in Paris, then across country by truck to her place at Este."

Owen frowned. "She had a house of her own in France?"

"Of course she did. Este. Didn't they tell you that? God Almighty, you could have got it from the books. I grew up here, young man, my wife was English, too, a Cavendish. Her family had owned Este since Waterloo, one of the spoils of war. That's it over there—"

A mottled hand stabbed out towards the door. Owen walked across. A large oil painting. Browns and golds of autumn. At the center the chateau, gray, weathered, set in misty acres of park. There were paddocks and rails behind with a single white horse cantering, slow and stately, in the distance.

"It's very beautiful."

The old man snorted, a harsh, dry, angry sound. Owen's remark had touched some nerve, although he had no idea why.

"Well, that's Este. Went to Marie when my wife died, although Marie didn't use it much—spent most of the year with me in Brussels. But it came in very useful then, headquarters of the whole thing, I suppose you could call it."

"And from there?"

Owen had returned to the fire.

"From Este? A chain of houses—safe-houses—right down to the Spanish border. Guides across, peasants, bloody scoundrels they were. Caused us more trouble than anything else. Used to take the pilots up into the mountains and then say they wouldn't go on unless they were paid double. After that another truck over northern Spain to one of the consulates. Finally a boat back."

Silence. The logs crackling in the fire. He was thinking about the guides, Owen guessed. In that jagged old mind it was the details that came back: the boorishness of a German officer, a game of chess, the petty deceit of a mountaineer.

"So that was the Orion line. Got that Thompson fellow through and dozens of others too. Frankly, I had damn all to do with it. I was just the respectable front at the Brussels end. Never moved from the house once. Marie ran the whole thing. And then, of course, in '44 they got her."

"I'm sorry."

"Sorry? What the hell have you got to be sorry about? Nothing to do with you, was it? Headstrong girl, always was. Just did what she thought needed doing, that's all."

A total lack of sentimentality, even of pride. Yet there was something almost chilling too.

The person had been his only daughter and the consequences of what she'd done had proved inevitable. The Gestapo had caught her, they'd tortured her for a month, then they'd killed her. And he could talk of it as calmly, as objectively, almost as irritably as that.

"Callous? That what you're thinking—?"

Maybe something had shown in Owen's face. The old man shook his head.

"Rubbish! Simply happened to be necessary at the time,

35

nothing more. But what happened afterwards, that's a different matter. The George Cross, the Légion d'Honneur, the books, every bloody thing you can think of. Even tried to make a film. I'd realized by then and I put my foot down. Lawyers and injunctions all over the place. It worked but it was too late—"

Suddenly, the defiance against age, the abrupt crusty language, the vigor and strength, all of them were gone. In their place was weariness.

"What's your name again?"

"Owen."

"I'll tell you something, Owen. When I was a child we had a saying: never buy a horse or marry a woman with their eyes set too close. Either way you'll get the devil's issue. Well, I discovered there's something worse. Don't sire a heroine—"

Flames and rain against the glass and the dregs of the brandy swirling in the firelight.

"She married, Marie, the year she died. Had a child, a daughter, the month before they picked her up. That's her—"

A photograph on one of the tables. Around it others, many others, a record over the years of a child growing up. In a cradle first, the anonymous smudged features of any baby. Next on the grounds of the Brussels house; playing with a gardener, mounted—curly-haired and chubby —on a small fat pony, standing in the shadow of a tree, diving, adolescent now, strong and balanced, into a pool.

Lastly, a studio portrait of a young woman. A wide powerful face, tumbling chestnut hair, dark eyes—direct and watchful—the steady arrogant gaze of privilege and wealth.

If she was born in 1944 she'd be just over thirty now. The likeness to her mother—there were photographs of Marie on the tables too—was unmistakable, uncanny. Yet, of the pair, Owen decided he'd have infinitely preferred Marie. In the mother the strength of the mouth was tempered by laughter; in the daughter there was only boredom, sullenness and disdain.

"She's called Hélène. And for her it was all too much. The idea for that bloody film was the last straw. She was at school, seventeen, when it came up. She read about it in some paper, she wrote me a letter, then she walked out and that was the last I saw of her for nearly three years."

He stopped, the little skeletal head with the tendons wire-tight at the neck slumping onto his chest. Owen shifted his weight awkwardly from one leg to the other and cleared his throat.

"And she blamed you?"

"No doubt the young, like the heart, have their reasons. But, yes, she did,"—a nod that was almost imperceptible. "Don't know what the hell she got up to, where she spent those years, nothing. To be honest I don't even want to. She came back eventually, not to me—to Este. Well, God knows, it's hers. From my wife to Marie and from Marie to Hélène. That's the way it's been ever since. I live here, much more my country than Belgium ever was, and she stays at Este."

And the two never met. Owen understood now. It explained the snort of anger when he'd commented on the painting. To both, grandfather and granddaughter, the chateau stood for everything that had driven them apart —the Orion line.

For him the line hadn't only claimed his daughter's life;

its legacy had been to permanently estrange his only grandchild too. She, Hélène, the daughter of a heroine, a cult figure, of a mother she never knew. The pressures must have accumulated relentlessly; the fingers pointing on the street, the press photographers waiting outside, the endless curiosity and questions and gossip.

Finally, like Meg, she'd rebelled and run away. Yet Meg had never really blamed Owen; it was London and the loneliness she couldn't endure. Hélène, on the other hand, had blamed her grandfather—blamed him bitterly and resentfully. For the line itself. For her mother's death. For the way he'd kept her memory alive, exploited it almost, as she saw it, and burdened her with it ever since.

"Still—"

The Count put down his glass, empty now, and shook his head, dismissing the subject.

"Can't have my problems intruding on yours. You want to know about the Orion line and that's about as much as I can tell you. Frankly, it left a bad taste in the mouth. And not just to me either; if those stories are right, to some other people too. Which is probably what you're really after, isn't it?"

Owen nodded.

"Can't help you there either. Read about what happened, of course, but never knew the fellows, never knew any reason for them even to have been connected with the line—"

He broke off, then leaned forward suddenly and gazed up into Owen's face. Briefly vitality came back to his voice and the rimmed eyes were penetrating again.

"You're wasting your time, young man. It's all gone now, long gone. Save your energy for something worthwhile.

That's my advice. Only, I know you youngsters, you're stubborn, you won't take it. So you'll probably go on. And because I can't stop you, I'd ask you just this—"

Something, some urgency in the words, some fleeting vulnerability in the old man's expression, made Owen listen intently.

"If you learn anything, come back and tell me. You see, the Gestapo arrested Marie on a Friday night. Twenty-four hours later they'd smashed the whole line right across France and up to Brussels. Marie was willful, difficult, impetuous. She was also very brave. I have never believed—"

He paused. Flames and silence once more. When he spoke again he was frail, exhausted, almost inaudible.

"I would like to know."

"I'll come back, I promise."

Owen went out. There were no taxis in Eaton Square and he had to walk to Victoria Street before he found one. By then the rain had seeped under his collar and was running down his neck. He gave the driver the Bayswater address and sat watching the blurred lights on either side.

It had taken the Gestapo only twenty-four hours after they caught Marie de Sourraines to roll up the entire Orion network. There were only two possible explanations. Either she'd cracked and talked instantly under torture. Or the Germans had penetrated the line before her arrest—long before.

"What about another?"

"Thanks."

Owen pushed his glass across the table and watched Blair stand up and thread his way through the crowd at the bar towards the counter.

Midday on Tuesday. Outside a convoy of yellow newspaper delivery vans rumbled up Fleet Street, splashing dirty water against the leaded windows. Inside the room was dusky, warm, thronged with its raucous daily gathering of journalists filling in the early afternoon hours before their copy deadlines.

Blair. The second on Wintour's list. One of the most famous names in contemporary journalism. Owen had never met him until now but he'd read him ever since he was a child. The caustic eloquent voice, understated yet passionately committed, which had recorded every major event in world history since the thirties.

He was coming back now, a glass in either hand. Tall, emaciated, hollow cheeked. He had long gray sideburns and he was wearing a fawn cardigan, baggy and antler buttoned, and he coughed constantly.

"Here—"

He handed Owen the drink. Then he sat down and lit another cigarette from the butt of his last one.

"God knows if it'll be any help but I'll try—"

Blair ran his hand across his forehead, holding it there for a moment as the smoke curled up.

"One of the paradoxes of working in words is that we, the paid recorders, don't keep any records. If you want to remember, it's all there for you in the back-numbers files. Your autobiography gets published for you at 4:15 every day on the dot. Unless—and that's the problem—there isn't a story, or not one worth printing. Still, let's see—"

The hand, shaking slightly, lowered as it tipped the ash into the glazed Martini saucer. Then it was back resting against his head again.

The two murders—Mathieson's "unfortunate incidents" —of senior members of the department. Both of them brutal, wanton, unexplained—and therefore charged with all the ingredients of a major headline story. The first had been in 1958. Blair had covered it.

"Strangely, I'd met him once. About a week after the

Falaise beachhead. We'd been attached—I mean the press corps—to some joint armored division. I went to the mobile communications HQ, got the day's handout and repaired to the nearest bar to see how many inconsistencies it contained. Walpole was the only other person there—"

Walpole. Sir Roger Walpole as he became later. (He'd been given his K, just as Mathieson would get it, when he retired from Baker Street.) At the time of the Allied invasion, 1944, he'd been with SOE preparing a local support network for the landings. Blair had found him just after he'd linked up with the D-Day forces.

"In a way, I suppose, it gave me a personal interest. Anyway, when I saw the flash on the teleprinter a dozen years later, I flew straight out—"

The teleprinter "flash" had announced that Walpole and his wife had been found murdered in the Garnes gorge two hundred miles south of Paris.

"'Good money's the heart of good journalism: good luck's its soul—'"

Ash piling in the saucer and a lopsided smile, under the lined forehead, at the old Fleet Street aphorism.

"My luck was with the *inspecteur judiciaire* in charge of the case. He'd been Monet's chief of security at the Geneva conference after Dien Bien Phu; I'd bought him a couple of jars then; and he remembered me. He drove me to the gorge and we walked out his reconstruction of what had happened—"

The Garnes gorge. In winter a lonely upland valley carrying the southern highway around the *Massif Central* towards Toulon. But that May evening, when the Walpoles reached it, clear and still and bright with spring flowers.

There'd been just the two of them, Walpole and his wife.

To celebrate his retirement from Baker Street the year before Walpole had bought what he called his "new toy," a trailer. A lifelong connoisseur of wine, he'd told friends they were going to motor slowly down through the center of France and spend a month pottering around the vineyards of the Rhône.

They reached the gorge at about 6:00 P.M. on May 7th, the fifth day of their holiday. There was a small grassy plateau to the left of the road, a copse of beeches beyond, a stream falling to the valley below and, high in the distance on either side, the snow-covered peaks of the mountains. As a place to camp for the night it must have looked perfect.

Walpole parked the trailer fifty yards off the road in the lee of the trees. His wife prepared a light dinner which they ate inside.

Afterwards Walpole went out and lit a fire by the stream to make coffee. Possibly he liked the taste better brewed over an open fire—he could have as easily used the gas stove in the trailer. Possibly it was just some impulse of pleasure at the fine night, a return to the schoolboy delights of open air and flame and darkness.

Whatever the reason, the coffee was never drunk—although miraculously, in the violent confusion of the next few minutes, the pot remained balanced on the fire and boiled away. As Walpole squatted there someone appeared through the trees. (More then one person? The conjecture started now.) Or maybe Walpole himself noticed a man lurking by the trailer; that was a later theory, that he caught a Peeping Tom watching his wife undress.

Walpole stood up, perhaps shouted, walked a couple of yards from the fire, then grappled with the intruder. There was a ferocious fight in the dark; even at sixty-one Walpole was a strong, healthy man and he'd been trained in unarmed combat during the war. But the stranger had a knife and after Walpole had been stabbed eight times—a dozen square yards of turf was stained with blood—he fell to the ground. Even then he wasn't dead.

As he lay there his wife appeared at the trailer door in her dressing gown. The stranger didn't only have a knife, he had a shotgun too—a double-barrel twelve bore. He fired once at Walpole's wife, then turned and fired the second cartridge at Walpole. The shots were aimed at their chests; both must have died instantly.

"Reconstruction, yes," Blair said, "and while I'm certainly no detective, it made sense. Only that, of course, was just the start of the mystery—"

The police had arrested the farmer five days later. Owen remembered his face from the newspaper photographs. An unforgettable face even through the gray filter of the newsprint. Massive, implacable, carved from the upland granite of the hill slopes, as secret, as durable, as impenetrable as the mountains themselves.

"Well, you probably know what happened then. The confessions, the recantations, the trials, the conviction, the appeal—it lasted for seven years and ended in bloody nothing. The old boy dying at eighty-four, still technically under sentence of death, and the case still unresolved. No—"

Blair stretched out his hand as Owen rose to fill their glasses again.

"Let me—"

He stalked through the crowd. The same greetings, the same laughter, the same hum of talk. Then he came back.

"What interested me, of course, was whether there'd

been a political motive. Walpole. SOE man. Working with the maquis in central France. The long roots going back, maybe, to a little pile of shit under someone's bed—"

Yes, he would call it that, Owen thought. A little pile of shit: fascism, corruption, collaboration, everything Blair had stood against and tried to expose all his life. It had been inevitable that the case had fascinated him.

"If there was, I didn't find it. In fact I got nowhere. Sullen peasants. Walls of silence. No beginning, no middle, no end. So I came back. No story."

"But you must have formed some idea after ten days—?"

Still watching his face, Owen turned in the chair so that he could stretch out his leg. Blair laughed.

"Best parlor game ever invented, isn't it, guessing the solution to an unsolved murder? But, yes—"

He leaned back, tilting the glass so it caught the light as he thought himself back to that day in the gorge with the French police inspector.

"Night. Stars. Water. Walpole by the fire, his wife undressing, the trailer lighted. And in the trees, in the darkness, people watching them. The old boy, certainly. I see him having come down the hill with his gun, a standard twelve bore like the one that killed them. Only he's not the only other person there. There's someone else, someone quite unconnected with him—the killer—"

The glass tilting further, the ash lengthening on his cigarette as he frowned, concentrating, framing the scene in his mind.

"Who was he and why? Robbery's the obvious motive, maybe he was another thieving farmer like the old boy himself—he's got previous convictions which didn't help. And yet, and yet—why the knife *and* the gun?"

Owen frowned. "Meaning what?"

"Meaning I've spent a lifetime reporting conflict—global war, tribal feuds, political assassination, domestic murder. One of only two patterns characterize them all: calculated aggression or the impulsive attack. Here, whether it's the old boy or some other anonymous thief, one's got to assume murder on impulse. But with a knife and a gun? In my experience only a professional killer, like a soldier, carries and uses both. And a soldier's function isn't impulsive, it's calculated—to kill."

In the background more laughter, the clamor of voices, a stout man in a spotted bow tie lurching towards the door. At the table silence. Owen finished his glass and pushed it aside.

"Someone intended to murder Walpole?"

Blair smiled. "As a scenario, why not? Our unknown attacker who meant to kill him with a knife and create a scene for a petty robbery. Walpole surprised him or certainly was far stronger than he'd thought. Then his wife appeared. And because our man was a professional, because he'd brought a gun too, he's forced to use that on them both. Finally, before he can stage the 'robbery,' the old boy turns up and he has to run."

"It still leaves the question of a motive."

"If I believed in fairy tales I might even believe in the existence of the white list. Only no one from Baker Street's going to say anything about that, are they?"

Owen shook his head, grinning. "No."

"Though not." Blair laughed and gestured at the empty glass. "One more?"

"No thanks. I must be going."

"Well, you owe me three doubles. I'll settle for a word on the side if you turn anything new up."

The reporter coming out in him at last. Owen smiled again.

"I'll let you know."

He thanked him once more, collected his raincoat from the rack by the door and went out onto Fleet Street.

Along with the four names, Wintour had given him a schedule of all the known safe-houses on the Orion line. Owen hadn't mentioned it, he didn't even know if Blair knew, but the Garnes gorge, where Walpole and his wife had died, was only fifteen miles from one of the most important staging points in the network.

The white list was something different. Even now no one was sure that it had ever existed. But if it had—and if it still existed somewhere—then the white list was dynamite. Allegedly compiled by an unidentified British SOE agent, it was supposed to contain the names of all the major French collaborators with the German occupying forces—and the Gestapo.

Whatever had happened along the Orion line, the white list alone would have been more than enough motive for killing. Not just in 1958 when Walpole was murdered, not even just three years ago when the second death took place.

It would be worth killing for now.

5

"Owen? That wouldn't be G. P. R. Owen, now, would it?"
Owen frowned. "Yes."

"Don't often make a mistake."

He nodded contentedly. Detective Chief Inspector Miles. A big man, burly, wide shouldered, self-contained. The third name on Wintour's list.

"Have we met before, then?"

Owen looked at him, trying to remember. They were sitting in the Old Bailey canteen—he'd gone there straight from the Fleet Street bar—during an adjournment in a case at which the chief inspector was giving evidence. A scratched Formica-topped table. Owen on one side, Miles on the other, cups of coffee between them. At the next table a group of counsel—black gowned and wigged with their briefs stacked casually on the floor—were finishing the *Times* crossword, arguing over the clues in loud, cheerful upper-class voices.

"Wouldn't call it 'met,' exactly. More of a collision, I'd say—"

Miles smiled. Behind him at the self-service hatch a defense witness kept glancing furtively in their direction.

"City Police grounds. Roehampton, 1952. Thames Valley cadets against your lot, Welsh schoolboys. Right?"

Owen nodded. It came back now—not Miles but the occasion. A game of rugby twenty-three years before.

"Well, it's my job, isn't it?" Miles was still smiling, "Names, faces, places, dates. Don't know why, but I always had a knack for it. You played a blinder that day, too. Gave you a lovely write-up in the *Gazette*, they did; keep all the cuttings at home as souvenirs. 'Another in the long line of the boy wonders from the valleys,' that's what they said."

Owen smiled back. The *bachgen dawnus* again. He couldn't recall who'd won but he remembered the day. Golden October sunlight. The leaves yellow and scarlet on the trees. Young men in long colored scarves and cheering boisterously from the single stand. The first time he'd been outside Wales.

"You didn't go on, though?"

"Go on?"

"Playing, I mean. They had you tipped for the national side."

Owen shrugged. "I got a knock, ligaments in the knee. I had to give it up."

"Ah." The slow, ponderous nod again. "Often wondered what happened. Anyway—"

He reached for his cup. It was a lock-forward's hand, broad and splayed and powerful.

"Didn't come here to talk about rugby, did you? Baring. Robert Charles Baring. So what can I tell you?"

"Whatever you can."

Bobby Baring. The second member of the department to be murdered after retirement. And one of Baker Street's rare scandals long before it happened.

Owen had known him slightly in the period after he came back from Algiers. "Known" was perhaps too strong a word—no one really knew Baring—but at least he'd met him often and, like eveyone else, he'd listened to him talking.

Baring had been fifty-eight, deputy controller of the European sections and a couple of years from retirement. In one way his "decline"—it had passed from office gossip into accepted fact well before Owen returned—had been fast, classic and predictable. Drink, the occupational hazard of all stress professions, not least espionage. Many of the older generation drank heavily. Handley-Reid, who headed the Middle Eastern side, had a lengendary capacity for alcohol.

On most of them it had no noticeable effect. In Baring's case it was all too obvious. The lurching movement, the slurred voice, the long rambling monologues, the hand shaking as he fumbled for a cigarette, the gaps in memory when he'd break off and stand in silence for minutes on end, oblivious to the embarrassment of his audience—and then pick up the thread of some totally different anecdote. People would edge away when he came into the bar but with the half-remembered skill of some punch-drunk boxer he could always head them off, back them into a corner and hold them trapped there while the slow arcs of his punches, the interminable stories, swung vaguely around their heads.

Yet there was more to Baring's drinking than just the effect of a lifetime in espionage. Baring was a man with a grievance, a grievance strongly enough based in fact to mingle guilt with distaste in the other members of the department when confronted by him. At his best, in the field during the war, he'd been brilliant.

Baring's province had been the Low Countries; apart from French he spoke perfect Flemish, Dutch and German. The network he recruited there, and ran personally at immense risk for three years, had been the department's greatest single intelligence triumph. And not only the network. Many of the systems he created—the slipped cutout, the rolling courier chain, the open—letter box system—had become classics of organized resistance, fundamental principles in the training manuals that were still used.

Perhaps when the war ended he'd expected to be seconded to the Foreign Office and raised eventually to ambassador. No one knew. The grievance—and the bitter stories in which he expressed it—was somehow vague, unspecific, hinted at but never stated. Whatever the truth behind it it remained Baring's secret. He'd stayed on with the department, organized an elaborate new section for the Ruhr, handled cyphers for a while and finally ended up with Europe—and the runaway decline had set in.

How his career actually finished no one, again, was really sure—although it happened with brutal speed. One Friday evening his brass nameplate was being polished by Wilson in the hall; on Monday the first arrivals noticed it had gone. Five days later someone, fortified by a couple of whiskies to celebrate the coming weekend, had been bold enough to ask Wintour where he'd gone.

Indefinite sick leave, Wintour said, doctor's insistence. Might last until retirement, poor man—and Wintour, umbrella in hand, had shuffled by on his way to the door. Accounts confirmed—pigeon-breasted Mrs. Baker plied with sherry at the Christmas party—that his salary was still being paid quarterly. But that was all anyone knew.

Until France ten months later.

"Well, you got to remember several things—"

Miles hunched himself forward over the table.

"First, I came into it a month later, when the whole bloody case was cold. Then I was working, far as I was working at all, right outside my manor—don't even speak their lingo come to that. And lastly the only reason I was there was politics, politics pure and simple—"

Baring had bought a van. Smaller than Walpole's but in essence much the same. He'd taken the Newhaven–Dieppe ferry, spent one night at Reims, the next at Chartres and the third far down the Loire valley.

Baring had stopped for the fourth night at a municipal camping ground outside Moulins. Apart from traveling a different route, the pattern of his journey until then had been almost identical to Walpole's. The similarity continued grimly that night.

Sometime after dark someone had kicked down the van's door, taken an ax to Baring and killed him where he was lying in the bunk bed.

"They'd put a damn great tarpaulin over the van on account of the rain. Pouring down, bloody cats and dogs, it had been ever since it happened. Trouble was the cover had only intensified the humidity. Made any serious forensic a right old waste of time—"

Miles sniffed contemptuously. He'd done his Home Office path labs course early in his career and he knew what you did—and what you didn't do.

"Still, you could see the general picture and it looked more or less the way they said. Someone had tried the door and found it locked. So they'd thumped it with the butt of an ax and the whole thing had caved in; well, cardboard really, aren't they, those van doors? And then they'd just done him over, hacking right through the blankets and all—"

Baring's body had been discovered in the early hours by the site's warden making a routine check of the camp. He'd telephoned the local gendarmerie and by dawn the couple had been arrested. An English boy and his girlfriend. Both of them nineteen, long-haired, dressed in caftans—"les hippies anglais," as the French press had called them.

They'd been traveling by motorcycle with a small tent which they'd pitched near Baring's van. The warden claimed to have seen them talking to Baring the evening he arrived. When the French police searched their tent they found a pair of sheepskin gloves whose woolen fibers seemed to match others they found later in the van. They also discovered a quantity of cannabis.

"Damn all in the way of anything we'd call evidence. That's why the English papers took it up, why I was sent out there after all the hoop-ha. But you got to admit it looked plausible. Right scruffy pair they were, too, dirty little tykes. And of course they made it worse for themselves by telling a pack of lies. On account of being scared about the drugs, that's what they told me—"

Miles had stayed there a week, interrogating them for

two days. Soon after he left the murder charges were struck off and instead the pair were given a short sentence for narcotics possession. The British press was satisfied and the story dropped from the newspapers.

"And that was all?" Owen said.

"Far as I was concerned, yes." Miles nodded. "Sent in my report and that was that."

"What did your report say?"

"Put it like this. First off, if it'd happened here I wouldn't even have bothered to send the file to the DPP—not on murder charges. Wasn't even circumstantial, they'd got nothing, bloody nothing. That's being technical, mind you. As a copper, a British copper that is, you need facts. You try that fancy Maigret stuff on your average beak. Laugh you out of court, he would."

"What about practically, then?"

"Not a chance." Miles shook his head firmly. "Those kids, they'd nick a few things, con a bit if they're bright enough —which I doubt. But do someone in with an ax for nothing? Never!"

The voice was flat, emphatic, utterly confident. It was like his contempt for the French police procedure over Baring's van. Miles had been a copper for thirty years. He knew which villains would kill—and which wouldn't.

"So who did it?"

"Who?" Miles laughed. "You get a murder inquiry as isn't a family job—like most of them are—and you know what you do? You draw a damn great circle around where it happened. And then you start with every single bloody adult inside, all of them equal. Case I had up in Bolton couple of years ago we finger-printed forty thousand men. We got him too. But that was easy. Sex assault on a kid,

54

so it had to be a fellow, and he'd left his prints on the wrench he knocked her off with. No sex assault on Baring, meaning you couldn't rule out a woman, and no prints. Just a quarter of a million frogs and nothing to go on."

"All right," Owen insisted, "but say it had happened here, say you'd been in charge, what would you have done?"

Miles put down his cup, rubbed his jaw, stared out of the window. Across the roofs, the dome of St. Paul's huddled forlornly under a dark, lowering sky.

"Tell the truth, I'd have been dead worried—"

He was speaking more slowly than before and although the smile was still there, the laughter had gone.

"Someone in your manor gets carved up with an ax, and I mean carved. Not family, you've established that. So what are you left with—?"

The defense witness had gone back upstairs and the barristers were getting to their feet, black robes floating like nun's habits around the white plastic chairs.

"I'll tell you. A psychopath, that's what. A psychopath with a fancy for wielding a chopper. Get a taste for it and he'll do it again—and again. That's why I'd have been worried—"

Miles stopped. The canteen empty now. Only a West Indian cleaning woman pushing a trolley towards them across the tiled floor.

Then he added abruptly, "Unless someone just wanted to kill him. But they'd have to have been a very bad enemy to do what they did to Baring. No, I'd settle for your psychopath. Well—"

He stood up.

"I must be getting upstairs, I'll be on in ten minutes. Mind you, they got some good ones, haven't they?"

"Good ones?"

"Sorry." Miles grinned. "Thinking of the game again. The French. That Astre—that the way you pronounce it? —right little devil he is if they're getting possession and going forward."

"He's good," Owen nodded and stood up too, "Thanks for your help."

"Anytime. And if you turn anything up, I'd be interested to know. Curious, that's what coppers are, always bloody curious."

He laughed again, shook hands and left. Owen walked down the worn, echoing steps and went out onto Warwick Lane.

Rain again. It had been raining in Moulins when Baring was killed by Miles's psychopath—or someone who wanted him dead so urgently and viciously that they'd used an ax for the job.

Moulins was the site of another of the safe houses on the Orion line.

"Where would you like me to start?"

"Perhaps with how you first made contact with the line, sir."

"Well, that was simple. I knew the de Sourraines family—"

He put his fingers together, resting them in a neat pyramid on the desk, and began.

Air Marshal Bouverie. The last name on Wintour's list. (And from the moment he saw it there Owen knew exactly why Mathieson had taken him to the joint intelligence meeting; it was simply to make the introduction and

pave the way for this, the final one of the four interviews—
"Sizing up the background," as Mathieson had put it, "before you make up your own mind.")

They were sitting in Bouverie's office in the Ministry of
Defense. The room was like the man himself: small, purposeful, scrupulously tidy, utterly masculine. Two upright
chairs, the bare desk, a single gray telephone with a scram-
bler button, only one object decorating the walls—a framed
letter from Churchill that had come with the second bar to
his DFC. There was no filing cabinet, no correspondence
tray, not even a note pad; it was as if he held everything in
his head—and considered it a weakness, a lack of self-
discipline in others that they couldn't do the same.

A very formidable man, Owen thought as he watched
the unblinking varicolored eyes. Mathieson had been right
—even at fifty-five Bouverie had far to go.

"In fact, I'd known the de Sourraines family all my life.
There was almost a family connection; the Count was my
sister's godfather. So when Brussels was no longer tenable
for the activities I was carrying out, I contacted his daughter Marie—"

Until the briefing Owen had assumed that Bouverie was
purely English. He wasn't. Like the Count he came of an
old Anglo-Belgian family. Like him too, although a generation later, he'd been educated in Britain. When Belgium
was overrun by the Germans he'd been twenty, a student at
Brussels University, from which he'd planned to go on to
Oxford.

The war of course had changed all that. With a group of
fellow students, Bouverie had formed a resistance cell.
Amateur, unequipped and uncoordinated at first, they'd
eventually linked up with an SOE network. Afterwards
they'd spent three years sabotaging Nazi communications

and transport—the munitions trains pouring into Belgium from the German industrial heartland.

"Precisely how we were penetrated, I don't know—"

A small shrug of his shoulders in the close-fitting tunic.

"The Gestapo probably picked one of us up by chance, tortured him on the general assumption they might get something and acquired the names of the rest. It's impossible to tell. So many people disappeared then that no one will ever be sure. In any event they started arresting us—"

Bouverie had had an arrangement to meet the cell's radio contact with SOE at an agreed rendezvous in the city center every Friday. By luck that particular day he reached the rendezvous an hour early.

While he was waiting he saw trucks of plainclothes Gestapo officers arrive at the rendezvous and stake it out. Then, when his contact appeared, he saw them arrest him. Bouverie turned and ran.

"I went straight—which of course meant with the greatest care—to the de Sourraines estate. Not because I knew the family or even because of the Orion line. At the time I had no idea it existed. We had an inflexible rule to stay clear of other cells; so that if one was penetrated the rest wouldn't be too. Contrary to popular belief, torture, then as now, is an immensely effective weapon—"

The quick, thin smile. Yes, Owen decided, but not against this man. You could break him in little pieces, take him apart slowly toenail by toenail, testicle by testicle, and he'd never say a word.

"No, simply because I knew Marie de Sourraines had been given travel passes and she'd used them several times to visit her place in France. Also, of course, that she'd shared my views about the occupation. So if anyone was able and likely to help, it would be her—"

Marie was in the house when he got there. Bouverie explained what had happened; his cell had been blown and he had to get out of Belgium. She took him up to the nursery wing—the same wing where her father had hidden the first pilot, Thompson, and five days later she funneled him into the Orion line.

Bouverie had been one of the last to use it. A few months after he crossed the Spanish border the Gestapo uncovered the network, arrested Marie and closed the line down.

"By then I was flying, so I didn't hear about it until much later—"

Owen started to frown. Bouverie noticed instantly. He paused, smiled again and explained.

"I wasn't a de Sourraines but I was what I suppose one would now call privileged. My father was fanatical about the air, he held the seventh Belgian pilot's license. I had my last lesson at fifteen, so I was fully qualified well before the war started. When I arrived in England there was a desperate shortage of pilots. Naturally I volunteered for service, they sent me to the Allied fighter command wing in Norfolk, and I was airborne within a matter of weeks."

The DFC and the two bars he'd won in a single month. An extraordinary achievement, as Mathieson said. It had required immense courage, immense skill—and money. Bouverie had them all.

After the war he'd decided to stay on in Britain. Already holding an RAF commission, he'd given up the Belgian side of his dual nationality and made the Air Force his career.

Owen nodded and said, "Did you ever form any idea of how the Germans penetrated the line?"

Bouverie shook his head. "None whatsoever. A paid informer? A full-time collaborator? A routine check at a roadblock? A chance arrest and interrogation under tor-

60

ture? The possibilities are limitless. It was like the way they penetrated my own cell—it's impossible to tell."

"What about Sir Roger Walpole and Robert Baring, did you know them?"

"The two who were killed? I met Walpole a few times socially long after the war, but that was all. Baring never."

Silence. The fingers still resting in the neat little pyramid on the desk, the medal ribbons glowing against the dark cloth, the eyes steady and unblinking.

And on the other side Owen puzzled, uncertain, frowning.

"Can you tell me precisely what you're after?"

That was exactly the problem. Owen couldn't. The instructions had been so vague, so unspecific. "An archaeological job really," Mathieson had said. "Take a couple of days and see what you think.'"

Well, he'd taken the two days and he'd done his digging in the past. The Orion line. He knew how it started, how it had operated, how it ended. He also knew that both Walpole and Baring had been murdered near safe-houses along the line years after the network had been rolled up. Nothing more.

It was all so long ago now—the phrase cropped up constantly. Owen didn't know—and he was no closer to knowing than when he started.

"No, sir. Well—" Owen qualified his answer—"It's more a question of not being quite sure what we're looking for than not being able to say."

"But it involves those two members of your department?" Bouverie suggested.

Owen nodded. "Possibly. And maybe some link between them and the line—"

He stopped. Bouverie took his hands off the desk, folded

them in his lap and leaned back. The movement was so slight it was almost imperceptible. Yet in some way he'd relaxed, lowered the stiff functional shield, opened himself to Owen in a way he hadn't done during the thirty minutes they'd been talking.

"As you know I came down that line. I was trundled down it like a piece of baggage, a very grateful piece of baggage—"

The smile once more. Not the quick, thin one as before but the one Owen had seen when he first shook hands. Warm and frank and strangely attractive.

"So I saw it all. The confusion, the deceit, the fear, the courage, the conflicting loyalties—the whole tangled response of millions of people, an entire continent of different languages and cultures, caught up in the nightmare of global war. That was thirty years ago. People die, memories blur, ideas change—"

The same small shrug and the smile still there.

"Personally, I would not ask anyone to try to unravel even one strand of the truth now—especially the truth about an organization as complex, as fragmented, as elusive as the Orion line."

"Thank you, sir."

Owen stood up, smiled in return and left.

For a time—it lasted throughout the taxi ride back to Baker Street—he felt confident, almost light-hearted. Delicately and obliquely Bouverie had confirmed what he already knew himself and hadn't until then accepted. There was no point in going back and no shame in acknowledging the fact. The Orion line was dead. It had been dead for thirty years, three-quarters of his life.

Whatever had happened, whatever the truth about Marie

de Sourraines, about her embittered arrogant daughter, about Walpole and Baring, it didn't matter now. It didn't matter simply because there was no way of establishing it.

Owen paid off the driver, walked into the hall and stopped.

Everything was the same as on the countless occasions he'd come into Baker Street before: the radiators gurgling, Wilson polishing the nameplates on the letter racks, the deep bay of *Diomed,* with the turquoise sky behind, above the circling banister. Yet he stood at the foot of the stairs for over a minute, cold and immobile, suddenly remembering what he'd forgotten in Bouverie's office.

Mathieson had said the Orion line might mean going out again. When he'd said it—gazing levelly into Owen's face—Owen had realized he was lying. Not about going out, but about the reason for it. There was something else, something Mathieson hadn't told him, something even Air Marshal Bouverie didn't know, something that even after thirty years had opened the line again.

Owen shook his head quickly and started to climb the stairs towards the top floor.

7

"Yes, an excellent summary. Very much what we thought, very much indeed, I may say—"

Mathieson's scholarly voice. Resonant and reassuring. The words drawn out as his head nodded gravely like a metronome in agreement. The voice he used with such devestating effect on the Treasury officials.

Owen waited.

Tuesday evening. The light fading in an April London sky that would have exposed Turner not as a fantasist, but a photographer. Rain and mist and cloud with a dying refracted sun behind and even steam rising from the home-going traffic on the street below. Wintour squatting hunchbacked on the grille by the window, smoke from Mathieson's pipe plucked away by the drafts from the passage door, Owen sitting upright in the creaking leather chair.

He'd told them everything. The old Count barking out the story of how the Orion line began, how his willful impetuous daughter had set up the chain of safe-houses, how she'd channeled the pilots down them, how he'd maintained the respectable front in Brussels—and how even now, suddenly tremulous and frail, he still wanted to know the way it had ended.

He'd told them about Blair, the gaunt, asthmatic journalist with a lifelong nose for little piles of shit, who hadn't been satisfied with the authorized version of the first murder—but as an alternative could only offer a parlor game of guesses. About the burly chief inspector who loved rugby and had been worried, dead worried, at the thought of a psychopath loose in his manor. About the compact little air marshal who'd traveled down the line, who'd witnessed the vast turbulence of the time and who was adamant that not one single strand of truth about it all could ever be unraveled—least of all now.

He'd told them and they'd listened. Wintour rocking slowly, Mathieson fussing with his pipe. He'd made his report. If there was something else, they'd tell him: for the moment he could only wait.

Owen went on waiting.

"Yes. Well, I must confess we haven't been totally fair with you, Owen—"

Still Mathieson's donnish voice, but the pitch had changed. There was something else.

"James, perhaps you'd get it—"

Reluctantly Wintour dropped off the radiator. He shuffled across to a cabinet behind Mathieson's desk, rummaged in the top drawer and came back with a small metal box which he put down on top of the heaped papers.

Mathieson waved with his pipe and Owen opened the box.

There were index cards inside, about ninety of them, pink and oblong, with ruled lines. Owen drew a few out at random; they weren't numbered and they didn't seem to be in any particular order. Someone had written on them all in pen or pencil; the handwriting, a jagged angular script, was the same throughout but the entries seemed to have been made at different times. Most contained a name and address, others just a name, a few a single word that looked like a code name.

"Tell Owen the story, would you, James."

Owen turned and watched Wintour as he went back to the window.

It had started by accident, Wintour said. Six weeks before, in early March, the Belgian resident, Marc Lestain, had been summoned by the chief of the Belgian security police. A furious row was going on between them and their Dutch counterparts over the ownership of some documents which had been found in a field on their common border. The documents, Lestain was told, were a collection of index cards.

Lestain was shown a sample of six and asked if he could identify the writing or cast any other light on them. He examined them carefully, memorized the names and addresses, and said no. In fact, Lestain hadn't been telling the truth. He'd recognized the distinctive writing instantly as that of his wartime SOE instructor, Paul Jarvis, who'd been killed in the parachute drop at Arnhem.

As soon as he returned to the section house Lestain had a check run on the six names. Predictably their owners all turned out to be dead—which was why the sample had been chosen. But one of them had died in prison only a year after the war ended; he'd been tried and convicted of collaborating with the occupying forces.

If Lestain needed any confirmation that was it. In fact he'd guessed what he was looking at the moment he'd seen the cards: some entries on the legendary white list.

Yet the cards he'd been shown were carbons. Obviously top copies had once existed—and not just of the six now valueless entries but of the entire collection. It was just conceivable, too, that they still existed. Lestain started searching.

"Took him only three weeks, actually," Mathieson interjected. "Sounds impossible, the proverbial needle in the haystack we've all been after for years. But Lestain's been a Europe man all his life, knows every rope there is. Very bright, too. And of course, for the first time, he'd got an idea of what he was looking for—"

Lestain knew the size of the cards, four by six inches. He acquired a library copy of a prewar trade directory, made a list of all the major Dutch and Belgian office-equipment suppliers of the time, contacted them (most were still in business) and obtained the names of the printers who produced their catalogues.

"Got a set of old catalogues from the printers, they usually keep some file copies, and found what he was after right away. Four-by-six-by-eighteen-inch leatherine cabinet—"

Mathieson tapped the box with his pipe.

"Just like this one except they put a fancy covering over it. Standard then, almost the only model in fact. And then he went straight to Avenue Cinq—"

Owen nodded. Avenue Cinq. The great rambling warehouse of a building on the outskirts of Brussels, called after the name of the street on which it stood. The original idea had been General Patton's.

1944. The German counteroffensive in the Ardennes had just been thrown back. Allied armored columns were lancing through the lowlands. Resistance groups were coming out into the open everywhere. Men who for five years had fought—or who claimed to have fought—underground. Couriers, saboteurs, radio operators, safe-house owners, armed guerrillas. Elegant men in dark suits, bearded men with ancient rifles, farmhands, bankers, liars, thieves, confidence tricksters, black marketeers, opportunists—and heroes.

All of them, for a myriad of motives, anxious to jump on the victory bandwagon—and all with a myriad of stories to tell. Stories of unrecorded operations, of hidden weapon caches, of German atrocities, of betrayals and feats of valor. And most of them with material, spurious or real, to support what they said: photographs, records, posters, diaries, drawings, newspaper reports.

Patton commandeered Avenue Cinq and instructed that everything "in print and whether visual or verbal including as relevant oral recordings" (the order had been specific) should be deposited there for processing. Much of it was used later in the Nuremberg trials. Much—because of the sheer volume of what arrived—was never even catalogued. It had stayed there in vast moldering piles ever since, an archive, part truth, part fantasy and part downright deceit, of the history of European resistance.

"Lestain was working on guesses—"

Wintour's hoarse voice as he took up the story again.

"First, of course, that there had been an original. Second,

that Jarvis had given it to a member of his network with in-structions to hand it over to the "proper authorities" if any-thing happened to Jarvis himself. Third, that the man had seen Patton's order—they put it out by radio and on posters —and turned the cards in to Avenue Cinq. And fourth that the only way he'd ever find them there was by looking for the cabinet—"

As Mathieson said, it had taken him three weeks to sift through the heaps of dusty papers, the crates and bales and suitcases and cluttered racks of shelves. But the guesses had been right. Lestain found the cabinet.

"And then, sensible fellow, he stole the cards!" Mathieson chuckled happily. "Put them in his pockets and walked out cool as a cucumber. Only thing he could do, of course. Get-ting stuff out of there—in spite of the fact they've no idea what they've got—is still an absolute nightmare. And if they'd known what these were, they'd all have been spin-ning around in high-velocity ever-decreasing circles—"

Still chuckling, Mathieson broke off to relight his pipe and swore as the maverick beacon of flame from the lighter touched his thumb.

"Lestain sent them over two weeks ago with his report. He also sent something else—"

Mathieson leaned back, shaking his hand.

"To get into Avenue Cinq you need accreditation first, then you have to sign the register. The register's a damn great book they keep at the entrance. The first day Lestain went there he had to wait for ten minutes while they tele-phoned the embassy to check him out. The register was out on the counter. While he was waiting Lestain flicked through it. They don't get many inquiries now—a couple of pages cover the applications for a year. Lestain got back to '71 and saw a name he recognized. Bobby Baring's. For five days in a row in September that year Baring had signed himself in at Avenue Cinq—"

September 1971 was two months after Baring had been sent on what Wintour had called "indefinite sick leave." Five weeks later he'd been murdered.

Owen sat forward, watching Mathieson's face now.

"At this point, like Lestain, I have to confess one's got to start guessing," Mathieson went on. "But I think the outline's clear enough. Both Walpole and Baring were SOE colleagues of Jarvis. God knows how many times afterwards we discussed whether Jarvis had compiled a white list before they got him. The subject was a real bugbear of his, everyone in the department knew it. Anyway, we didn't get anywhere—all we could do was speculate. Jarvis was dead and the rest of us soldiered on. Then Walpole retired, made that trip to France and got murdered."

"Why that particular trip?" Owen asked. "Why down the route of the Orion line?"

"To be quite honest I haven't the slightest idea—"

For once Mathieson's frankness, and the smile that went with it, seemed to be what it was. Frankness. He didn't know.

"All I can do, again, is guess. He was very proud of the Orion line, Walpole, frankly so were all of us in the department then. Marie de Sourraines set it up originally, but we funded its operations after we linked with her and the whole thing ran like a dream. I imagine for Walpole it was a sentimental journey back which happily coincided with some of his favorite vineyards. Not so Baring. Baring, I'm afraid, probably had a motive for the route he took—"

Mathieson glanced at Wintour who, nodding bleakly on the grille, seemed to share his distaste at the memory.

"I don't usually make a practice of discussing members of the department, Owen, not even former ones. But I should tell you there was a very unpleasant scene here when Baring left. He felt, quite wrongly, he'd been cheated. Over many things, but particularly over money—"

Mathieson gestured irritably with his pipe.

"It was a running feud he'd carried on with Accounts and Treasury for years. I'm sorry to say it made him very bitter, so bitter that when we were eventually forced to ask him to retire he started making threats."

Owen frowned. "Threats?"

"They weren't explicit, Baring seldom was himself. But he hinted he knew something and if Treasury wouldn't pay his 'compensation,' he had another way of getting it. At the time we simply ignored him. His grudge had become obsessive, he was drinking heavily—"

The expression of distaste on Mathieson's face once more.

"Bluntly, I thought it was a thoroughly discreditable—and unsuccessful—piece of bluff."

"And later?"

"Later?" Mathieson paused. "After he was killed we ran a routine security check here. Normal practice in the circumstances; just to see if anything was missing or he'd been behaving unusually in his work before he went. Nothing had gone and there wasn't really anything unusual in what he'd been up to over the last few months. Except—"

The slight hesitation again. And again Owen sensed it was real. Mathieson wasn't playing games; he was trying to piece together a jigsaw puzzle without a picture to guide him to what it represented.

"Well, just before his departure he'd asked archives for

every single file dealing with Jarvis's network. No reason why he shouldn't, of course; he was D.C. Europe and all the files had been duly signed back in. We noted it, but nothing more."

"Until his name turned up on the register at Avenue Cinq?" Owen suggested.

Mathieson nodded. "In the overall context of what happened and what Lestain found there, the incident does assume a rather different significance, doesn't it?"

All three of them were still now. Wintour no longer swaying on the radiator, Mathieson silent behind the desk, Owen as before sitting stiffly on the edge of the chair.

There were still gaps of course, but the rest of it had fallen into place. The white list of wartime collaborators hadn't been a myth after all. Compiled by the long-dead SOE agent, Paul Jarvis, it had existed in two copies. One, the carbon, incomplete and rain-sodden, had surfaced in a windy March field on the Dutch-Belgian border. The other, the original, had been ferreted out by the astute Lestain after a three-week search through the ghost-ridden depository of Avenue Cinq.

The two men who'd died later, Walpole and Baring, had both been SOE friends and colleagues of the list's creator. Walpole, the elder, had returned to France on his retirement and had been brutally murdered. "A sentimental journey," Mathieson had called his trip and he was probably right. Walpole's interest was claret—not the white list. His killing was an unnecessary precaution, an accident, a mistake.

Not so in Baring's case. Baring was a man with an all-consuming grievance, a grievance like a cancer. Denied what he believed was his rightful due, he'd hit on another way of acquiring it. *If* the white list existed, then it would be worth a fortune in blackmail. He'd started to hunt for it by meticulously combing through the old files of Jarvis's network. Something there had taken him to the Avenue Cinq. After a week in the depository he'd bought a van, crossed to France, followed Walpole's route south and finally, like his predecessor, he'd been killed.

The exact sequence of events between Baring's initial decision and his death didn't really matter now. He hadn't found the list itself. (Unlike Lestain, he'd no idea what he was looking for.) Quite possibly, in that tormented, alcohol-blurred mind, he wasn't even sure himself what he was going to do. Ask questions? Trace people involved in the line? Insinuate he had certain information? Suggest that "arrangements" could be made for safeguarding it?

The answers were unimportant. All that mattered was Lestain's discovery in the Avenue Cinq. Laughing in the Fleet Street bar, Blair had suggested that the white list, if there ever was one, would have been more than enough motive for Walpole's death. The same applied in even greater measure to Baring.

The white list had existed—it still did. And both the killings had occurred along the route of the Orion line. Whatever the source of the nasty smell in the line, it was not only connected with a name on the list; it was still there today.

"These have presumably been analyzed, sir?"

Owen pulled out the single drawer until all the cards were exposed.

"We haven't exactly been twiddling our thumbs since Lestain sent them over. Those are the originals. Over there—"

He indicated the large filing cabinet from which Wintour had taken the box.

"We've got five duplicate sets, all of them annotated and

cross-referenced. Ninety-six separate entries altogether, aren't there, James—?"

Wintour nodded.

Archives would have done it, Owen guessed. Archives— with a contribution from Library and the field checks carried out by the heads of local stations. The exercise must have carried a "Director Only" instruction; no word of it had reached him at the French desk.

"Unfortunately, didn't yield much," Mathieson added. "Of the eighty-odd names in clear, about sixty are dead and the rest were working way outside the territory covered by the line. In fact, all we were left with were fourteen code designations—"

A single word or occasionally two, hyphenated. Owen had noticed some of those when he'd riffled through the drawer.

"Eliminated nine of them—dead or other territory again —from Cabinet Office records. What we finally ended up with were these five. No residual identification, no trace, no cross-reference, nothing. Just five pseudonyms which may or may not have belonged to people involved in the Orion line—"

But if they did, even if one of them did, it might explain why the entire line had been smashed in the twenty-four hours after Marie de Sourraines's arrest. Whether she'd talked or not. The reason for Walpole's and Baring's murders. So much else.

Owen took the cards—Mathieson pushed forward a set of copies in a folder tucked away among the papers on his desk. Studied them one by one.

"Jo-Jo" and "Soldat"—he'd seen those already among the originals. " 'Guette"—possibly a diminutive for the name of the music-hall star, Mistinguette. "Bien-aimé"—well-beloved, maybe because the man (the woman?) had used it as his or her standard greeting; maybe ironically because he'd been universally disliked. "Charlot"—little Charles, the French name for Chaplin and his tramp.

Owen put them down. One of them, perhaps, concealed the identity of someone so deeply compromised by what he'd done during the war, of what had happened along the Orion line, that twelve and then again twenty-five years afterwards he'd been prepared to murder—twice, viciously, wantonly—to keep the secret inviolate.

Owen didn't know. The names were meaningless now. Again and again the phrase came back: it was all too long ago now.

"Not to him, it isn't—"

Mathieson had guessed what Owen was thinking. Him. The man behind one of those five innocent-sounding covers. The collaborator who'd betrayed Marie, exposed the line to the Gestapo, killed again and again a generation later.

"He could have been over thirty when the war ended, and he'd still only be in his early sixties now. In his prime, I'd say—"

The smile came and went quickly.

"I have a distinct aversion to members of my department being killed, Owen. If it's humanly possible I would at least like to know who did it and why. Armed with those names there's at least a possibility of learning that now—"

Mathieson glanced down and applied himself to his pipe, studiously avoiding Owen's face.

"It does, of course, mean going out and traveling back down the Orion line."

Owen said nothing for a moment. The light had gone from the sky and the sound of the traffic had faded and even Wintour's husky breathing had quieted.

Then he stood up. "Yes, sir."

He walked stiffly to the door and went out. On the stairs he thought of what had happened to the last two people who'd tried to retrace the course of the line.

"Rue Gabrielle right?"

Owen peered up into the darkness. As the car slowed at
the intersection the lights of a passing bus briefly caught
the blue-and-white lettering on the sign: Rue Gabrielle.

"Yes."

The old man chuckled. He was blind and he was sitting
in the back of the Simca, hands clamped over the white
cane between his thighs, next to Béchaud, the head of the
Paris station. Owen was in the front beside the old man's
daughter, who was driving.

"Stop for a moment, Elise. Remember I used to tell you?
Listen—"

She braked and drew in to the pavement. In the half-silence they all heard the patter of falling water.

"The fountains of Place des Écoles, around the corner on the right. The boches never turned them off even when they blacked out the whole city. That's how I used to know where I was at night. Now—"

The old man was still laughing happily.

"Go straight over the Porte de Charenton, left at the next lights and after that straight again for about half a kilometer."

The car moved forward. Owen stretched out his leg and leaned back, watching the headlight beams waver over the grooves of the old streetcar lines.

The outskirts of Paris at ten o'clock on a clear April evening. Five days after he'd walked out of Mathieson's office. Five days since he'd tacitly agreed to make the journey back down the Orion line.

Meg, as he'd guessed, had been furious—he'd telephoned her the same night. He was very sorry, he said, but something had cropped up which meant going abroad for a while. So he wouldn't be down on the weekend, nor probably for the next two or three Saturdays either. Would she please explain to the children, send them his love and say he'd see them again just as soon as he could.

"You make promises, Gareth, you keep them—"

Her voice, cold and angry and defying contradiction, after he'd finished. And he could see her at the sink—the telephone was on the wall above—just as he'd seen her the first time he'd walked into her mother's kitchen all those years ago.

The sleeves rolled up to the elbows above the suds. The long dark hair, raven's-wing in color, gathered in a clip at the back of her neck. The green catlike eyes. The face, thinner now but still in essence the same, which had made her the beauty of the village—and had captivated Nantynth's *bachgen dawnus* as it had captivated so many others.

"You know what a few weeks are to a child? A few weeks are a lifetime. When you came back you said you wouldn't have to go away again, right, Gareth? So what's happened now? Why—?"

Owen hadn't been able to answer. He apologized again and rang off. But Mathieson knew the reason. Mathieson had known from the start why it wouldn't be remotely necessary to force him.

Mathieson knew what had happened in the hotel bedroom outside Algiers—and what still remained to be settled.

Owen had left the following morning, flying straight to Brussels. As the de Sourraines estate outside the city had been the start of the line, it was the logical place to begin. Yet the chateau had been sold—it housed a business administration school now—and the staff had long since dispersed. The only person Owen managed to trace was a former gardener, who still lived in a cottage in the park.

Yes, of course, he remembered the line—*le groupe,* as he called it. The government had even given him a medal after the war; he proudly tapped the little pink ribbon on his lapel. But all he'd done was sometimes carry food from the kitchens to the pigeon loft, where they hid the pilots if there wasn't room in the nursery wing. He didn't know what happened after they left the chateau and he was certain he'd never heard any of the five names Owen mentioned.

He was very sorry. Maybe his cousin, another gardener,

would have recognized them. Unfortunately his cousin had died last year. Still, since the monsieur had bothered to come all this way, perhaps he'd care for a glass of wine?

Owen thanked him politely and left. It was a futile, meaningless beginning and at Mons, the border point with France and the next staging post along the line, it was even worse. The safe-house there had been a small hotel near the station run by an old widow—a staunch and lifelong opponent of the Germans. She too was dead and the hotel had long since been demolished to make way for a new office block.

Owen spent a frustrating day trying to find someone who remembered her. No one did. The area had been part of the old town—and the old town had gone. Shops, restaurants, bars, hotels, all bulldozed flat and, as they'd vanished, so had their former owners. New Belgium, modern, prosperous Belgium, was courteous, friendly and utterly unhelpful. The past had been buried with the rubble of the war. Their concerns now were with the price of common-market butter and whether Herr Schmidt would continue the *Ostpolitik* initiatives.

But since Monsieur Owen had taken so much trouble to so little effect, the hospitality of Mons demanded he be compensated. Would he care to visit the new town hall and afterwards dine at the new convention center—as a guest of the *Syndicat d'Initiative*, of course?

Again, Owen politely declined and instead went on. Paris was next—and Paris was different. Warned by telex from Baker Street, Béchaud, the station head, had done his homework. For the first time he'd come up with someone who'd been an important link in the network and was happy to talk about it. The old man.

"The Quai d'Austerlitz," his granddaughter said.

They were in the heart of the city now and traveling along the left bank of the Seine towards the Pont Neuf.

"Pass the bridge, start counting the lampposts immediately until you get to the ninth, then stop—"

The old man leaned forward and tapped Owen on the shoulder.

"When the Germans turned off the lights because of your air raids, they put cat's-eyes on all the lampposts. They were meant to guide their street patrols enforcing the curfew, but they had other uses."

He was laughing again as they pulled into the side of the road.

"Right—"

They'd all got out and were standing on the pavement watching him: the girl, Béchaud with his trim brown mustache, Owen in his raincoat.

"Up there—"

The old man indicated the Pont Neuf.

"They had a mobile canteen. That was for the patrols too. They did four hours around the streets, a thirty-minute break, then another four hours. When the break came they went there for coffee and *saucisson*—*Wurst* they called it. By midnight, right down to here—"

The white stick made an arch through the darkness until it was pointing at the eighth lamppost from the bridge.

"There'd be patrol trucks parked. All of them empty, with the soldiers around the canteen getting their coffee. We used to draw in right here behind the last truck—"

The old man had been a baker, employed by the famous French *pâtisserie* Le Cochon Rouge—The Pink Pig. The route they'd taken that night had been the one he'd driven every evening throughout the war; from the site of the bakery on the outskirts to the center of Paris.

"And they let you stop here?" Owen said.

"Soldiers!" The old man snorted. "Everywhere in the world the same—and the boches the worst, the most stupid. Passes, whores and food, that's all they understand. Girls, no, we didn't have. But passes, because we delivered to the German commandant, yes. And food, of course, too, the day's baking we'd just collected from the ovens. There'd be two of us in the van, Marcel and me. One of us would go forward, didn't matter which—they knew us both by then. Hey, we'd say, du Kamarad, Johann—"

The old man mimicked it, stepping towards the canteen's invisible counter, waving his hand and shouting in jovial fractured German.

"Du like a cake, Johann? Give us a caffee, Johann, caffee fur me, cake fur du—right from the pig to the pig." The deep-throated chuckle once more at the ancient joke. "Said the last part in French, of course. They didn't understand, they just laughed, the *salauds*—"

Owen smiled. He could visualize it clearly. The bakery van drawing up behind the trucks, one of them walking forward to the canteen with a tray of cakes, joking, engaging the soldiers, asking for coffee—while the other remained behind.

"And the one who stayed here?"

The old man didn't answer. Instead he turned, rattled his stick along the pillars of the pavement balustrade and found the opening.

Even with the street lamps burning Owen hadn't noticed it, a break in the stone railing with a flight of steps beyond. They walked behind him as he tapped his way down to the quay.

"They say things change—"

The old man was standing by the water.

"I tell you, one thing does not change and will not change, then or now. The good red wine of France and what it can do—"

He stopped and smiled. In the distance the floodlit towers of Notre Dame soared against a starry sky. On either side couples were wandering slowly hand in hand. Murmuring, dreaming, pausing to watch their reflections in the ripples. A small boy sat fishing, hunched in fierce silent concentration over his line. A *bateau mouche* passed, strung with decorative colored lights. An accordion echoed from a boulevard café and the smells of the Seine lifted in the night wind.

Spring in Paris. The eternal changeless lovers' city. As unchanging as the good red wine of France—and the *clochards*, the drunks, it remorselessly claimed for victims. Owen looked at them. They were everywhere, bundles of tattered coat and ragged newspaper lying immobile in wine-stenched torpor among the pools of shadow.

They had been there during the occupation. They were there now. The pathetic human detritus of the capital. Pathetic, filthy, untouchable—and anonymous.

"The van had a false floor, I fitted it myself. We could take two a night, no more—"

He was climbing back to the road. Owen behind him, then the girl, then Béchaud. The white stick, flickering in the moonlight, drummed across the stone as he probed for the steps.

The border town was a hundred miles northeast.

After they'd crossed from Belgium the pilots were put onto one of the forced-labor trains that ran daily into Paris. The trains' terminus was the Gare du Nord, two kilometres upriver from the Pont Neuf. A courier would meet them at the station, guide them down to the wharves and smuggle them on board a barge carrying cement for the fortifications at Falaise.

After the barge had passed beneath the Pont Neuf, it would swing into the quay and drop its "passengers" before continuing on its journey to the sea. The pilots would wait there for the old man or Marcel to collect them, indistinguishable from the derelicts.

"Then, with a couple of the boys under the floor, we'd do the deliveries—"

They were back in the Simca, the girl at the wheel again, retracing the van's delivery run.

The Cochon Rouge itself first, the elegant shop in the Rue de Rivoli where the wives of the German officers had bought their millefeuilles and éclairs. Then the house of the German commandant on the Avenue Foch. Two or three more buildings where other senior officers had been quartered. Finally Les Halles.

"That was the bread and butter, so to speak. But it wasn't the only thing we delivered—"

They'd stopped for the third time and were standing grouped around him once more in the darkness.

Les Halles. The food market of Paris for over a century. Once a vast cavernous structure of iron and glass where four generations of Parisians had come to buy their groceries, prod sides of beef and mounds of vegetables, haggle at the ranks of stalls, make their purchases and eat bowls of onion soup before they went home.

No longer. The building had been torn down two years before and the market moved outside the city. Now Les Halles was an immense empty construction site, muddy, desolate, pitted with half-completed foundations, ringed like watchtowers by the silhouettes of cranes and derricks. Office blocks would rise here soon. There'd be no more meat and cheese and fruit, no more good-natured haggling, no more onion soup.

"But it was different then. Well, you probably saw it yourself—"

The old man turned and looked at Owen, identifying instantly where he stood in spite of the blindness.

"I saw it later, but I imagine it was just the same."

The old man nodded. "It didn't change in the war. The trucks brought in the food from the farms. Whatever didn't sell that day, they'd load up again at night and drive south to the markets in the smaller towns. They'd sell it there next morning. Less money, maybe, but they'd still get rid of it—"

The Cochon Rouge used to sell loaves to the drivers, the long crusty baguettes they baked on the other side of the capital. It was the steady reliable staple of the business, as opposed to the delicate *pâtisseries* which the wealthy trade of the Rue de Rivoli might, or might not, buy on whim.

And at the same time that they delivered the loaves, they'd deliver the pilots. Transferring them from the false floor of the van to one of the trucks heading south after midnight, so that it reached some little market town in the Loire before dawn.

"By then, of course, they'd be out of our hands. What happened afterwards—"

He shrugged. His section of the line had started on the

banks of the Seine and ended here. Here in what had been a noisy diesel-smelling concourse of trucks and black-bereted drivers, and now was a silent cratered field.

"There are some names," Owen said, "five of them. Maybe you remember—"

He recited the list slowly: Jo-Jo, Soldat, 'Guette, Bien-aimé, Charlot. Then he waited.

"Here—"

The old man had listened in silence, head bowed over the knob of the stick. Now he waved the girl back and walked forward, beckoning Owen to follow.

"All of that time was bad, some parts were worse. There were things you had to do then, but afterwards, maybe because you change as you grow old, you're not proud of. I would sooner she didn't know—"

They were out of hearing of the other two. Underfoot the turf was soft with the recent rain. In front twin tracks glowed against a patch of raw earth.

"Yes, there was a man we called Soldat. He said he'd fought in the first war. Who knows? A trucking foreman, he was, big fellow, about fifty, laughed a lot. They, the boches, conscripted some of the drivers here to service their armored cars at the Neuilly depot. The boys worked on them nicely."

"Worked on them?"

"Sand in the axle bearings, slipped leads, little things you couldn't tell were sabotage unless someone told you. Some-one told them. They took all the boys out one morning and shot them. We found out it was Soldat. He'd told them many other things too; they'd been paying him for a year."

He paused. They'd reached the two tracks. An excavation pit gaped beyond and the wind was rattling the cables of a hoist.

"What did you do?" Owen asked.

The old man lifted his stick and felt for the nearest rail. He found it and tapped three times, slowly, gently.

"The loaded trolleys ran along here into the market. They were big and heavy, big as a truck, with metal wheels. The night we discovered, we brought Soldat out and talked to him. He cried, said they were threatening his family, oh, much more. Maybe it was all true. But we also knew he'd had money and a lot of the boys had died. So we held him down on the track, just his legs, and waited for the next trolley. It cut them off clean at the knees. He was still alive, moaning, when we went away, but he bled to death in the night—"

He touched the rail with his stick again. Then he shook his head and turned back towards the car.

"Necessary, yes. Men, good men, were being killed because of him. But to deal with it in that way? Now I'm not so sure. You understand why I don't want my granddaughter to know?"

Soldat. The big laughing foreman. The family man who claimed he was being blackmailed—and probably was. The man who'd been taken out and held down over the track and had his legs scythed off at the knees—dying in agony hours later from shock and loss of blood.

"Yes," Owen said, "I understand."

Even for traitors there were other, easier ways to pay the price.

"Did he know about the Orion line?"

"Of course. He was in charge of one of the loading gangs who helped us hide the men in the trucks."

"So he almost certainly told the Germans about it?"

"Maybe—"

The old man hesitated. They were close to the other two now. Owen could see the girl standing by the car door and the glow of Béchaud's cigarette above the hood.

"I don't think he did. We offered him his life for everything he'd passed onto them. It wasn't a true offer; we'd have killed him anyway. But he was terrified and we wanted to find out all the damage he'd done first. He admitted many things, not that. He said he was too close to the line, that if he'd told them and they started arresting people, we'd guess how they'd discovered. He said they hadn't even asked him about escape routes. It made sense. And the proof was, the line went on running after he died, they didn't touch it. To me that was enough. He'd lied and deceived and betrayed many things—but not the Orion line."

They went on, got into the Simca and drove back through Montparnasse and out of the city.

Soldat claimed he'd collaborated with the Gestapo over everything but the Orion line. The old man, crouching above him as he lay spread-eagled and terrified by the rails in the darkness, had believed him. The old man was probably right. But there could have been another explanation.

Soldat said they hadn't even asked him about escape routes. Escape routes—and the maquis networks that ran them—were the Germans' main counterintelligence priority. If they hadn't questioned Soldat about the line, it might have been because they knew about it already.

There were still four unidentified names left from the card-index file Lestain had unearthed in Avenue Cinq.

Either the woman was deaf or the clamor had drowned Owen's voice. She screwed up her face, ancient and wrinkled above the shapeless mourning dress, cupped a hand to her ear and shouted at him again.

"*Quoi?*"

A bank of heaped vegetables separated them. Owen leaned across it and shouted back for the second time.

"Pierre, Pierre Faure."

"Ah—"

She'd finally understood. Nodding slowly, she wiped her hands on her apron and methodically started to rearrange a pile of cauliflowers.

Owen waited.

The covered part of the market—he was standing at its center—was low-roofed and iron-beamed, a tiny country version of Les Halles with the same skylights and the same sea-green glass in the panes. All around them, thronging the narrow aisles between the stalls, Wednesday morning shoppers were gossiping, arguing, laughing, scolding screaming children, quarreling with the stall owners as they bellowed out the merits of their cut-price charcuterie or their dairy-fresh camembert.

Les Halles might have been demolished. The market at Nevers was still raucous, alive and well.

"You want Pierre, do you?"

She'd finished with the cauliflowers and the question was a long-practiced screech above the tumult.

"Yes."

"Try the garage. Rue Danton, over there—"

A hand like a claw stabbed towards an open archway. Distantly, over the uproar, Owen could hear the cackling of trussed chickens, the grunts of pigs and the wavering cry of a lottery-ticket seller.

"Anyone will show you."

"Thanks."

Owen turned and headed for the space of bright sunlight. He passed a gleaming counter of oranges, stepped between crates of tomatoes, shouldered his way through the crowd at the entrance, then he was on the street—with the smells of meat and fruit and garlic behind.

It was 9:00 A.M. and the fourth day after he'd left Paris, driving south in a rented Peugeot along the routes the trucks had taken. Like the start of the journey the three days had been fruitless. There'd been safe-houses in half a dozen small towns within a two-hundred-mile radius of the capital where the drivers used to leave the men for the next stage of their trip to the Spanish border.

Owen had visited five of them and discovered that, like Belgium, France had changed almost beyond recognition. The buildings had gone, the members of the network had died or moved away, and he hadn't been able to find a single person who'd even heard of the line. In fact it had been worse than Belgium. At least in Brussels and Mons he'd been listened to politely. In France, as soon as Owen raised the subject, people became evasive, reluctant to talk, denying any knowledge of the occupation—although he knew that all the older ones he'd spoken to must have experienced it in one way or another. To them "resistance" might almost have become a dirty word.

Puzzled and frustrated, Owen had risen early on Wednesday and driven to the market at Nevers. Nevers had been the sixth and most distant of the dropping-off points. It was also the home of Pierre Faure.

Owen had chosen the woman because she was old. It turned out, as she'd said, that anyone in the town could have told him. Even thirty years later Faure was famous —famous enough to be known instantly by a boy lounging by a handcart outside the market.

Pierre Faure's garage? Up there on the left, maybe a hundred meters down the turning. Owen couldn't miss it.

The boy was right. Owen followed his directions and found the garage a few minutes later—a large dusky shed with runnels of oil on the stone floor and cobwebs glistening across the roof. A battered Citroën van, its engine half-stripped, blocked the doorway, and bundles of used tires hung from iron hooks in the walls. There was a torn

Pirelli calendar, a jumble of rusting spare parts and, incongruously, at the back a plastic bust of Lenin with the symbol of the French communist party tacked to the wooden boards above.

"Bon jour."

For a moment Owen had thought the place was deserted. Then trolley wheels squeaked and a man pushed himself from under the van's chassis.

Owen looked down.

"Monsieur Faure?"

The man levered himself up, wiped his face quickly with a rag and nodded.

"Yes—"

He was in his mid-fifties. Small, even shorter than Owen, but spare and wiry where Owen was broad—a grizzled little whippet of a man with cropped gray hair, narrow eyes and a fierce tight mouth. There was a crumpled yellow Gitane tucked behind one ear and his dirty mechanic's overalls reeked of diesel. Standing by the van, balanced on the balls of his feet with his wrist tendons jumping out as he flexed his hands, he looked like a bantamweight fighter ready to move in for the kill.

Hard, fanatical, loyal and dangerous, Owen thought. A good friend and, as the Gestapo had found out, a relentless enemy.

"What can I do for you?"

"If you can spare the time," Owen said, "I'd like to talk to you. About the war and the occupation, but particularly about the Orion line—"

It took Owen ten minutes. He explained what he wanted slowly, deliberately and specifically. With someone like Faure there was no choice; he'd been trained in the same game and he'd have instantly seen through any cover story.

In the end Faure accepted him. Not out of nostalgia for the past, not because he believed anything would come of it, least of all because he thought they shared any common political ground—Faure was a dedicated hardline communist and Owen was merely a hireling of British imperialism.

Instead the reason was simple: he recognized and accepted Owen for what he'd once been himself—a fellow professional in the trade of espionage.

"Marie de Sourraines asked me to run the transfer here. You've heard of her?"

Owen nodded. They'd gone to a café up the street and were sitting under the awning, glasses of milky-white Pernod on the table between them.

"Silly, vain girl but she had guts, I'll say that for her—"

The voice was like the man; harsh, uncompromising, shaded always with anger. By all accounts Marie de Sourraines had been neither silly nor vain. It was just that to Faure every aristocrat was automatically endowed with those characteristics.

"Anyway, she arrived here one night and explained her setup. We already had our own group by then, a big one. Handling the transfers for her line was just one of the things we did. There was much else."

Nevers was one of the first and best-organized centers of the maquis. Like almost everywhere else in France where an effective resistance movement developed, it was started and controlled by the local communist party. Faure, a cobbler's son, had joined the party as a youth member two years before the war broke out. By 1940 he was organizing secretary of the Nevers branch—and the driving force behind a network that harassed the Germans mercilessly until the Normandy landings.

During that time, as Owen had learned from the Baker

Street files, he became something of a folklore hero—a youthful latter-day Scarlet Pimpernel with the difference that Faure was hell-bent on destroying any enemy of the working classes. At that moment the occupying forces just happened to be the most immediate and threatening manifestation of everything he'd dedicated his life to overthrow.

The Gestapo put a bounty on his head—the largest they offered during the entire occupation. The little cobbler's son contemptuously slipped through every trap they laid for him and ruthlessly continued with his private war: arson, sabotage, ambush, assassination.

And intermittently, between the night attacks and the detonated bridges, the transfers of the pilots who came down the Orion line.

"They arrived in the early mornings, usually a pair of them once every few weeks. One of the drivers would leave a message in advance warning me they were on their way. So when the camions pulled in, I'd be there at the market to meet them—"

Faure finished his Pernod, tossed the ice cubes into the gutter and abruptly stood up.

"Come on, I'll show you."

As they went out Owen asked the café proprietor for the bill. The man smiled and shook his head.

"Not for a guest of Pierre," he said.

Owen didn't argue. Even if he'd spent the generation since the war in a futile embittered pursuit of his dream—that the party would take over France—to the population of Nevers, Faure was still a hero. His drinks were on the house. They always would be.

Owen followed him back down the Rue Danton to the market.

"It's bricked up now—they use fork-lift machinery to put the vegetables into crates outside. But you can see where it was—"

They hadn't entered the still-crowded and noisy building. Instead Faure had led him down a flight of steps at one side and into a cavernous cellar below. Now they were standing at its far end. Looking up at where Faure was pointing Owen could see a lacework of splintered light, the gaps in the mortar that had been used to seal off the aperture above the chute.

The chute itself was still there, a massive wooden trough angled from the ground to the cellar floor. Owen reached out and touched it.

"And they were tilted down this?" he asked.

"Turnips, potatoes, carrots, men, all tangled up together—"

Faure whirled his hands like a windmill and made a deep rumbling sound—imitating the truckloads as they were deposited down the chute.

"Bruises too"—for the first time a quick smile. "We patched them up right here under the feet of the boche guards outside. Then I took them back to the salon for the cosmetics—"

He turned and Owen followed again.

The "salon" was a storeroom—barely larger than a cupboard—beneath the cellar stairs. Inside it a member of Faure's network, a young hairdresser, applied what he called the "cosmetics" to the pilots who'd been painfully dumped down the wooden trough.

"Moroccans, Algerians, Tunisians, *merde*, who knows what they were—"

He shrugged dismissively, uninterested. Owen watched as he struck a match against his thumb and peered into the musty airless closet. Chauvinism obviously wasn't the prerogative of the right.

"Arabs, anyway. Cheap immigrant labor. We've got a thousand of them on register in Nevers now, we had twice as many then. The Germans used them and so did we—"

The Germans had built a munitions plant fifty kilometers to the west. They requisitioned the aliens' register from the local gendarmeire, and every Friday they'd post a list of two hundred Arab laborers who were required for a week's shift work at the plant. The Arabs gathered in the market square at dawn on Sunday, their identification cards were checked against the register, then they'd set off on bicycles to cover the distance between the town and the plant so they were there to start their week's work early on Monday morning.

"Say Marie sent us a couple down the line. We'd bring them in here, strip them, dye their skins with walnut juice, crimp their hair, dress them again in djellabahs, then Sunday morning we'd send them out into the square. Meantime I'd have picked two of the Arabs on that week's roster—"

Faure tossed the charred match into the dust.

"They'd agree, they always did if you reasoned with them sensibly—"

He smiled again, as quickly as before but grimly now. Owen walked behind him up the steps to the square.

"And that was it. They had the right cards, the boches just checked them against the list, then they set off on bicycles with the rest. There wasn't any language problem, of course. The Germans didn't speak Arabic and the Arabs didn't speak German."

"What happened the other end?"

They were back in the square, warm and dusty and dazzling after the darkness of the cellar.

"One of us rode with them as a guide—we could get passes to move around too. A few kilometers before the plant we'd drop out of the column, wheel the bikes across a field and rendezvous with another guide from the next section of the line. They'd take them on from there—to Moulins."

Moulins. The place where Baring had been murdered.

"He tried to see me, the one who was killed, did you know that?"

Owen looked at Faure, startled. He'd told him what he was after in the garage—to find out as much as he could about the line and whether the two deaths could have been connected with it—but Faure hadn't mentioned Baring until then.

"Baring tried to see you when he came through here three years ago?"

"Was that his name?" Faure shrugged. "I can't remember. An Englishman with a van, a fat belly and drunk— *sacre dieu*, but drunk! I was out fixing a van somewhere. I got back to the garage and he'd paid a kid to stay there and say he wanted to talk—he was waiting for me at the station bar. I went there, took one look and walked out. He was worse than a *clochard*—snoring on a table with broken glasses at his feet. Two days afterwards I read in the *Sur* he'd been murdered."

"So you didn't even speak to him?"

"Speak to him—?"

Faure spat contemptuously at the ground.

"I probably wouldn't have spoken to him even if he'd been sober. It's changing now, the truth's coming out at last. But even three years ago? *Merde!* It was like it was since the end of the war. Everyone wanted to talk about the resistance, to write books, to show their medals, to boast about what they'd done. You'd think every Frenchman had taken part, but you know what it was really like—?"

He glanced at Owen, ferocious, challenging, an aggressive little gamecock with the Gitane still drooping behind his ear.

"Just a handful of us—workers—fighting fascism. That was all. For every hundred people who used to say they'd fought with the maquis, ninety-nine were lying. And if they were the bourgeoisie, they were all lying. Collaborate to protect their precious capitalist system, that's what they did. Now at least they're learning to keep their traps shut."

Owen nodded. Even if Faure saw it in exclusively doctrinaire terms, what he said went a long way to explaining the evasion and hostility Owen had met over the past few days. Now that the records were being released and the reality of what had happened during the occupation started to be documented, there must be many who wished they'd held their silence—and even more with good cause not to talk.

"Do any of these mean anything to you?"

They'd returned to the garage and Owen was back on the subject of the line. He recited the remaining four names from the card index.

"The first two—" Faure shook his head. "But Bienaimé and Jo-Jo, they're the same. You mean Joseph Bienaimé, don't you? He called himself Jo-Jo sometimes. Yes, I knew him—who didn't around here?"

As Faure explained, Owen guessed how the names had

become separated. Drawing on many sources as he built up the list—some at two or three removes and often reaching him by word of mouth alone—the agent Jarvis had probably assumed they referred to different people. In fact they belonged to the same person, and Bienaimé wasn't an alias—as Owen himself had thought—it was the man's surname.

However it came to be split, Jarvis was right on the only point that mattered: Joseph Bienaimé had been a traitor.

"He was a *concessionaire*," Faure said, "a rich man who held many agencies. At the start we thought he was useful to us. He'd made friends with the area commandant, the commandant had licensed his salesmen to continue traveling and we used them as couriers. Then we found out Gestapo headquarters at Lille had a copy of everything we sent twenty-four hours after it went out. So we went and we reasoned with him, like we did with the Arabs, except with Bienaimé we were firmer—"

He paused but he didn't need to finish. Owen remembered what the blind old man in Paris had done to the other traitor, Soldat. It had almost certainly been merciful compared to the vengeance Faure had taken as he "reasoned" with Bienaimé.

"But the line went on running afterwards?"

Faure nodded. "We worked on a cell structure. Every part of the Nevers network was separate from the others. The Orion transfers were just one link. Nothing about it had gone through Bienaimé's salesmen, the line was clean, it continued as before."

"Right up to the end?"

"Yes—"

Faure stopped and frowned. Then he finally took the cigarette from behind his ear, straightened it, struck another match and propped himself against the van—blowing smoke up into the cobwebbed shadows.

"Well, almost. Before we learned about Bienaimé, we had a hundred percent record in getting Marie's pilots through. It was the same after except for once. A pair of them as usual. They were dropped down the chute, we disguised them as Arabs under the market, then the next Sunday we pushed them off on the bicycles. I went with them as the guide that day—"

The small stubborn face, suntanned and hollow cheeked, creased as he thought back.

"We rode fifty meters apart in the column. Me first, then one of the pilots, then the other. Halfway between here and the plant the boches had set up a checkpoint—the only time it happened. They let me through and they let the second pilot through. But the one between us they picked up. He wasn't the only one; for once they'd got an Arab translator and they took out a dozen others too. Who knows—?"

Faure shrugged again.

"Bad luck, I'd guess. It was almost at the end of the war, the maquis was really strong then and to hit back they'd got a new system of making random checks all over France. That time they hit lucky. The one they got, he'd flown pathfinder for your raids over Dresden. You'd given him —what do you call it—you know, the big medal—?"

"The Victoria Cross?" Owen suggested.

"Right." Faure tapped the Gitane against the van's open hood. "They found out who he was, they made a big propaganda in the papers, then they sent him back to Colditz—the prison camp he'd escaped from. That was later of course. The day they stopped us, I went on with the other pilot, made the transfer, then I came back to Nevers. We did maybe a couple more runs over the next month and *fini!* It was summer, 1944. The boches smashed everything they could lay their hands on, like they meant to smash Paris. Marie's line? Well, they stamped on that too. But that was just spite, a *truc*—they'd had the Americans in Normandy to think about then."

"And you?"

Owen was standing in the garage doorway. He could feel the sun hot on his back and the coolness coming off the oil-smeared stone floor inside.

"They got me as well. Maybe because someone cracked in the line, maybe someone else in another part of the network. *Merde*—everyone was giving everyone away then! *Sauve qui peut,* that's what it became then. But they made a mistake—"

The cigarette drummed quietly against the van's chassis again.

"Would you lock me up with a milk-tooth Gestapo boy, a kid they'd recruited when the roof was falling in?"

Faure was grinning now.

Owen smiled back. "No."

"They did. In a cell with a window over a back alley that ran straight into the city center. And except for a quick check they didn't even search me properly first—not down the sides of my boots where I had a razor that would go through a bull's throat like butter. It took me ten minutes after they shut the door. I hid up for a few weeks, then the Allies reached us—and it was over."

"Not that part?"

Owen gestured at the bust of Lenin on the wall at the back.

"That part's never over." Faure raised his shoulders slightly. "It takes time but we'll go on, we'll get there in the end."

Faure would always go on, Owen thought. Even on his deathbed he'd be battling—not just for life but for the party. A brave, dour, intransigent and, beneath the surface aggression, an immensely likeable little man. But above all honest.

He'd told Owen everything he knew about the Orion line. Nothing was being held back—Owen was certain of that. Yet apart from eliminating two of the names on the cards, it had got him no further forward. Along with all his other maquis activities, Faure had just run the Nevers transfer. He had no idea whether his eventual arrest was a result of that or stemmed from some other part of his network being penetrated.

Even with Baring he'd been no help. Faure had looked at him through the station bar window, seen the sprawled drunken figure and simply walked away. There was nothing more he could contribute now.

Owen thanked him, shook hands and went out. He'd left the Peugeot parked by the market. He got in and drove south through the city into the open countryside beyond. An hour later he passed through Moulins. There was no point in stopping. The safe-house, a fruit farm, had been sold to a property company and the land was covered with neat urban villas. Even the camping site where Baring had died was closed—it wouldn't open until the summer season started in a month's time.

After a further hundred and fifty kilometers Owen began looking for the sign. He saw it within ten minutes: blue lettering, the name St. Julien and an arrow pointing up a side road to the left. Owen took the turning and began to climb upwards.

St. Julien was a small medieval fortress village. There was a single church, a cluster of white houses below the ruined walls of the keep, a maze of winding cobbled streets and two tree-lined squares—earth-brown and deserted in the early afternoon heat. Owen parked the car in the lower square—the streets were too narrow for traffic any higher —and carried his suitcase up to the second one.

St. Julien hadn't been the site of one of the Orion line's safe-houses. Owen had chosen it simply because it had the nearest hotel to the place he'd decided to visit next. According to the map the hamlet of Este—and the de Sourraines chateau which the old Count had called the "headquarters" of the network—was less than twenty kilometers away.

Owen checked into the hotel and returned to the Peugeot.

10

The wrought-iron gates, massive and topped with a gilded coronet, were padlocked. Owen left the car on the verge, went in through a side door and walked towards the house along the half-mile drive through the park.

It was even lovelier than he remembered from the painting in the Count's apartment. Great elms on either side, the leaves sharp, spring green in the sunlight. Below them thick sweet-smelling grass fenced at intervals with white wooden railing. He passed one of the paddocks and a foal followed him, a slender dapple-gray shape stepping like a unicorn through the bowls of sun and shadow before it turned suddenly and galloped away.

Then the graveled courtyard with a fountain at its center, a marble lake surmounted by a leaping dolphin. Behind, through the glittering curtain of water that soared twenty feet into the air, the house itself. Faced with stone that time and weather had made golden, mellow, sleepy. Immense but graceful—an old lion of a house resting securely beneath the trees that cradled it.

Owen walked up the steps and rang the bell. There were rooks cawing overhead and distantly the clatter of hoofs on a cobbled floor.

"Monsieur?"

A maid had appeared, small and young in a black dress with a lace apron and cap.

"Is Mademoiselle de Sourraines at home?"

"*Madame* is out riding at the moment."

Owen paused. The reference to madame had been instant and emphatic. He didn't know whether it meant that the Count's granddaughter was married—or that she was addressed like that as a courtesy, reflecting her status as the chateau's owner.

"Will she be long?"

"I'm not sure, monsieur."

"Perhaps I could wait. I've driven a long way to see her."

The maid inspected him in silence. Then she stepped back.

"This way, monsieur."

The hall was high, dark and hung with eighteenth-century portraits of ladies, gentlemen and hounds.

"I will tell madame as soon as she returns."

She pointed at a slender chair with a faded embroidery seat and went away.

Owen ignored the chair, which looked too fragile to bear his weight, and walked over to one of the windows. The sash was open and lavender was rustling against the sill, filling the room with its scent and the murmur of bees. He leaned back against the frame waiting.

"Claudine!"

It was five minutes later. The door had suddenly opened, a figure—silhouetted against the oblong of light on the floor—had appeared in the entrance, and a voice was calling out. The maid must have expected Hélène de Sourraines to come in through the back. Instead, she'd chosen the front.

Owen straightened up. For a moment she didn't see him. He had a brief impression of gleaming riding boots, white breeches and a bottle-green jacket. Then she turned, peered towards the window and stepped back, startled—an erect imperious figure with a strong face and chestnut wind-blown hair.

"Monsieur?"

Owen came forward as she stood there blinking in the half-light after the brilliance outside.

"I apologize, madame—it is Madame de Sourraines, isn't it?"

She nodded.

"The maid showed me in. I met your grandfather a few weeks ago. I said I'd be passing through St. Julien and he suggested I come to see you."

She hesitated, inspecting him as the maid had done, except with a steady condescending gaze. Visitors to the chateau were obviously rare and not particularly welcome.

Then she said, "Please wait for me in the salon."

She indicated a door on the far side of the hall and disappeared, shouting for Claudine again. Owen walked through.

It was a long raftered room running half the length of

the west wing. Spring flowers, bright and fragrant in Provençal pots, were banked on every side and the waxed boards were crowded with furniture: cabinets, astrolabes, tables, bookcases—all of them dark and polished and worn with centuries of use. Owen picked his way carefully to the fireplace and stood in front of the empty grate; the mantel was a vast oak beam and the family arms were carved in stone above.

"And your name, monsieur?"

Hélène de Sourraines had come in from the hall. She'd taken off her boots but otherwise she was dressed as before. Owen saw that the green riding jacket was velvet and its silver buttons were engraved with the crest on the arms behind him.

"Owen, madame, Gareth Owen."

They shook hands stiffly, formally.

"So you're Welsh, are you?"

She'd switched from French to English, speaking it as flawlessly as her grandfather.

"Yes."

"Well, I wouldn't have known. I congratulate you."

She was tall, almost as tall as he was even without her boots. Her eyes were like her hair—deep chestnut brown—and her face, free of any make-up, was tanned.

"Thank you."

"Please sit down."

They sat facing each other on matching sofas—Hélène de Sourraines leaning back easily, Owen stiff on the edge of a cushion. Deliberately or unconsciously, she made him feel like a traveling salesman being afforded the unusual honor of an interview in the drawing room.

"And how is my grandfather?"

The question was crisp and disinterested. She took a cigarette from a silver box and lit it without offering him one.

"He seemed very well."

To Owen, small talk, even in the surroundings of the Nantynth pub, had always been agonizingly difficult. Here it was almost impossible.

"That's good."

Silence. The traveling salesman's interview was clearly going to be as short as she could make it.

"And you're doing what—you're touring, are you?"

A token gesture of interest, like the mayor's wife at prize-giving, stopping for a few seconds to ask him his hobbies.

"Yes, well more or less, then."

"There's some attractive countryside around here. You've probably got your own maps but if you're staying awhile and want any suggestions, please don't hesitate to telephone. I'm afraid I'm almost always out myself, but do ask for my butler, Etienne. He's a fund of local knowledge."

She looked up, smiled briefly, patronizingly, ground out her cigarette and leaned forward. The most fragmentary of the necessary courtesies had been afforded and the interview was over. Owen, if he had the slightest sensitivity, would take the signal and get up to leave.

Owen did not get up.

"I'd be grateful for your help, madame."

"I've said—"

"I'm not interested in talking to your butler. I'd like to talk to you."

For a moment the interruption and the sharpness in his voice silenced her. Traveling salesmen weren't expected to answer back. She picked up another cigarette and held it unlit in her fingers.

"What do you wish to talk to me about, Mr. Owen?"

"The Orion line."

Another silence, much longer than the one before. Then she lit the cigarette, got to her feet and walked to the window. Standing there, outlined against the sunlight, her body was strong and athletic.

"Do you know how old I was when the Orion line ended, Mr. Owen—?"

Her voice was flat and dispassionate, all emotion held in by a wall of self-control.

"I was exactly eleven months. And however precocious any of us are—for example, you, I'm sure, were a child prodigy in learning French—the fact remains that few of us remember much from that age."

Owen ignored the irony.

"I know that. I also know this house was the operational center of the Orion line in France. I thought it possible that your mother might have left something here. I'm not sure what. Maybe a diary, maybe something she gave one of her servants, I don't know. But something that might help me in my inquiries."

"Your inquiries?" She turned to look at him. "May I ask what you do, Mr. Owen?"

"I work with the Foreign Office."

"The Foreign Office? I do apologize—"

There was the same insulting patronage in the words as she eyed his brown shoes and rumpled fawn suit.

"I thought you were from a newspaper. Please forgive me."

Again Owen ignored her, but she went on before he could say anything.

"Listen to me, Mr. Owen. I do not really care whether

you come from the *News of the World* or the Queen herself. The Orion line ended thirty years ago at the finish of a war that even you—let alone myself—are probably too young to remember. My mother died because of it. I'm told before that happened she was raped repeatedly and tortured slowly for a long time—"

She walked back to the fireplace. The self-control had suddenly dissolved and she was white cheeked, trembling with anger.

"I've lived with that memory and much else ever since. I live with it still. That is my concern and mine alone. For the rest, the past is gone, put away forever. I've not the remotest interest in what you call your 'inquiries'—"

"We believe people are still dying because of the Orion line."

Owen was standing now too. This time it was her turn to ignore him. She'd stopped, feet apart, and was gazing into his face.

"You arrive here uninvited. You use my grandfather to wheedle your way in. Then you start to ask me prurient, salacious, prying questions like a gutter-press hack. Even by their standards your behavior has been despicable—"

There was a woven bellpull by the side of the mantel. She reached out and caught it.

"Will you please leave my house now. The corridor to the servants' entrance is on the right at the end of the hall."

Owen went out.

He could smell the new grass as he walked down the drive. The dappled foal kept pace with him until he reached the iron gates.

11

Owen's anger started the moment he got into the car again. Like Hélène de Sourraines, he'd held it back. Unlike her, when it came it was silent, cold, contained. Her rage had been open and flaring, an outburst of fury expressed in the acid voice and the tense, shaking body. In Owen the only sign was a tremor in his wrists as he gripped the steering wheel.

Only once before in his life had he felt anything like it. He'd been sixteen, playing his third game for Nantynth —the youngest first-team player they'd ever picked and the first time he'd been exposed to deliberate systematic harassment. Word of his prowess must have reached the other side in advance because they'd detailed their flanker to mark him.

Owen could see the man's face still. A greyhound's face, dark and keen and fast, with a five-stone advantage in weight and a decade more in years and experience. He'd rested on the set-pieces, crawled around the blind side and hit Owen almost before the ball came back.

Nine times in the first quarter he'd come through illegally and gotten away with it. The tenth time Owen went cold with rage—as cold as he was now. He accepted the ball, held it a fraction longer than necessary, then he spun it out. By then the man had him by the waist and Owen was on his knees. Owen stretched forward as if to prevent himself falling, stiffened his arm and drove it back.

The point of his elbow caught the man at the center of his forehead. The blow split his skin from his hairline to the bridge of his nose. It also knocked him unconscious. Afterwards, until the Llanelli game, no one had interfered with him again.

Yet at least on that occasion he'd been able to release the surging anger—after the game he was almost sorry for the ferocity of his retaliation. Now there was nothing. Hélène de Sourraines, arrogant and contemptuous, had first received him like a door-to-door hawker of cleaning brushes. Then, deliberately and calculatedly, she'd insulted him. Finally she'd thrown him out—with the explicit instruction that he use the servants' entrance and the implication he'd be tossed through it if he didn't leave of his own accord.

Owen started the Peugeot, turned and headed back for St. Julien.

Even in Baker Street, where most of his contemporaries were on the waiting list for White's or Boodle's and, like Mathieson, wore Brigade of Guards ties, no one had ever spoken to him like that. Owen settled down at the wheel and concentrated fixedly on the road, watching the green hedges—starred with hawthorn blossom—on either side and the fields of rising wheat beyond.

He came to the main highway south, with the sign pointing towards St. Julien, hesitated and suddenly turned left —back in the direction of Nevers.

He'd excised the memory of Hélène de Sourraines, the anger had drained away and he was thinking clearly again —about the Orion line. Baring had arrived in Nevers, tried to see the little mechanic, Faure, and had failed—not least because he'd drunk himself into a stupor while waiting in the station bar. Two evenings later he'd reached the camping site outside Moulins. Some time after midnight he'd been murdered.

Moulins was only fifty kilometers from Nevers—barely an hour's drive as Owen had found out that afternoon. It meant that after missing Faure on the first evening Baring had spent two nights and forty days in Nevers without apparently having attempted to contact him again—if he had tried Faure would certainly have said so.

Owen guessed why Baring hadn't tried—or rather what happened. If he was right, for a completely different reason he could also guess why Baring had been killed.

"Monsieur Faure—"

Driving fast Owen had covered the two hundred kilometers back to Nevers in under three hours. He was only just in time.

Faure was on the street outside the garage. He'd rolled down the metal shutter, padlocked it and was about to walk away. He turned as Owen drew up, called through the car window and got out.

"Yes—"

The voice was as uncompromising as before, but the morning's bond remained and the antagonism had gone.

"I'd be grateful if you could give me a few more minutes—"

Owen stood in front of him under a darkening sky.

"The man who wanted to talk to you, Baring, the one who was murdered. You said you read about it?"

Faure nodded, puzzled, frowning.

"In the *Sur*?"

"Yes—"

Faure paused, still frowning. Then he understood. He threw back his head and laughed.

The *Sur*—and Owen had stressed the name—was published and distributed exclusively in the south. If Faure had seen Baring's death reported there, he'd either been reading an old copy which had somehow filtered up to Nevers—or he'd been a long way south of the city when the news broke.

"It's the *deux chevaux*—"

He jerked his thumb towards the closed garage where the old Citroën van had been resting on chocks when Owen came in that morning.

"No market for them here, people just want the big new 'economy' models. But way down the Rhône it's different. Reconditioned with a good few years left in them, you can still get a price. So that's what I do. Buy them here for scrap, tart them up and take them south myself."

"How long are you away?"

"To deliver and sell one? Depends." Faure shrugged. "Five days maybe—but that's being lucky. Normally I allow a week."

"And that day, the day Baring tried to see you, you had one ready?"

114

"Took it the same night—"

Faure had another Gitane tucked behind his ear. He reached up for it and chewed on the tobacco seeping out of the butt.

"Far as I remember I left after supper, drove to Ville-franche sur Saone and then down to Les Roux. I must have read about him somewhere around there—although they still had the story in the local papers here when I got back here again a few days later."

Owen nodded. He couldn't prove it, of course—there was no need to prove it—but he had been right.

Baring had tried to see Faure again. He might even have made his second attempt that same night, perhaps only just missing Faure as he set off for the south to sell the van. Almost certainly he'd spent the next two days waiting, maybe even as they were now—on the street outside the padlocked doors of the garage. Finally he'd given up and driven on to Moulins.

And Faure, of course, away far down the Rhône valley for the whole week, had known nothing about it. But if Faure didn't, someone else, Owen was certain, did.

"There's just one more point," Owen said. "Back in the occupation, when the line was running, you said there was one occasion when you'd cycled with a pair of pilots as a guide and the Germans picked one of them up. Can you tell me a bit more about exactly what happened?"

"Well—"

Faure broke off, glanced at his watch and thought for a moment.

"It's early enough. I'll show you the spot if you like. It's only a few kilometers outside the town. You can see for yourself."

"That would be better still."

They both got into the Peugeot and Owen drove back through the dusk along the route he'd taken that morning. Ten minutes after the lights of Nevers had disappeared behind them, Faure told him to stop.

"It was right here—"

He'd got out of the car and was standing on the grass's edge. Owen joined him.

If one was going to set up a checkpoint in territory where maquis units were operating, this was the obvious choice. Until then the road had run straight between thick woods. Now it angled sharply to the left, there were high banks on either side and the countryside had abruptly opened out into wide flat fields. No one coming from Nevers could see the block until they rounded the corner. Even then, if they tried to evade it by climbing the banks, they'd find themselves without cover beyond.

"It was like every Sunday," Faure went on. "We were checked out of the square, the Arab work shift and a handful of us with passes, we rode down to here, then we came around the corner—and there they were! A couple of dozen soldiers, a Gestapo captain, his intelligence group, a clerk with the file and the two translators sitting behind a trestle table. They'd even put a white cloth over it. *Merde!* It looked like a bloody picnic—!"

Faure chuckled. It was almost dark now and a soft night wind had risen. A few trucks went past, heading back for the town, and across the fields a homegoing tractor rumbled distantly.

"I was up towards the head of the column. One of the Gestapo intelligence men stopped me. '*Francais ou Marocain,*' he said—the only two words most of them knew round here. 'French,' I said, obviously—I wasn't wearing a djellabah but they had to go through the ritual like parrots. *Mon dieu!* I've known enough idiots in my time, but the Germans, they're unbelievable—"

As he flicked his cigarette into the ditch, Owen remembered the blind old baker in Paris describing them in almost the same words—and with identical contempt.

"They pushed me over to the French translator. He asked where I was going. I told him—Moulins to visit my uncle's farm. The clerk checked my pass against his file. It was correct, they let me through and that was it."

"And the Arabs—the *Marocains?*"

"Just the same except they went to the Arabic translator —or I guess it was the same. As their questions were in Arabic I don't know what they were asked."

"But you're sure they had to answer too?" Owen insisted.

"The ones being processed while I was at the table, yes. I couldn't understand—but I heard them speaking. The others behind?" Faure lifted his hands. "Who knows? I'd been cleared and I was back on my bike then. I just went on, I couldn't hang around. I found the second pilot after they let him through, I made the transfer, then next morning I cycled back to Nevers."

"Yes—"

Owen stopped. Then he thanked Faure again, they got into the car and he drove back to the town.

Faure lived in a pension a few blocks from the garage. Owen dropped him there, waved goodbye as the stiff little mechanic turned towards the door, and for the third time that day took the southern highway out of Nevers.

He'd been right about what Baring had done during the two days before he died. Now he'd been proved right again —at least to the extent of knowing the reason for his murder. Quite unwittingly Faure had been the cause—Faure and his knowledge of what happened at the German checkpoint.

As far as Faure knew everyone in the convoy had been interrogated by one of the two translators. Faure himself, with a legitimate pass, had been allowed through. One of the pilots had been stopped and arrested. That was inevitable. Asked questions in Arabic, the man would have been helpless to answer. Yet it wasn't the first pilot they'd caught, it was the second. That meant they'd still been making oral checks when his colleague was processed at the table. And they'd let him go on.

Faure hadn't realized and Owen hadn't pointed it out. But to Owen—and to anyone else searching for evidence of a leak in the Orion line—the inference was inescapable. The line, or at least Faure's sector of it, had been penetrated. The Germans knew in advance who was being funneled down it and when. They'd decided to recapture the second pilot because he held the Victoria Cross and he'd escaped from their "escapeproof" prison camp at Colditz. It was probably a matter of Gestapo pride—as Faure said, they'd made a big propaganda issue of the arrest afterwards.

The first man, for reasons of their own, they'd ignored—almost certainly as a smokescreen to cover the fact they knew of the line's existence. For the same purpose they'd taken out the other dozen Moroccans at random. Whatever the reason, for the moment it was irrelevant. All that mattered was what Owen had learned as he stood with Faure at the angle of the road fifteen kilometers outside Nevers.

Someone had betrayed the Orion line. To that person Faure was still a walking time bomb. So dangerous because of what he knew that even the possibility of his being questioned—as Baring had tried to do—was reason enough to kill.

It was nine o'clock when Owen left Nevers and just before midnight as he turned into the lower of St. Julien's two squares. He parked the car and got out. On the level earth beneath the trees old men were playing *boules* in the glow of the floodlights reflected from the church tower. He heard the click of metal balls, laughter and a wheezing curse: he smelled cigarette smoke and the scent of magnolia: he saw a puff of dust coiling over the low wall, a hunched shadow moving with painful slowness across the ground, a constellation of moths revolving beneath the leaves.

He also saw the man sitting on the bench.

"Right, this bird as isn't wearing no skirt nor knickers nor nothing. Spot her quick as flashing, wouldn't you all, then, even old nancy-boy at the back—"

Eighteen years before. A bleak January day in the drafty hall of the Wiltshire house. Five of them in the high-backed chairs with the slide flickering and the instructor's voice—a chirpy nasal Cockney—salivating over the mildly pornographic image he'd imposed on the scene. A naked girl on a bustling London street.

"Only this one—"

A tap of the pointing stick, a blur and the slide had changed. The same street, the same midmorning bustle, the same girl—except she was dressed now.

"Looks tight as a nun's cunt, doesn't she, chastity belt and all? Only she's not wearing bleeding knickers neither, and it's the first pint tonight for the one as can tell me why."

The scrape of five chairs as they leaned forward intently, concentrating, studying, thinking.

"*Jesus—!*"

The same voice, exasperated and contemptuous now after the silence.

"*You lot, you wouldn't need two hands to get it in, let alone one—you'd need the bloody monkey god's arms. Look at where she's standing now!*"

In the first frame the girl had been on the edge of the pavement in the sunlight. In the second she'd demurely drawn back under the shadow of a shop awning.

Girls who wore no knickers didn't silhouette themselves against the light. Men who read newspapers didn't read them in darkness—least of all when there were lamps on either side.

Owen locked the car door, turned, strolled around to the offside wheel and bent down to examine the tread on the tire. The man was about forty-five, burly, bald-headed, wearing an open-necked shirt, gray trousers and rope-soled shoes. He'd glanced up uninterestedly as Owen got out, then returned to his copy of *France-Soir*. Owen unscrewed the valve cap, licked his finger and put it against the metal nozzle. Then he listened—head cocked on one side—for the whistle of escaping air.

He saw the second one instantly. Much younger, in his late twenties, possibly Algerian, with oiled black hair and a thin mustache. He was about fifteen yards beyond the bench, leaning over the parapet around the square with his chin cupped in his hands as he watched the game of *boules* inside. The third was more difficult. (There had to be a third, there always was. Two for muscle and one, the control, to monitor and direct, as the bald-headed man would do—from where he was sitting he could scan all the alleys that led up to the hotel.)

Owen had to move around and check the nearside back tire before he located him. He was younger still, a big heavily built teenager in a farmer's donkey-jacket, examining the racks of newspapers in the *tabac* stall opposite the car—its roof had hidden him from where Owen crouched down first. From there, watching the reflections in the glass, he'd be able to see—and take instructions from—the man on the bench.

Owen replaced the second valve cap, walked around to the front of the car, prodded the other two tires speculatively with his foot, then stood for a moment thinking.

Three of them. Not surveillance but a strike—for surveillance two, working a box pattern, would have been more than enough in that tiny village. So, as he'd guessed, they wanted to cut him. That meant hitting somewhere along the hundred meters of winding alley between the square and the hotel.

"Never matters what story we tell so long as we all tell the same story—"

The same caustic voice in the same wind-riddled hall.

"Which, being interpreted for the benefit of such gits as haven't had the privilege of collecting Her Majesty's shilling, means like the prophet said: 'Take them on together and they'll sod you—split them and you've got a chance.' So if it's them doing the arguing, don't let them argue at the same fucking time!"

Owen kicked one of the front tires again. The youngest of the three, the raw-boned youth in the donkey-jacket, would be the easiest to separate first.

He strolled across the square and stopped in front of the

tabac window. There was a cigarette-vending machine on the left. Owen dug into his pocket, found a five-franc coin and pushed it into the slot marked "Camel." The man was older—and larger—than Owen had thought. A great sullen-faced peasant with massive hands that fumbled indecisively through the chained racks of paperback books as Owen stood beside him.

The pack dropped into the chromium tray, Owen scooped it out and walked away. There were three cobbled alleys leading up to the hotel—all of them, Owen remembered, converging on a passage beside the northern wall of the church that opened into the upper square. He chose the first one. Ripping the cellophane from the pack, he turned casually into the tunnel of darkness, pulled out a cigarette and, stumbling over the curbstone, dropped it.

The man in the donkey-jacket had left the *tabac* stall and was following him a few yards behind. Owen stood up with the cigarette in his mouth and patted his pockets —searching unsuccessfully for a box of matches.

"Excuse me, have you got a light, monsieur?"

The man had had no choice but to keep walking and he was level with him as Owen spoke.

"Oui—"

He produced a Zipp-lighter from his pocket and snapped on the flames. Owen leaned over it, inhaled, blew out a cloud of smoke and smiled his thanks.

"You ever got it by sitting on your arse and waiting? You must be jokin—!"

Even eighteen years later the voice was unforgettable. The voice—and the instructions it rasped out.

"Turn it around, take the initiative, go out to her—or him as the case may be. Make him give you a light. Guar-

*antee a poke it won't, begging nancy-boy's pardon, that is.
But two things it will. First, you'll discover which hand
he favors. Second, if he isn't a pro, he'll put it back in his
pocket—"*

This one was right-handed, he wasn't a pro and he put
his hand back in his pocket after he'd lit Owen's cigarette.

Owen rocked forward, grasped the jacket lapels and
jolted his knee into the man's groin. His body jackknifed
down and his mouth opened to scream. Before any sound
could come out, Owen dipped his head and butted him in
the face. Then as he started to crumple, he let go of one
of the lapels, swiveled on his hip and smashed his elbow
into the man's neck. Finally Owen swung him, limp and
sagging now, and drove his head against the stone wall.

Then he stood up. He was breathing quickly and a warm
smear of blood was trickling down his face—he must have
broken the man's nose as he butted him. That was all.
From the square, hidden by the corner of the street, the
click of the *boules* was still echoing up the alley. There
was no other sound.

Owen hesitated for an instant. It was guesswork now.
There were three alleys—and there'd been three men. The
alleys met at the church and there weren't any lights in the
lane beyond. That was where they'd planned to take him,
pushing him up like a rabbit through a warren. This one,
the one behind in the gutter, was meant to block the exit; if
he'd taken a different alley, one of the other two would have
done the same. So both of them would be ahead of him
now, waiting.

Owen turned and walked back to the square. If he moved
quickly he could circle around the perimeter of the village
and reach the hotel from the back before they realized what

had happened. He stepped into the lamplight—and stopped.

He'd guessed correctly about the Moroccan, who'd vanished. But he'd been wrong about the bald-headed man on the bench. He was still there—not even pretending to read now but looking straight at the entrance to the alley. He saw Owen the moment he came through it and he didn't hesitate. He stood up and ran for the western corner of the square—cutting Owen off both from the Peugeot and the route around the back of the village.

Now there was only the alley again. Owen swiveled and set off up it once more.

He walked fast, keeping to the center of the cobbles, passing the unconscious body of the youth in the donkey-jacket, clearing his mind of everything except what would happen when he reached the church wall. Somewhere beyond it in the darkness the Moroccan would already be waiting. The bald-headed man—every pretence had gone now and his footsteps were echoing behind him—would hold back until he closed on Owen. Then he'd move in too.

Concentrate. Remember. *"Even snot's a weapon if you get it in his eye."* The voice coming back again and again. A weapon. The keys in his pocket. Owen pulled them out, three of them including the trunk key and the spare for the ignition, and spread them between his fingers—the fretted ends protruding from his knuckles like razor blades. Jacket. Take it off and sling it over your shoulders—that way they can't drag it down and imprison your arms. Belt. Check it's firmly buckled with the flap tight in the loop—a man with his trousers around his knees is as immobile as any circus clown.

Calculate the distances. The bald one about thirty yards

back and walking. Almost a standing start. Maybe five seconds from the moment he started to sprint. That was all. Five seconds after the Moroccan hit and then there would be two of them and if they were good that would be enough. And with the Moroccan he'd have five seconds at most.

Owen reached the end of the alley, crossed the tiny courtyard where the others joined it and forced himself to keep walking into the space of total darkness by the church wall beyond. Nothing now except a faint haze in the distance, the lights of the upper square, the smell of urine and an owl calling from the tower above. He'd taken a dozen steps and then the Moroccan came at him—and he'd been wrong again.

Not from the front but the back. He'd let Owen pass, stepped forward and lashed out at him. Owen heard him an instant before he struck—the scuff of a shoe and the quick hiss of breath. He didn't have time to turn but he managed to drop to his knees. Something, a short wooden club, whipped past his head, arced down against his chest and clattered away.

"Salaud—!"

The man's momentum had left him sprawled over Owen's back. As the club rolled across the cobbles his hands probed for Owen's neck and he shouted at his colleague behind them. Owen crouched lower, ducking his head between his knees, curling himself up like a hedgehog. Then he suddenly heaved upwards. The Moroccan, spread-eagled and unbalanced, pitched forward and somersaulted against the wall.

Now. Still kneeling, Owen jerked sideways and jabbed out with the keys—not punching but in a short dragging movement down the Moroccan's face. *"Go for the nose, al-*

ways go for the nose, because the nerve links can temporarily blind the eyes with what we in the medical profession call responsive tears." Owen found the nose, the man screamed, his head twisted convulsively in pain, Owen clawed at him again—two, three and four times—then there was blood seeping between his fingers.

He'd been fast—but not fast enough. As he tried to stand up, the bald-headed one reached them. All Owen could do was kick out, hook his foot around the man's ankle and tug it towards him. He toppled over and all three of them were on the ground—the Moroccan moaning, Owen pinioned, the new one grunting.

"Laisse-moi le faire, Jean."

The bald-headed man broke away and got to his feet. He plucked at his belt, a spring snapped, then there was a sudden, thin gleam against the stonework. A switchblade, long and dagger-shaped. He crouched and came at Owen again, not stabbing but slashing, fast and professionally, to disable him. Owen felt the blade, just missing the knee tendon, bite deep into his thigh, then twice against his rib cage, then into his shoulder.

The man stepped back, balanced himself and came forward again. As he did so Owen's right arm, trapped under the weight of the Moroccan's body, at last came free. The blade flickered, he could see the shoulders above him tilted to strike, then Owen dived forward—his hand going for the man's groin. For an instant he was totally exposed. His fingers touched the cloth and almost slipped off. Then he found what he wanted, locked his fingers and gripped.

The man's testicles. Owen held them tighter than he'd ever held anything. The knife dropped, the man moaned like the Moroccan, doubled over in agony and started to scrabble desperately at Owen's palm. Owen held on, pulling him forward inexorably until he was lying sideways on the cobbles, his back humped and his nails still tearing at Owen's skin.

Then Owen suddenly let go, clasped both his hands together and chopped them down across the man's neck. It was over. The Moroccan was huddled by the wall, a whining bundle with his hands covering his lacerated face, the other one was limp and motionless beside him.

Dizzy and trembling, Owen stood up. Blood was pumping from his thigh and shoulder, his ribs burned from the cuts that had been sliced across them, and his shirt hung around his waist in sodden tatters. He stumbled, steadied himself and focused on the haze of light at the far end of the wall—the upper square. By now it would be deserted and the hotel desk clerk would have gone to bed. He could cross it unnoticed, use the night key to get into the hotel, climb the stairs to his room and set about binding up his wounds.

Stooping, he fumbled in the darkness for his jacket, found it, succeeded in putting it on to hide the blood-stained shirt and set off. He reached the square, leaned against the wall panting, then collected himself again, looked out—and froze.

He'd assumed there were only three. There weren't. There was a fourth—heavyset, wearing a Breton beret, leaning against the war memorial at the square's center, unmistakably covering the hotel entrance.

Owen swayed, drew back into the shadow, turned—and afterwards it became a blurred nightmare. Limping and staggering he got back down the alley to the car, unlocked the door, fell into the driver's seat. There was a map—

dimly he remembered that later because of the blood that kept dropping onto it as he tried to work out his route. Lyon, one hundred kilometers to the east. He'd pass by Este again, take the Mauvergne road, swing left at Grille and arrive at Lyon in two hours.

At Lyon there was a British consul with Baker Street accreditation, a member of Laval's network whose reports occasionally reached Owen at the French desk. He'd be able to take Owen in and get him a doctor without involving the police.

Owen started the car, took the road down to the main highway, crossed it and drove on between the fields of spring wheat he'd passed in daylight that morning. He didn't reach Lyon—he didn't even get as far as the Mauvergne turning. Fifteen kilometers after the crossing he saw a light ahead, a single lantern above some iron gates. Shaking with pain each time his foot pressed down on the accelerator, weak and confused from loss of blood, he decided to check his route once more.

He drew in under the light, groped for the map, spread it out across the steering wheel, leaned forward—and fainted.

12

Lavender and bees and the movement of sunlight like water overhead.

The scent came first, strong and fragrant and circling in eddies as the wind moved the bushes outside. Afterwards the murmur of the insects, constant through the open window. Finally, when he opened his eyes, the ripples of light across the ceiling.

Owen lay very still. He could feel three separate belts of pain; across his leg, his ribs and his shoulder. They ached steadily but distantly—almost as if they were detached from his body. Other places hurt too; a swollen eyelid, part of his jaw, the instep of his left foot, the back of one of his hands—where a small fire seemed to flicker from his wrist to the tips of his fingers.

None of them mattered against the smells, the sounds, the warmth.

He turned his head—there was a pillow underneath, soft and white and lavender-scented too. He could see a stretch of waxed oak floor, a cupboard, old and dark with linen-fold paneling, a billowing curtain and, through the window frame, a square of parkland—green and hazy in the sun.

He shifted onto his back again and watched the checkered ceiling.

Later—he didn't know how much later—someone came into the room. The door creaked open, footsteps crossed the floor, there was the rise and fall of someone breathing, then the steps tapped away and the door closed. Owen didn't move.

Later still the door opened once more.

"Are you awake?"

The voice clinical, abrupt, uninterested. Vaguely, he thought he'd heard it before. He concentrated, slowly, carefully, and remembered—Hélène de Sourraines.

"Yes."

His own voice was soft and faint and he had to clear his throat twice before he could answer.

"How are you feeling?"

Owen considered the question for a time. Like the belts of pain across his body it was somehow irrelevant. What mattered was that in speaking he'd found his mouth was dry.

"Can I have a drink?"

A small clatter. Then his head being raised and a glass of water, cold and sweet, against his lips. Somewhere close to him green velvet and the glitter of silver buttons.

His head was put back on the pillow. He rinsed the water around his mouth and wondered about the crest on the buttons—a heart with a row of jewels beneath.

"How are you now?"

He must have gone back to sleep. It was much later this time, almost dusk. The bees had stopped but the lavender was still thick in the air, there were grains of dust hanging golden in the last of the light and the turf glistened with evening dew.

"Can I have some more water, please?"

This time he could lift his head himself. Hélène de Sourraines gave him the glass, he drank thirstily, then he propped himself up further so he could see the whole room.

"Where am I?"

"On the ground floor at the front. It's one of what we call the lavender guest rooms."

Lavender, yes. But just *one* of them—with the unstated observation that there were other series of guest rooms too, rose and lilac and magnolia, maybe?

Owen thought of the little flintstone house in Nantynth, with its single cramped parlor and the attic, where he slept beneath the eaves. Then he smiled. It hurt—his jaw was still stiff—but he realized he was better, much better.

"How did I come to be here?"

He could remember the fight in the darkness, the man in the Breton beret outside the hotel, the blood pooling on the map after he'd struggled back to the car. But after that just wavering images of the drive, the lamp above the gates —and then nothing.

"My groom found you—"

She was sitting on the windowsill by the undrawn curtain. Owen could barely see her in the shadow but he sensed the same tension, the same rigidity in the set of her body as before—her face hard and blank as she gazed over the park.

"I ride every morning very early. There's a new colt we keep in the pasture on the other side of the road. Jean-Marc, the groom, was going over to bridle him when he saw your car—he recognized it from the day before. He came back and told me and I got them to bring you in."

Owen nodded. That's what they were called—"them." People. People with children and hopes and fears and beliefs, people who liked wine and looked at sunsets and loved olive trees, horses, laughter and the grain rising after a wet spring. Except if you happened to own the land where they lived—and had owned it forever—they weren't people any longer. They were "them," appurtenances and possessions like the gatehouse or a new combine harvester.

"Why did you get 'them' to collect me?"

"Why—?"

A shrug, her shoulders barely moving against the curtain as the sun died.

"No doubt it will sound quaint, even absurd, to you, Mr. Owen. But to all intents and purposes you were found on my land. That's why."

She'd turned towards him. Owen, raised on one elbow, looked across the floor at her—and suddenly everything came back.

The irony, the patronage, the arrogance in the insults. A wounded stranger on one's doorstep? He was no different from a traveling salesman. You'd afford him the same meticulous perfunctory courtesies—courtesies you'd give an animal. A shotgun-sprayed fox or a man carved up in an alley fight, they'd get the same treatment indiscriminately. And when they were healed—more or less healed, either of them —the duty would be discharged.

You'd smile, accept no thanks and show them the door—the servant's door. And if they didn't go, fox or man, you'd reach for the embroidered bellpull and have them thrown out.

"I want to get out of this bed," Owen said. "Get out and fucking leave."

"I think you should go back to sleep, Mr. Owen; you're very tired."

She stood up, filled his glass of water and left.

Owen tried to knock the glass over as she went out. He couldn't. She was right. He was tired—helplessly, hopelessly tired. The spasm of anger—even as he'd looked at her—had spent itself in the words.

He dropped back on the pillow, the ceiling spun, he shut his eyes and slept.

"Who sewed me up?"

Exploring with his hand, Owen had found groups of stitches over the three main wounds.

"The local vet."

"The *vet?*"

For the first time Hélène de Sourraines laughed. It was the next morning and she was sitting on the windowsill again, still dressed in the green jacket and the white breeches.

"Don't worry. He used to be a doctor, a very good one. Then he decided he liked the country and working with animals better," she paused. "I called him in because I know him well and I trust him."

Owen discovered he could sit upright now. He pushed himself back against the brass bedrail.

"What did you tell him?"

An unconscious foreigner with multiple surface abrasions and a series of deep knife gashes could hardly be explained away as the victim of a road accident—least of all when his car was undamaged.

"For the record I said you'd had an accident with the wheat thresher. In fact it was his own suggestion—the cuts were just about consistent. Anyway, it'll give him something to say if anything comes out and he's asked why he didn't report it."

"And what did you think yourself?"

She shrugged but didn't answer.

"I don't know the law in France but in Britain it could get you into trouble—they can even put people in prison for not telling the police about something like that."

"In France they're not in the habit of putting the de Sourraines in prison."

Owen shook his head. The arrogance, the mind-reeling arrogance. Yet she was probably right. In Britain or France people like the de Sourraines weren't necessarily answerable to the laws of the land—they made and kept their own laws.

"What about my car?"

"I told them to put it in the stables."

"There must have been a lot of blood on the seat."

"There was blood everywhere," she said. "Your jacket's been cleaned but the shirt and trousers had to be burned; they were too stained and torn to be used again. I imagine the car itself has been hosed down. I don't know but it doesn't matter. There won't be any questions—they'll have done exactly what I said."

"They" again. The apparently mindless functionaries who served her and whom she owned like so many cattle. It was extraordinary. Listening to her, Owen felt he might have stepped back nine centuries into an early feudal world. Yet she hadn't lived then. She'd been born at the end of the war. Like Owen himself she'd grown up in an age of hydrogen bombs and men walking on the moon and politicians more corrupt—and more sophisticated in their corruption—than at any time in history.

Unbelievingly he shook his head again and opened his mouth. She *had* to be curious about what had happened, she had to make some response.

"You're probably hungry. I'll tell the maid to bring you something."

She was gone before he could speak.

The "vet"—a bandy-legged unsmiling little man with partridge eyes—came the following day.

As Hélène de Sourraines had said, he seemed capable and experienced. He examined Owen quickly, pronounced himself satisfied with the way the cuts were healing, and left saying he'd be back in another three days to remove the stitches. He didn't ask any questions and his visit must have lasted under five minutes.

In the afternoon Owen went out for the first time. The butler had brought him some clothes and a dressing gown. He dressed and opened a door at the end of his room, limping and feeling the wounds grate under the bandages. The door gave onto a walled garden with a stretch of close-mown lawn running down to a line of peach trees. It was another brilliant day and there was the scent of late blossoms in the air.

Owen moved slowly across the grass. The silence, the stillness, the timelessness were almost tangible. He'd forgotten —if he'd ever known—that places like this existed. In London there was the constant background roar of the traffic. It had been the same in every posting he'd had; the dock sounds in Marseilles, the planes landing at Templehof in Berlin, the street-market clamor of Casablanca and Algiers. Even in the valley there'd been the day and night clatter of the colliery.

Here a horse whinnied occasionally, the chapel bell chimed the hours, once a white dove flew down onto the wall and sat there for a moment cooing in the sunlight. In between there was nothing. As on the evening before, Owen had the sense of a world set apart—only now it was set apart in space as well as time.

After a while he felt tired, went back to bed and slept.

Hélène de Sourraines didn't visit him that day or the next. But in the evening a maid came through with a message. If Owen was well enough *madame* would be pleased to have him join her for dinner—eight o'clock in the salon.

Owen hadn't shaved until then. He did so now with difficulty, his arm still stiff and painful from the shoulder wound as he raised it to his face. Then he dressed and went in—conscious of his half-stubbled cheeks, open-necked shirt and the borrowed trousers flopping around his feet. He was even more conscious of them when he saw Hélène de Sourraines by the fire.

She was wearing a black velvet trouser suit with a white lace jabot at the throat, and she'd put on some jewelry—a heavy diamond bracelet and a diamond brooch pinned casually above it on her sleeve. She turned as he came in, her arm moved and for an instant the stones, flashing in the firelight, almost blinded him.

"Mr. Owen—"

They shook hands formally as they'd done when he'd first arrived at Este. Then she led him through to the dining room —huge and paneled, with a great silver bowl of flowers at the table's center. They ate in almost total silence, three courses with a separate wine for each, served by a butler and a footman.

Owen glanced at her over the coffee, wondering if it was the same every night—this extraordinary silent ritual with the silver gleaming in the candlelight and the shadowy figures moving noiselessly behind the chairs. Her face was expressionless and he looked away bewildered, wincing as a nerve in his shoulder grated when he lifted the cup.

"Would you like a cognac?"

The meal was over, they'd gone back to the salon and Owen was standing awkwardly—trying to decide whether it was time for him to return to his room. On the last occasion the signal to leave had been unmistakable and he'd deliberately ignored it.

Now it was different. Whatever else, she'd taken him in and seen he was looked after. That she'd have done the same, with the same condescension, for a wounded fox found by one of her gamekeepers wasn't important. Owen was still a traveling salesman; he was also briefly a guest— and had a guest's responsibilities.

"Thank you."

After she'd poured it for him she poured a whiskey for herself—almost half a tumbler, with only the smallest splash of soda on top.

"Please—"

Owen took the glass and sat down. She didn't sit. Instead she stood in front of the fire and drank quickly, finishing the glass in less than a minute and pouring another.

Owen sipped at his brandy. Perhaps there was something vulnerable in her after all, something she needed to blur and forget through those huge measures of almost neat alcohol. Or maybe the drink was just another link in the chain-mail armor of arrogance and indifference. He didn't know—and her face was as blank as before.

"You don't like me, do you, Mr. Owen?"

She'd moved and Owen had to turn to see her. She was leaning against the mantel and her chestnut hair was almost scarlet against the flames.

"I owe you a great deal."

"That isn't what I asked."

"Then it's not a fair question. What you've done for me should overrule anything I feel personally—"

"Should—but doesn't!" She laughed. "Even four days ago you'd have walked out of the house if you'd been strong enough."

She stopped and drank again. Owen sat on the edge of the sofa with the brandy glass between his knees. She was right. If he hadn't been too weak to get out of bed, he'd have gone the evening she came to his room. But he'd stayed, accepted her hospitality and now he didn't know what to say.

Then she asked suddenly, "Tell me what happened, please."

Before, when he'd been astonished at her lack of interest in why he'd come to be lying bruised, slashed and unconscious in his car outside her gates, Owen hadn't been sure what he'd have told her. Certainly, after her adament refusal to talk about the Orion line the same morning, not the whole truth—perhaps just that he'd been attacked by a gang of thugs after his wallet.

Now, confronted by the abrupt question and without understanding the reason, he told her everything. The unanswered questions about the murders of Walpole and Baring. The discovery of the white list in the border field. The five code names. Belguim, Paris, Nevers. His two conversations with Faure. His return to St. Julien, the men waiting for him, the fight by the church wall.

"How old was he, the one with the bald head?"

It had taken Owen twenty minutes. She'd listened in silence, he'd finished, now she was into her third whiskey—still rock-steady and her voice as hard as ever.

"Somewhere between forty-five and fifty," he said. "It was difficult to tell because of the lamplight in the square. But certainly not more than fifty."

"So he could have been involved—?"

Owen nodded. If the man was, say, forty-eight he'd have been seventeen in 1944, when the line was rolled up—old enough to be a courier at least.

"But not the other two?"

"Definitely not. The first one, the one in the donkey-jacket, wouldn't even have been born. The Moroccan might have been a few years old—at most—when the war ended. It just leaves the other."

"Except—"

She paused but Owen knew what she was thinking. He'd realized it himself as he'd lain in bed and tried to piece together the significance of what had happened.

The bald-headed man. Even if he had been part of the Orion network, it was inconceivable he could have known

—or done—enough to warrant him organizing that vicious attack thirty years later. As a seventeen-year-old he wouldn't have been given enough responsibility or intelligence to make his collaboration with the Germans anything more than a teenage expression of weakness, fear or greed. And even that assumed he had been a collaborator.

No. Whatever he'd done, behind him there had to be someone else. Older, more important, more powerful—much more powerful. Connected, perhaps, with the bald man in the chain of betrayal all those years ago. But with a reason still, a real reason, to kill if anyone threatened to expose him even now.

"There's an attic upstairs—"

Hélène de Sourraines finished her glass and pushed herself away from the mantel.

"It contains some of my mother's possessions. In the morning, if you like, you can look through it."

She tugged at the bellpull and walked towards the hall door. As before, the signal was unmistakable. This time Owen accepted it. He stood up, limped to the passage that led to his own bedroom, reached the connecting door, stopped and turned around.

"Why now?"

"Why—?"

She was standing at the far end of the salon, her hand on the doorknob too. Outside, the butler's footsteps were echoing on the stone floor.

"Could you not just accept something, Mr. Owen, without constantly asking questions?"

"I can and, if you don't want to say, I will." Owen's voice was quiet but stubborn. "Only, my business is not just answers—but the reasons behind the answers."

"Un moment—"

She called out in French as the handle turned—the butler coming in to switch off the lights and bank the fire. Then, as the man waited beyond the door, she looked back again.

"When I was a child, Mr. Owen, my grandfather insisted among other things that I learn first aid. I went to the local hospital and I was trained by the nurses. So after you were brought in here and Duclos, my 'vet,' came, I helped him while he treated you—"

Owen had been right about the whiskey. There was something vulnerable behind her cold, imperious facade. The voice hadn't changed, she was as erect as before—yet it still came out.

"I saw those cuts on your body. I did not like them. My mother, I imagine, died from much the same sort of wounds—although no doubt there were more of them and they were inflicted with greater care over a longer period of time. I do not like that people can still do those things now. So I've decided that if there's something here which will help you stop them, you are welcome to it. Good night."

The door opened quickly, she had gone and the butler was coming forward.

Owen went back to his room and lay awake in the darkness.

13

"These two here—"

She was standing by a pair of brass-bound trunks near one of the small dormer windows. Owen picked his way carefully across the cluttered floor to join her.

"I had all her books and papers, her small personal things, packed away when I came back. My grandfather had left them just as they were."

"And you returned ten years ago?"

She nodded. "Everything else has been here since God knows when."

She waved around the attic. If the journey down the

Orion line was an exercise in what Mathieson had called "human archaeology," this was like standing in a past that had been frozen in amber.

It was a long, low room, beamed with oak like a ship's timbers, thick with dust and draped in cobwebs. There were little pools of dim light and everywhere, in the half-darkness, the accumulated detritus of generation after generation of the de Sourraines.

Stored portraits, one of a man in seventeenth-century hunting dress, another of a child in a crinoline. Rolls of parchment with faded yellow ink, probably the title deeds to outlying farms. Mounds of books with monogrammed black leather binding. An old rocking horse, chipped, its mane moving slowly in the breeze from the stairwell. A tall cupboard with its door open and the scarlet epaulettes on a military greatcoat glowing inside. Crate after crate after crate, all of them sealed in wax and stamped with the de Sourraines crest.

An entire cross section of the life of a family and a house. And at the end, these two trunks, the leavings of a mother she'd never known.

Owen knelt down and opened the first. Letters on top, six bundles of them tied with pink ribbon and each with a small posy of long-dead lavender stuck under the bow.

He began to untie one but she interrupted him.

"I doubt you'll find them useful. They're from a man called Claude le Vosges when she was eighteen. It came to nothing and he married someone else."

Embarrassed, Owen put the packet aside. Below the letters, photographs, stacks of photographs, some in frames, others in albums, others still loose. Portraits of her mother and her father, the old Count. Groups at house parties, shooting parties, riding parties, yachting parties. Young men in straw hats. Girls in ball gowns or giggling in bathing costumes on a beach. A visual panorama of the life of a young girl in the thirties.

Finally, at the bottom, the contents of her dressing table —silver boxes and brushes and toilet sets. Owen put everything back and closed the lid. There was nothing there to help him.

The second trunk was more interesting. Another layer of letters and photographs first, but below that was a box file. Inside was her passport—the same obdurate, high-cheeked face as her daughter's—and her wartime documentation: driving license issued by the German commandant in Brussels, ration books with the stamps torn out, warrants to cross the Belgian-French border, a *laissez-passer* from the Civilian Adminstration Center in Paris.

Owen held them up to the light and studied them carefully one by one. The dates and stamps fitted what he knew about the pattern of her movements as she set the line up, but there was nothing new. He put them away and tried again. Some folded propaganda posters next, put out by the occupation authorities: *Warning to the local population! Any person found assisting enemy personnel will be executed immediately.* Across one of them, scrawled cheekily and defiantly, the Churchillian two-finger gesture followed by an exclamation mark.

Her private joke, a souvenir to be framed and maybe hung in a cloakroom when the war ended. Except she'd died too soon.

A few paperback books, some little Sèvres porcelain figures wrapped in tissue paper, then, right at the bottom, an expensive leather-bound Michelin road atlas. Owen flipped it open. It was a touring guide to Europe for the days when the rich traveled in convoy. Two chauffeurs and two cars, one for the owner, the other for the servants behind—it even listed hotel prices for staff accommodation.

Owen turned the pages and stopped. He'd come to a section of northern France. Someone had annotated it by hand. In the margin there was the word "Sirius"—the code name of the fifth safe-house on the line.

"Can I take this?"

"Take what you want."

He packed the second trunk and followed her back downstairs.

"Is it any use?"

Owen closed the atlas. It was fifteen minutes later and they were sitting on a bench in a walled rose garden that led off her private drawing room—she'd told the butler to bring morning coffee there and had asked Owen to join her.

"I can't be quite sure, but I'm afraid not."

The maps had been annotated with the code names and locations of all the safe-houses. There were a few other comments about times, distances and routes, and about a dozen references which appeared to have nothing to do with the line—they'd probably been made for motoring trips before the war started.

But there was no mention of " 'Guette" or "Charlot," the last two names on the white list unaccounted for, and nothing else that he didn't know already.

"I'm sorry."

"Thank you for helping anyway."

"What are you going to do now?"

"Go out again, go back to where I left off and continue down the line until I get to the Spanish border."

The "vet" had been back that morning and removed his stitches. Some of the wounds were still raw at the edges, but Owen was ready to move again.

"And you'll leave—?"

"Tomorrow morning early—that is, if I can stay another night."

"Of course—"

She stood up, walked away, removed the dead heads from a rosebush, then she came back.

"I'm sorry I wasn't able to be of more help. I hope you find what you're looking for."

For an instant, before she spoke, Owen felt she'd been on the point of saying something quite different. But she didn't add anything; he thanked her again and went inside.

Hélène de Sourraines was dining out that evening. Owen —daunted by the thought of facing the ritual in the dining room alone—asked instead if he could eat in his room. The footman brought him a tray and by ten-thirty he was in bed with the light out. To test his leg he'd walked in the park for an hour during the afternoon. It had stood up well but the exercise had tired him.

He was at the point of falling asleep when he heard steps in the passage and a knock on the door.

"Yes?"

Owen sat up and switched on the bedside lamp.

"I'm sorry, I hope you weren't asleep—"

It was Hélène de Sourraines' voice. For once the authority had gone and she sounded not so much hesitant as indecisive.

"That doesn't matter. Would you like me to come out?"

"No, not if you're in bed," she paused. "Perhaps I could come in for a moment?"

"Of course—"

Owen pulled the dressing gown around his shoulders as the door opened.

She was wearing the same black velvet suit as the night before but this time with a single pendant ruby hanging from her neck.

"I hope you won't think this strange, Mr. Owen."

"Not at all."

"It's a beautiful night, isn't it?"

"Yes, it is."

Owen watched her, amazed. She'd sat down on her favorite seat—the windowsill overlooking the park—and she was gazing out, smoking a cigarette.

Perhaps this was another prerogative of the very rich, that you could come into a stranger's bedroom at night, settle yourself down and smoke a cigarette with only the barest apology—and no explanation—for what you'd done. Outwardly she was as coldly composed as she'd been ever since he'd first met her, apart from the one occasion when she'd flared with anger after he'd mentioned the line.

Yet, as he'd done that morning, once again Owen sensed something was churning under the icy surface.

"That motoring map you found in the trunk. I was looking at it just now after I came back from dinner—"

She'd turned to face him and she was speaking quickly. Owen had left the atlas in the salon before he went to bed.

"On the last page, the page showing the border country around Perpignan, there's the name 'Diana' in the margin and an arrow to the town of Larras—"

Owen nodded. "That's right. 'Diana' was the code name of the last safe-house before the Spanish border. Larras was where it was."

"Yes, I thought so." Silence as she drew on her cigarette. "Larras was where the Germans arrested my mother, wasn't it?"

"I'm afraid it was."

"And you'll be going there?"

Owen shifted in the bed.

"I'll be going there eventually, as I told you today. First, of course, I'll follow the line south from here—"

"Mr. Owen—" she cut him off—"I would like to come with you."

For a moment Owen was so startled he just sat gazing at her blankly.

"Please," she went on before he could speak. "I've been thinking about it all day. I believe I could help you considerably. Listen to me. However well you speak French, you're still a foreigner here. Also, forgive me, you look a little like a policeman. The French do not like foreigners or *les flics*. I'm not a foreigner and I don't think I look like a policeman, even a French one—"

The smile was forced but briefly it was there.

"You've been trying to talk to people who were involved in the Orion line. You told me last night about this mechanic, Faure, who was prepared to speak. But apart from him, and the old man in Paris, have you had any success—?"

She was right of course—and Owen shook his head acknowledging the fact.

The blind old baker and little Pierre Faure, yes, they'd talked to him. Two honest men who, for different reasons, were proud—and rightfully proud—of what they'd done. Aside from them and the occasional garrulous boasting by someone whose role in the maquis, even if they'd taken part at all, was minimal, all he'd encountered was evasion, forgetfulness, lack of interest.

"I, on the other hand, am Marie de Sourraines' daughter. The daughter of a heroine. De Gaulle insisted that he personally present my mother's posthumous Légion d'Honneur to my grandfather. From Jeanne D'Arc onwards the French have loved their heroines—"

The cigarette stub curved into the darkness and her lighter flickered as she lit another.

"Believe me, Mr. Owen, they will say things to Marie's daughter that they would not say to you in a thousand years. That isn't vanity—that's fact."

She paused and Owen spoke for the first time since she'd announced she wanted to come with him.

"I may not have learned much yet, except that the line was almost certainly penetrated in the Nevers sector and possibly in other places too. But one thing I have proved for sure. Whatever it is they've got to hide, someone who took part is prepared to kill to keep it hidden. They killed Walpole and Baring. They've tried once for me—and they'll try again."

"And I can protect you—"

Until he saw the seriousness in her face, Owen thought she was joking. Then she explained—and he understood.

"To attack an unimportant foreigner, whose employees would disown him anyway, is one thing. But to do the same to a de Sourraines—let alone the heroine's daughter—that would be to assure an outcry, a scandal, the length and breadth of France. If I was with you they'd never dare."

The conviction was absolute, unchallengeable. But once again she was probably right. Owen shrugged helplessly.

"Why, then?"

It was all he could think of to ask. The same question as when she'd told him the night before that he could look through her mother's trunks in the attic.

This solitary embittered intractible woman who, as a child, had so violently resented the past that she'd done everything she could to escape from it. Running away first. Then after her grandfather had given her the chateau, walling herself up there with her horses in a little self-contained feudal world.

What had changed now that after ten years' isolation—during which she'd refused to communicate even with her grandfather—she'd decided to come out? It wasn't because of Owen himself. She'd said she hadn't liked the way he'd been slashed, and he'd believed her. It was a reasonable explanation for showing him the trunks, not for joining him on the journey down the line.

Owen was still the traveling salesman, the wounded fox, who'd been taken care of as her code required—and who would leave as soon as he was fit enough again. Well, his cuts had healed, he was ready to go on, he'd expected to be ushered out with barely concealed relief on her part. Only now there was this sudden inexplicable reversal. Instead of showing him the door, she was insisting on coming with him.

Why?

"This house, as you've no doubt observed, is very old, Mr. Owen. They say in Este, in the village, that it's haunted, that it's full of ghosts—"

She'd stood up and was walking around the room—rearranging the flowers in the bowls on the tables and cabinets.

"Oh, they tell extraordinary stories from the time of the Bastard of Orleans on. I've never seen a ghost here, but I have lived with one all my life—"

She swung around towards him. Hostile and impatient

again, demeaning herself in giving any explanation for what she'd decided to do. The de Sourraines didn't explain; they simply acted. Yet for once someone else, Owen, held the higher hand and she had to answer.

"The ghost of my mother. I'm tired of living with that. Perhaps it's time it was laid—"

Another cigarette curved out into the darkness. Then she went to the door.

"You'll be called at seven. There'll be croissants and coffee in the morning room. Afterwards we'll leave. We'll take one of my cars. Yours is known, mine are more comfortable and I'm used to driving them."

The door closed and she was gone.

Owen waited for five minutes. Then he got out of bed, walked down the passage and went into the salon. The lights had been turned out—the butler must have come in after she'd gone upstairs—but he found the switch by the glow of the fire.

He walked over to the drinks table, chose a bottle of Armagnac and poured a large measure. He took a couple of sips, thought for a moment, then tossed the rest of the glass into the embers. The brandy ignited in a sheet of white flame.

Afterwards he swore and returned to his room.

14

"Where first?"

They were sitting outside the front door, in the car, a magnificent old black Citroën with hand-stitched leather upholstery. Hèléne de Sourraines was at the wheel, Owen beside her with her mother's motoring atlas on his knee.

"La Motte," he said.

She started the engine and drove down the drive. As they reached the park gates the chateau vanished behind them in the morning mist. One moment it was there, tall and graceful through the whiteness with the fountain playing in the forecourt, the next it had gone—disappearing so suddenly that it might almost never have existed.

Owen put the atlas on the shelf under the dashboard and settled back in his seat.

La Motte. He didn't have to refer to the map now—he knew all the code names and sites of the safe-houses on the line by heart. La Motte, the "Great Bear" of the network, was two hundred kilometers to the south. A distribution center for the wines of the Rhône valley; the pilots had been taken there in small farm vans from Faure's transfer point outside Nevers—winding through the lonely country lanes beside the highway. When they reached it they'd been hidden in the storage vaults beneath the warehouses around the main depot.

Then, as soon as a truck was ready to return to the vineyards, they'd been put inside the large hogshead barrels—empty now after the wine had been delivered—and driven further south still. Afterwards there was only the final run to the border.

"What are you going to do in La Motte?"

They'd just turned onto the highway. Apart from asking Owen where to go first, she'd hardly spoken since he'd joined her in the morning room half an hour earlier.

"I want to find the man who hid the pilots in the vaults and arranged for them to be put into the barrels."

"He could be dead, he could have moved away, anything."

"That's possible." Owen nodded. "But even so we should be able to find someone who'll confirm what I'm damn sure about already—that he was still there in 1958. And that's what matters—"

She listened in silence while Owen explained.

Baring, obsessed and resentful, had followed the route of the line systematically down from Paris, just as Owen had done himself. Like Owen he'd learned nothing until he got to Nevers. In fact even there he'd been no further forward, squandering his one chance of talking to Faure by being drunk in the station café when the little mechanic came to see him.

But Baring had still spent almost three days in the town. The night after he left he'd been killed. For someone determined that Baring not meet Faure—and uncertain whether he'd done so the first evening—the possibility alone was reason enough to murder him immediately afterwards. That at least had been Owen's guess as he drove out of Nevers. If he needed any confirmation, it had come only hours later by the church wall in St. Julien.

Owen *had* managed to see Faure. Not just once, but twice. And by midnight he was almost dead himself.

In Walpole's case, sixteen years before, the pattern could have been the same. Unlike Baring and Owen, Walpole hadn't followed the line down from Paris. He'd driven straight across central France, reached the head of the Rhône valley, turned south, spent a night outside La Motte—and the next evening he and his wife had been murdered too.

"So you think only certain points along the line are dangerous? Nevers is one, La Motte may be another—?"

"Nevers I'm certain about," Owen said. "La Motte's a guess. We can test it several ways. First, whether the man who ran the safe-house in the vaults really was there in 1958. Second, whether Walpole spoke to him when he came through—after the police inquiry there are bound to be people who remember that. And third—"

He paused.

"Third, what?"

"If anything happens to us."

She laughed quickly, contemptuously, dismissing the suggestion with the same total confidence she'd expressed the night before. Unimportant foreigners might meet with "accidents." Nothing could happen to a de Sourraines.

Owen shrugged and watched the road, a pale, dusty ribbon uncoiling in front of them in the morning sunlight.

She drove fast and well, handling the powerful car and its stiff gearshift with a strength Owen had expected—but with a gentleness and a hairline accuracy through the many bends he hadn't been prepared for. He'd never seen her ride. But glancing at her from time to time—she never once looked at him—he guessed she was a superb horsewoman.

They reached La Motte at midday, a little noisy bustling town with the hills rising beyond. The main wine depot was on the far side. Some new storage containers—gleaming silver-gray tanks—had been installed recently, but the old warehouses with the vaults beneath were still in use too. As they drew up, a trolley, laden with a chateau-bottled consignment, disappeared through a doorway and a clerk holding a clipboard followed it inside.

"You don't have a name or anything?"

She'd parked the car on the street opposite the gates.

Owen shook his head. "Nothing."

Like the other safe-houses on the line, the "Great Bear" had been listed in the Baker Street files, but not even Faure had been able to tell him who'd operated it.

"Well, I'll see what I can do. No—"

She stopped Owen as he began to open his door.

"I'll go on my own. It'll be easier. Wait for me in the café over there."

She got out and walked across the road towards the gates, an assured purposeful figure in oatmeal trousers and a crisp white silk blouse. Owen watched her for a moment. With her jacket draped over her shoulders and a Gucci handbag swinging casually from her wrist, she might have been setting off for a morning's shopping expedition on Bond Street or the rue de Rivoli.

Then he got out too, went over to the café, sat down at a sidewalk table and ordered a Pernod.

"There were two of them, brothers, David and Jean Betille—"

Owen looked up, startled. She'd been less than half an hour. Prepared for a long wait and reading a copy of yesterday's *France-Soir*, he hadn't even noticed her coming back until a chair scraped and she sat down opposite him.

"They had their own wine collection business and they did everything. Moving the pilots from the vans to the vaults, hiding and feeding them while they were there, putting them in the barrels when they'd got an empty truck going back, driving them down to the vineyards. *S'il vous plait—*"

She raised her hand at a passing waiter and ordered a coffee.

"They were among the first my mother recruited and they handled this part of the line right up to the end."

"And you learned all that in thirty minutes?"

Owen was gazing at her in disbelief. It had taken him as long just to find Faure—let alone the time he'd spent in persuading the mechanic to start talking.

"I think I told you people would speak to me, Mr. Owen. Perhaps surprisingly I can also think for myself—"

Her smile was quick and cool.

"My grandfather used to buy wine for Este privately. He chose the vintages he liked and had the bottles sent direct from the vineyards to the chateau. The Betille brothers collected the wine for him. Had you noticed you'd have seen their name as "*agents transporteurs*" on the label of a bottle we had with dinner two nights ago. It occurred to me they'd be logical people for my mother to approach. They had, if nothing else, a strong commercial allegiance to my family."

Yes, Owen thought, they would have done. It wasn't just the immediate dependents—the servants, grooms, farmers and shepherds—who were in thrall to families like the de Sourraines. It was the suppliers of their goods and services and luxuries too.

"And what else did they tell you, these brothers Betille?"

"They didn't tell me anything—"

Her coffee came as she answered. She pulled out a cigarette and beckoned for the waiter to light it.

"They were rounded up and killed when the Germans uncovered the line in 1944. A cousin inherited the business and he still runs it. He's there now—"

She gestured towards the depot gates.

"I asked the supervisor for the company office, he took me there, introduced me to the cousin and the man told me the whole story. He knew it all—he'd accepted a posthumous Légion d'Honneur on their behalf just like my grandfather did for my mother."

Owen frowned. "How old was this cousin at the end of the war?"

"Just a child. He had nothing to do with the line."

"So even in 1958 there'd have been no one to talk to?"

"No one. And I learned something else. On the way to the office I asked the supervisor if he remembered the murder of the Englishman, Walpole. He said of course, it had been a big story at the time. The police even came to the depot to find out if Walpole had visited it—his hobby was wine apparently. But he hadn't, he never came near the place. He just drove straight through La Motte, and next night he was killed."

She stopped and finished her coffee. Then she sat in silence watching him.

Owen knew what she was thinking—and he was baffled. In half an hour his hypothesis—a hypothesis he'd been convinced was correct—had been totally demolished. The safehouse at La Motte and the brothers who ran it had been destroyed in 1944. There'd been no legacy of the line here for more than thirty years. Walpole hadn't even paid a sentimental visit to the vaults. He'd gone straight through the town and continued his journey.

Yet twelve hours later he was dead. It made no sense at all. The next safe-house was a hundred and fifty kilometers further down the Rhône. Walpole had never reached it—the Garnes gorge, where he died, was halfway along the route. In fact between his arrival in France and his murder he couldn't have had any contact with a survivor of the original network.

"So what do we do now?"

Owen was shaking his head slowly, bewildered. He stopped and shrugged. For the moment he had no idea.

"We'll go on, I suppose. Then—"

"Well, whatever we do—" she cut him off—"we'll eat first. *Garçon—!*"

She snapped her fingers and called for the waiter again.

They had lunch in the café. Then they set off once more, following the road through the chalky-white fields of the plain beyond the town and later up into the hills.

At four they reached the Garnes gorge. They were three

thousand meters up then, the air was much cooler and in the distance they could see snow drifts on the peaks of the *Massif Central*. Before he left London Owen had bought a large-scale map of the area and marked the site of the glade where the murders had taken place. As they approached it he asked Hélène de Sourraines to slow down. She reduced speed without comment—like the morning she'd driven in silence.

"Here—"

She pulled into the side of the road and stopped. Owen walked across the grass while she stood beside the car.

It was exactly as the journalist, Blair, had described it. The spring grass, bushes of pale-rose mountain *Cistus*, a stream flowing under the road and tumbling, foamy and peat-brown, into the valley beneath, scattered rocks at the back and finally, curving around the rising hillside, a belt of trees.

Peaceful, silent, deserted, fragrant—there was wild mint by the stream and the scent rose as his feet crushed the leaves. Unchanged since that night seventeen years earlier except that then a trailer had been parked on the grass, someone had been hidden in the trees while Lady Walpole cooked dinner and later, in the starlight after dark, the grass had been trampled, scarred and stained with blood.

Owen paused in the center of the glade, closed his eyes and listened.

"I want to go back towards La Motte."

He'd returned to the car. She'd been watching him, almost amused as he stood, eyes closed, among the flowers. Now she nodded tolerantly, got in, turned the Citroën and drove back down the mountain road.

This time Owen didn't sit looking out ahead. Instead he

swung around, settled his arms over his seat and scanned the trees on either side behind.

It was a new Simca, the Gran Turismo model—ice-blue and shaped like a barracuda. He glimpsed it in a copse four hundred meters below the glade, a predatory metallic silhouette in the tree shadows. They were traveling too fast and the shadows were too deep for him to see how many there were inside. One, certainly, apart from the driver— the sunlight flashed on dark glasses in the passenger seat behind the windshield. Possibly others in the back. He didn't know. They'd rounded a corner, the copse had vanished and the road was empty in front of them.

He'd been almost sure they were there on the way up, several times catching the sound of gears changing at a steady distance behind them. Then in the glade he'd been certain; he'd listened for—and heard—the car stop, the engine reverse and silence as the driver cut the motor. Owen watched for another ten minutes. They'd be on the road again, but as before they were staying out of sight behind the bends.

As he turned towards the front Hélène de Sourraines asked, "All the way back to La Motte?"

"No. Do you remember Varençon?"

She nodded. Varençon, an attractive little village perched up in the hills above the plain, was the only place they'd passed through since leaving La Motte.

"Just as far as there. I'll show you where."

She didn't ask why and Owen would have found it difficult to explain if she had. Now it was pure guesswork—but there had to be an explanation and the image had stuck stubbornly in his mind.

"In there—"

He pointed, she swung off the road through a pair of

gates and they both got out. Owen waited, listening for the Simca but he heard nothing. They'd be able to track the Citroën by the sound of its heavy engine and they must have stopped out of sight again.

"It's extraordinarily like the glade—" She was looking around.

Owen glanced at her and said, "Yes."

It was another municipal camping ground just outside the village. He'd noticed it briefly as they passed on the way up. What had come back to him later—and what struck her now—was its resemblance to the little plateau in the gorge where Walpole had finally stopped for the night. There was the same belt of trees, the same rocks, the same bright, thick turf, the same stream running through the center.

The only difference was a warden's lodge on the left and a row of wooden service cabins beyond.

"And you're wondering why he didn't stop here instead—?"

They were walking towards the lodge. Owen nodded.

"He was getting on, he liked his creature comforts—they have hot showers and so on in these places. And they'd used proper camping sites for all their other stops. The first thing to do is find out if it was open in 1958—if it's even open now."

Unlike the site at Moulins this one had already opened for the summer. It had also been open in 1958. And Owen discovered why Walpole hadn't spent that night there.

"Some *gosse* started it, that's what I always believed, some silly spoiled little kid playing with matches—"

The warden grunted, leaned across the counter and rested his chin in his hand.

He was old and leathery and he only had one arm—the

other had been chopped off in a logging accident as a youth. It had happened just after the war. He'd had the job at the camping ground ever since and he'd been there on the May morning seventeen years before when Walpole drove his trailer through the gates and signed himself in.

Owen had learned all of that in the first few minutes after he opened the door. He'd introduced himself as Walpole's nephew and said he wanted to retrace his uncle's movements in the week before he died. The old warden, garrulous and bored—the site was still empty and he had nothing to do—had been delighted to help. He'd even insisted on finding the register and showing Owen Walpole's signature —with the date and time of his arrival alongside it.

Walpole drove in at 10:30 A.M. He parked the trailer, booked himself and his wife in for the night, and filled out his tourist registration card. Then he'd set off on foot for the village.

Now Owen was being told what had happened at the site between then and Walpole's return at six that evening.

"Late afternoon when it began. Right here when I first smelled the smoke, I was—"

He tapped the truncated arm against the wooden flap.

"I ran outside, but what could I do? They were solid timber, weren't they, just like the new ones we put up afterwards. Except now they've got a fire-resistant coating on top. But that lot, they had nothing. I ran back, called the *pompiers*, then I tried with the foam extinguishers. Hopeless! *Mon dieu*, it was like Bastille day—!"

While Walpole and his wife were away from the site, someone—a careless child if the warden was right—had set fire to the original complex of service buildings. They'd been gutted and burned to the ground within minutes.

Under French law the site had to be declared closed and everyone evacuated immediately. It couldn't be opened again until the services had been restored.

"Stupid, you could say." The warden shrugged. "The fire hadn't touched any of the trailers or the tents. But that's the way it is—and I had to tell them all to go. They got their money refunded, of course. Your Monsieur Walpole was the last back. I explained to him, he understood and he took his trailer out. Then up in the Garnes that night he and his wife were killed, *les pauvres.*"

He drummed a cigarette out of a pack on the counter, flicked a match against his thumbnail and lit it.

"You don't know where they spent the day," Owen said.

He shook his head. "In the village maybe. I don't know. When he returned the *pompiers* were here, the huts were still smoldering, there was water everywhere and the telephone going—it was impossible! I just said what had happened, the regulations and he left."

"Thank you, monsieur, thank you very much."

"Pas de tout."

Owen had put a ten-franc note on the counter and the old man was smiling contentedly as they went out. He'd probably have smiled anyway—there were obviously few people to talk to at the Varençon camping ground in the late spring.

"And now?"

They were back in the Citroën. Owen thought for a moment.

"We'll spend the night in the village. Tomorrow we'll try to find out just what Walpole did while he was there."

She started the car without comment and drove back onto the road.

Beside her Owen was only partly wondering what the genial wine-loving former Baker Street director might have done in the hours he'd been away from the site on the last day of his last holiday.

More immediately he was thinking about the ice-blue Simca somewhere in the dusk behind them.

15

As at St. Julien, there was only one hotel, and it too was on the main square.

By the time they checked in it was almost dark. Hélène de Sourraines, predictably, asked for the best suite while Owen took a single room on the same floor. After she'd gone upstairs he went out and walked slowly around the square. The inevitable game of *boules* was being played at its center, a gang of youths were gathered around some rainbow-painted motor scooters, a few couples strolled hand in hand under the trees, and the plate-glass windows of the late-opening shops spilled light over the cobbles.

There was no sign of the Simca, or of anyone else watching the hotel entrance.

Owen went in again, showered and, half an hour later, joined her in the dining room. She ordered promptly for both of them without bothering to consult him. Owen said nothing. The food was simple and excellent and they ate in silence as they'd done in the chateau.

Then, when coffee came, she suddenly looked at him across the table.

"How did you get those other scars?"

Owen frowned. "What do you mean?"

"That morning when they brought you into the house and I called Duclos, I saw them. The tissue on the knee and the hip. Duclos said the hip had been badly broken and someone had done an excellent job in mending it."

"I used to play rugby. One day I was tackled. I fell the wrong way and the ligaments went. That was the knee." He shrugged. "It happens to a lot of players. The hip—"

Owen stopped. Mathieson knew about the hip, Mathieson, Sayd Rifai and the American surgeon. No one else, not even Meg.

Yet now he told her too. He didn't know why any more than he knew why he'd told her the whole story about the mission after dinner two evenings before. Perhaps because the truth was the only possible response to her own bluntness, the disconcerting candor that was as much part of her as the arrogance.

He wasn't sure. He just remembered the way it had happened and he described it simply and directly.

Algiers. His source had been a procurements official in the Bureau de Défense, a weak, handsome man who'd

166

eventually found the cost of supporting both his wife and the two mistresses his vanity required more than his salary could stand. A Moroccan intermediary on a Baker Street retainer had steered him to Owen, he'd reached for the quarterly *"supplément"* like a drowning man for a lifebelt and they'd met every month in a *hôtel de passage* just outside the city.

Owen used to book a room for the night and arrive with a girl, one of the security-cleared secretaries from the military attaché's office in the embassy. The Algerian would do the same—although his companions, Owen guessed, also gave the service they were paid for. Owen would have sent him his room number in advance on a postcard and after a time there'd be a knock at the door. The man would come in—he'd have told his companion he was taking a bath—and give Owen the minutes of the Bureau's monthly meetings.

Owen gutted them fast, reading out the relevant parts to the secretary who'd take them down in shorthand. Then the Algerian would return, collect the papers and take them back to his own room. Owen and the secretary used to leave an hour later.

That particular night the Algerian didn't hand over the monthly minutes. Instead, he said, he had something more important. He'd brought with him someone else—his counterpart at the Home Ministry who was interested in the same arrangement. The man was waiting in his room but he'd only meet Owen alone. Owen agreed. The stipulation was reasonable enough; in any covert intelligence transaction a one-on-one relationship was axiomatic until trust had been established.

He sent the girl back to the embassy and waited. The

knock came again, Owen opened the door and there were five of them—coming through in a fast, silent wedge. He dropped the first, kicking instinctively at his groin, and he almost got the second with a stiff-arm jab to the throat. The man went down to his knees but the other three were too much. Owen didn't really know what happened because he was unconscious within seconds. But they worked him over systematically and viciously—apart from his hip five ribs and his jaw had been broken.

It was obviously meant to be a lesson—or they'd have used knives. But they did the job so thoroughly, the surgeon said afterwards that if Owen had been left there a few more hours the internal hemorrhaging would have killed him. It was solely due to Rifai, who'd checked when he missed the fall-back, that he was still alive.

"So when you said you worked with the Foreign Office, you really meant you were some kind of a *barbouze?*"

She was watching him with a polite, detached interest, like a specimen on a microscopic slide. A *barbouze*. One of the "bearded ones," the mindless criminal thugs De Gaulle had hired to fight the fascist underground army of the OAS.

Instantly Owen was furious with himself for having told her about Algiers. Until then there'd been a truce between them, fragile but enough to make her presence tolerable. Now she'd shattered it. Not deliberately—simply because it would never have occurred to her that he, any more than a young stable boy entered on a census form as "servant," might have resented the description.

Somehow her dispassionate curiosity angered him more than the open contempt when she'd first thrown him out of the chateau.

"Yes, I suppose you could call me a *barbouze*—except I

happen to shave." Owen smiled but his voice was flat. "Just like your mother, because she was a *barbouze* too. Only she didn't have to shave. Or did she?"

"I came with you to help. Not to hear crude, filthy insults—"

Her face was chalk white and she was pushing back her chair to get up. Owen rose first, swiveling on his seat, standing and backing away from the table into the shadow of an arch in a single fast movement.

"Stay where you are—"

No one at the surrounding tables had noticed him, but the urgency in his voice halted her. He stood quite still in the shadow and looked again.

To his right, on the far wall, was a mirror, an ancient Coca-Cola promotional giveaway, chipped and lettered in blurred gold with the lacquered silhouette of a girl curving around the rim. It was angled towards the street—Owen had deliberately chosen a chair where he could see it. Until then there had only been the lights and the trees and the occasional flicker of people passing.

Now there was an ice-blue metallic reflection at one side.

Owen walked around the edge of the dining room and into the hall. The official *Bureau de renseignements* board was in an alcove by the entrance. Above it was another mirror, new, clear, brilliant in the light of the chandelier. Owen stopped with his back to the square and studied Varençon's coming attractions.

The Simca was parked just up the street. It was the same as before—the Marseilles registration letters and the first two digits, after he'd converted the reverse image, matched those he'd glimpsed as they'd driven past the car in the tree shadows. He still couldn't see how many there were inside, but he recognized a silhouette in a black Breton beret smoking by a foutain. There was another, too, who would have been part of the team, a dark-skinned man in a sailor's vest pacing slowly under the trees.

Four of them almost certainly and probably another at the back of the hotel.

Owen returned to the dining room, slid back into his chair and pulled it up to the table. Hélène de Sourraines was frowning slightly but still implacably hostile.

"Your suite, how many rooms does it have?"

He was smiling as if they were having an ordinary after-dinner conversation.

"What do you mean?"

"We were followed out of La Motte this morning by a blue Simca with at least two men in it. It stayed behind us up to the gorge, turned when we turned, then followed us back to the village. The car's just arrived outside the hotel. I guess there are at least four men with it. One of them was in the group that attacked me in St. Julien. No—"

Instinctively she'd started to look around towards the window.

"Stay as you are. If they're watching I don't want them to know we've seen them. Just tell me how many rooms are in your suite."

"What on earth has that got to do with it?"

"Just tell me, please."

She shrugged. "If it's the slightest concern of yours, it has two. They're linked—a bedroom and a sitting room with sliding doors between."

"Fine—"

Owen poured himself another glass of wine.

"Well now, you've got three alternatives. Either I sleep in your sitting room. Or if that's too close for comfort, we'll change our rooms. We'll find two-singles with a communicating door and leave that open—"

"If you think I'm having a—"

"A *barbouze* sleeping with you? Of course not, I'm sorry I even suggested it. Because, as I said, there's a third possibility. You go straight back to Este and I go on alone. Take your pick."

She said nothing for a moment. Then she smiled icily.

"How very gallant of you, Mr. Owen."

He shook his head. "It's not gallantry. You asked to come because you wanted to learn about your mother. I agreed because I thought you could help me with what I'm after. You're what we call a 'high-grade' contact. And I don't want to lose my contact, do I, then?"

Her glass was still full and she looked as if she was about to throw it at his face. Then she suddenly stood up and walked out. Owen called for the bill, signed it and followed her.

"Yes?"

He'd gone upstairs and knocked on the door of her suite.

"It's me."

"Would you kindly wait until I'm in bed."

The same chilling, furious voice. Owen grinned and walked to the end of the corridor. A single small window above a well-lit side street. He tested the sash; it was welded to the frame with layers of paint and wouldn't move. If they came during the night they'd have to use the front door and the staircase.

He went back towards the stairwell and found what he was looking for: a heavy brass fire bucket full of sand. Rolling back the corridor carpet, he tipped the sand onto the floorboards, scuffed it flat with his foot, then replaced the carpet. Afterwards he lifted a picture from the wall—a framed print of Varençon at sunset, with the plain below—and unraveled the hanging wire from the back.

"You can come in now."

He'd returned to the suite with the empty bucket and the wire and knocked again.

Owen opened the door. A single light was burning in the sitting room, the bedroom through the arch was in darkness. With the door still open he lashed the bucket to the outside handle, winding the wire in knots that would need light, time and noise to untangle.

"What are you doing?"

She'd heard the bucket clanging when he shut the door, and the sheets rustled as she sat up in bed.

"Just making sure that if we get any visitors, we're ready to receive them."

Owen turned the handle to test it. On the other side the bucket boomed and clattered like a ship's bell. Then he pulled two armchairs together, settled back in them and crossed his arms behind his head.

"There's a perfectly good lock on the door, isn't there?"

She'd come out of the bedroom and was standing in the arch looking down at him. Owen glanced up. It was the first time he'd seen her in anything but a pants suit. She was wearing a long silk dressing gown and her hair was loose on her shoulders.

"That's right."

"Well, what's all this idiotic nonsense with the bucket?"

"The lock's an old Yale tumble-spring model. That means you can't leave the key at an angle. And if you can't leave the key at an angle, someone can push it through with another one from the other side. There just happen to be two other keys in the hotel; a passkey for the management and a third for the maid. So if someone really wanted to get in and got one of those—"

"It's melodrama!"

She shook her head, almost amused again. Owen swung his legs off the chairs and sat upright.

"Tell me something," he said. "When did you last leave Este?"

"I go out constantly—"

"That's not what I meant. Not for dinners and your social engagements and so on. But when were you last really away?"

She didn't answer—and Owen knew why. Hélène de Sourraines had moved back into the chateau ten years before. Since then she probably hadn't spent even a single night outside it.

"Well, let me tell you something then," he went on. "You asked tonight how my hip had been broken. I told you what happened, but not the reason for it. The reason was because for once in my life I wasn't 'melodramatic'—I didn't think and I wasn't ready. Because of that I almost got myself killed. Never again. Outside Este there are places where people like me work. No servants, no grooms, no butlers, no precious little castle to keep you safe. Just streets and alleys and open ground you cross in the dark without knowing whether someone's there waiting for you with a knife—"

He reached into his pocket, found a cigarette and lit it.

"You've come out to where those places are. Fine. That's your decision. But while you're out here, you'll work the way I do. And if that includes fire buckets tied to door handles, then believe me, you'll start loving fire buckets tied to door handles."

She waited for a moment without speaking. Then she

turned and Owen heard the bedsprings creak as she lay down.

He lay back again himself, cramped on the two chairs, and finished his cigarette. There were weeks on end when he didn't smoke, but he always carried a pack with him. It was a legacy of the training, the conditioning.

"Like your honorable Lord Baden-Whatever said to his bleeding scouts—be prepared!" The nasal voice coming back time after time. *"Into French letters, he was. I'm talking about fags. Take them everywhere. They can open a conversation, buy you a moment to think and very nasty they are, too, if stuffed hot end forwards into someone's boatrace."*

Owen wasn't smoking now for any of those reasons. He was using it to help him concentrate. Somewhere in Varençon seventeen years ago Walpole had found a man and talked to him. In the morning Owen would also have to find that man and persuade him to talk. To have a chance of doing that the bucket outside the door would have to stay silent all night.

He closed his eyes and slept lightly.

No one came to the suite during the night. In the morning Owen didn't even have to look for the man. The man found them.

Owen woke at dawn. He carefully unlocked the door and went down to the hall. Outside, the square was deserted in the gray light. The Simca had gone, so had the man in the Breton beret and the other one in the sailor's vest. They'd be somewhere close, he was sure of that, but for the moment there was nothing to worry about. The village was already coming to life; as he looked out a milk cart rumbled by and an old woman shuffled up to open a tobacco kiosk. Even if they wanted to try anything, they'd have to wait now until the Citroën was on one of the deserted country roads again.

He went back upstairs, removed the bucket and replaced it on the wall, then he walked along the corridor to his own room. Three hours later, after another sleep and a long bath, he went down again for breakfast.

The man was propped against the counter in the hall.

"Mister Owen, no—?"

His accent was thick and he made two attempts before he came out with an approximation of Owen's name.

"That's right—"

Surprised, Owen nodded and answered him in French. The man made a little bow and smiled.

"Ah, so you speak French?" He'd changed languages immediately. "Then on behalf of the *mairie*, may I welcome you and Madame de Sourraines to Varençon—"

He was about fifty. Small and shifty and grubbily dapper in a loud checked suit with the frayed ends of his shirt collar carefully tucked under his lapels. His hair was slicked down with scented oil, his breath smelled of garlic, his voice was wheedling, and the ingratiating smile never left his face.

Owen disliked him instantly.

"Let me explain, m'sieu. Varençon welcomes visitors. We like to give them every assistance in seeing the sights of the village and the surrounding countryside. I have the privilege of being our official guide—"

A discreet but self-important gesture towards a little brass badge on his jacket.

"There's much in the village itself. The church and the

abbey are both listed in the *Guide Michelin*. Just outside
we have a most interesting Roman aqueduct. Then, of
course, all around there are many famous vineyards. Maybe
you and Madame—"

"Thank you—"

Owen interrupted him. He knew now what had happened.

The man was a tout, making his living off the foreign
tourists who passed through Varençon on their way south.
He must have noticed the big Citroën parked outside the
hotel the night before. A few francs to the desk clerk and
he'd have gotten their names from the register. In the off-
season travelers in an expensive car were at least worth a
try for a guided tour.

Owen was starting to move towards the dining room
when he checked suddenly and turned back.

"How long have you been Varençon's official guide?"

"M'sieu, if you doubt my credentials please ask anywhere. The hotel here, the *mairie*, anyone in the village—"

The outspread hands managed to be incredulous, out-
raged and pleading at the same time.

"It's not your credentials," Owen said. "I'd just like to
know how long."

The man rubbed his jaw, a weak receding ferretlike jaw,
as he thought back.

"It's all of twenty-five years now."

"And there's no one else?"

"M'sieu!" The simulated outrage in his voice once more.
"If you believe I'm pretending to be what I'm not—"

"Please have coffee with me."

Owen cut him off again. They went through to the dining
room and sat down. Owen ordered two coffees and crois-

176

sants for himself. Before the waiter came back Hélène de Sourraines appeared in the doorway. She glanced around the tables and joined them.

"Madame—"

The man jumped to his feet, bowed obsequiously over her hand and introduced himself. Jules Bastaq. Officially appointed guide to the municipality of Varençon—and no doubt, Owen guessed, its pimp, procurer, car-rental agent, newspaper feed and all-purpose fixer too.

Only, Owen had been right. It was the reference to "vineyards" which had triggered it. Bastaq had been hanging around the hotel entrance that May morning in 1958 when Walpole and his wife walked into the village from the camping site outside. He'd latched onto them and escorted them for the rest of the day.

"Even if the tragedy hadn't happened, how could I ever forget them? He, the perfect English gentleman. She, so charming you would not believe it. And as a connoisseur of wine—!"

He broke off and lifted his hands as if words were inadequate to describe Walpole's knowledge. Then he looked at Owen.

"You English, m'sieu, you put us French to shame. No doubt you are such a one yourself—"

Owen thought of the beer in the Dragon's Arms at Nantynth and said nothing.

Bastaq had taken them to two vineyards, one close to the village and the other further back, on the edge of the plain. They'd sampled the wines, talked to the proprietors and in between they'd lunched at an *auberge* Owen remembered noticing on the road. Then in the late afternoon they'd returned to Varençon.

"We said good-bye right there." He pointed at the hall. "They walked back to the camp and there'd been a fire. So they drove on, they stopped up in the Garnes, then that night—it will stay with me for the rest of my life."

He lowered his head, shaking it slowly, and almost managed to produce a tear. Owen wondered how much Walpole had tipped him. There was silence for a moment.

Then Owen said, "What did you talk about during the day?"

"Talk about?" He sounded surprised. "Wine, of course; that was his passion. Vintages, the soil, the rain—"

"Not about the occupation, the maquis?"

"Ah—"

He'd understood and he looked up smiling again.

"No, the police asked me that later. But he never mentioned it. Until they came I had no idea he'd even been involved with the resistance. Of course, if he'd said so I'd have been happy to talk. Well, it would have been like old times, wouldn't it—?"

He paused, calculating rapidly, Owen thought, assessing Owen's question and redirecting himself to answer it.

"If you're interested in the maquis, m'sieu, then you've come to the right person. Yes, Jules Bastaq was there. No medals maybe, but he took part in the fight against the enemy. Young—I was little more than a boy then—but with all my heart and soul. You want to know what we did in Varençon?"

Owen said, "Yes."

"M'sieu, that isn't business, that would be a pleasure—"

The hands, little predatory hands with dirty fingernails, gestured expansively.

"I can tell you everything. It was almost a family affair.

Me, my cousin Paul and my uncle Jean who ran the group. Jean Duchamp, he was, a very famous man in Varençon, although he used a code name then—well, we all did to confuse the boches. I was 'Bobinet,' Paul was 'L'Ane' and my uncle called himself ' 'Guette,' after Anisguette, the liqueur we make here—"

Owen put his cup down slowly and looked at Hélène de Sourraines. Her face was expressionless.

"You don't know Anisguette? Then I insist you and madame taste a glass as my guests—"

Bastaq waved grandly at the serving hatch, the glasses came and the waiter poured three measures.

"*Salut*—and welcome once more to Varençon!"

"May I—?"

She'd drained her glass and was reaching for the bottle again.

"Madame, of course—"

She poured again and sat cradling the glass on the table, looking neither at Owen or Bastaq—but at the bottle between them. The label was pale green with an emblem of a unicorn in a wood, the arms of Varençon, and blazoned across the top the single word "Anisguette."

'Guette. The fourth name on the white list cards. The collaborator who could well have been responsible for her mother's arrest, torture and death.

"It's excellent." She sipped and smiled politely. "I must remember to order a crate. Meanwhile, please tell us about your uncle and the group."

Bastaq beamed and began.

It took him an hour. Much, Owen guessed, was fantasy, exaggeration, a heroic posturing account of his own role which had probably been limited to the occasional message errand. But the core rang true—true enough to explain why someone who knew Walpole's identity believed there was reason to kill him after his day with Bastaq.

The Varençon network, under 'Guette's direction, had operated one of the main "reception" centers for the Allied support program to the maquis in central France. The plain between La Motte and the hills contained a number of ideal night-landing sites. When a supply flight was planned, a message would be transmitted from London over the BBC's French-language broadcasts to occupied Europe.

'Guette, listening in at prearranged times, would hear the message, select a site and radio back its map coordinates in code. Then, on the chosen night, an RAF plane would take off from the south coast, follow the French coast to the mouth of the Loire, turn inland, skirt the *Massif Central* and drop over the plain. 'Guette and his team would be waiting on the ground. When they heard the plane's engines, two rows of kerosene lamps would flare briefly—marking the improvised "runway"—and the plane would land.

Five minutes later it would bump away into the darkness, take off again and head back for England. Sometimes it would carry with it an agent whose cover had been blown or an escaped prisoner of war. More often it would have brought in an SOE operative, a communications or explosives expert to link up and work with some resistance cell.

Invariably, whether it left or took away men, it would make a delivery of matériel. Weapons, gelignite, transmitters, ammunition, detonators, aerial intelligence photographs—and gold.

"You're obviously a man of the world, m'sieu, so I don't need to explain—"

The shrug and the lifted eyebrows as he glanced at Owen were complicit, deliberately flattering, acknowledging him as another experienced in the ways and weaknesses of mankind.

"But gold was all people believed in then. It came in canvas bandoliers, a sovereign in each pouch. We distributed it north as far as Paris, south right down to Perpignan. Oh, it was used to finance maquis operations everywhere. Sabotage, raids, counterpropaganda, escape routes—"

He broke off abruptly, frowned and thought for a moment. Then he stood up and solemnly bowed to Hélène de Sourraines.

"Madame, I am appalled. I offer you my most sincere apologies. Somehow, inexplicably, I had forgotten the name. You are, of course, her daughter—?"

"Please, it's so long ago now. I completely understand—"

She smiled and waved him back to his chair.

"But tell me what happened afterwards to your uncle, your cousin and the other members of the group?"

"My cousin Paul went to Algeria; he's still there farming. My uncle tragically died—a car accident just after the war. The others? I don't know. They just scattered, moved away, I suppose. As you said, it's so long ago. Certainly, in Varençon I'm the only one left. . . ."

He shook his head mournfully. Not so much, Owen thought, in nostalgia for the war or grief for his dead uncle. Rather, because if he'd realized sooner that Hélène was Marie de Sourraine's daughter, he'd have slanted his entire account of the Varençon network towards the contribution it made to the Orion line.

"Thank you so much, Monsieur Bastaq—"

They all stood up as she rose. Owen reached for his wallet, but she was already opening her bag.

"You must have a fund in Varençon for the orphans of the war. I'd be happy if you see they received this—"

She took out her wallet and put ten one-hundred franc notes on the table.

"In memory of your uncle—and my mother."

She smiled again.

"Madame is too generous—"

As they went out Owen saw Bastaq slip the notes into his pocket and rub his frayed sleeve across the badge on his jacket.

16

"What was it? The gold?"

Owen nodded. "I imagine so. There are markets for guns, for detonators, even for aerial reconnaissance pictures. But gold doesn't need a market—it created its own, then as now, wherever you go."

Midday. They were on the mountain highway again, already past the Garnes gorge and winding high up into the *Massif Central*. Owen had tilted the wing driving mirror on the outside of the car so he could see the road behind. There'd been nothing yet but he watched the mirror constantly.

There was still much he didn't know, but the general pattern was clear beyond doubt now. The Orion line had been systematically penetrated along its entire length. He'd guessed as much in Paris when the blind old man had told him it continued to run after they'd executed the traitor Soldat. What he'd learned from Faure in Nevers and now in Varençon had turned the guess into a certainty.

There hadn't been just one collaborator—there'd been a group of them. Soldat, 'Guette, Bienaimé, maybe more whose names hadn't reached Jarvis as he compiled the white list. All of them betraying their individual sectors of the network in return for payment in gold. The bright new-minted sovereigns in the canvas pouches that were hurriedly thrown out of some plane into the darkness of a La Motte field, before the aircraft took off on its flight back.

Yet behind them all there'd been someone else. The man who'd made the original deal with the Germans, who'd recruited the others and acted as their paymaster. The man who, for reasons Owen couldn't understand, was still so desperately anxious to keep the secret of the collaborationist ring that he killed when people contacted members of the line who, unwittingly, could provide evidence of its existence.

The others were dead. This man was still alive. He'd arranged the attack on Owen in St. Julien, he'd had them followed by the Simca yesterday. What he did now would depend on what happened in about six hours time. At the rate they were traveling they'd reach Orange, a small town at the foot of the Rhône valley, in the early evening.

At Orange the road forked. The left branch led to the resort towns of the Côte d'Azur, St. Tropez, Nice, Cannes, Monte Carlo. The right to Perpignan, the Spanish border—and the last safe-house on the line.

Owen concentrated on the mirror.

"That bastard—that contemptible little bastard!"

It had taken her three hours to comment on Bastaq. When she did her voice was as furious as Owen remembered from their first encounter in the chateau.

He grinned. "In his case it's like alcoholism—it runs in the family. And at least we were spared meeting cousin Paul."

"But that my mother had to deal with people like that, die because of them—because they'd been bought for a few gold coins."

She shook her head, tense, angry, momentarily bewildered.

Owen glanced across at her and understood. She'd come with him not just to lay a ghost, but thinking the ghost could be laid in the way she wanted. However bitterly she resented the inherited burden of her mother's role in the maquis, she'd believed the resistance itself was something noble, dignified, worth fighting and dying for. Now she was learning different.

The resistance had been greed, vanity, weakness. Men, ostensible patriots, being bought and sold like cattle. Rings of collaborators informing for money—and casually accepting the result would be torture and death. Tawdry little touts like Bastaq and his uncle 'Guette who'd taken the gold and told the Gestapo whatever they wanted to know. A shabby degrading world which her mother had demeaned herself by entering—and where she'd paid a final, vicious penalty.

Except it was not all like that.

"There were others who were different—"

Owen tried to explain. He told her about the old *pâtissier* in Paris who'd parked his van behind the German patrol trucks, and collected the pilots night after night from among the sleeping *clochards* on the banks of the Seine. About Faure, describing the little mechanic—inflexible, aggressive and finally humorous when he at last thawed. But honest, totally incorruptibly honest.

Both motivated solely, although in different ways, by a remorseless hatred of German fascism and a passionate intractible allegiance to their country. No money, no bribe, could suborn them. They loved France, they had taken every risk to win back its freedom—and if death had been the price, they'd both have accepted it.

"Two just men," Owen finished. "Traditionally there are meant to be four, although I'll settle if we can find a third. Whatever the number, your mother didn't only work with people like Bastaq's uncle—she had the others too. And any one of them is worth the rest, all the rest, put together."

She didn't say anything for a time. Then she nodded slowly.

"Maybe you're right. Maybe I've been away so long—"

She broke off, paused, then she added abruptly, "I'm sorry about last night, about what I said at dinner. I regret it."

Her voice was clipped and formal, there wasn't any softening in her face and she still hadn't looked at him—but it was an apology. Owen was so startled it was several minutes before he could think what to answer.

"I'm sorry too. Let's just agree there are good *barbouzes* and bad *barbouzes*—"

He grinned, embarrassed, trying to make a joke of it.

"We'll put your mother, the blind old man and Faure in the first category, the others in the second and leave me somewhere in the middle."

"It's a bargain."

She half-smiled and concentrated on the road. Owen went back to watching the wing mirror.

"Listen carefully—"

Three hours later. They'd lunched briefly at an inn high in the mountains. Now they were running down through a deeply cut valley. There was a river, still and clear, on the right of the road and the hillside rising almost sheer on the left. Owen had stopped looking at the mirror and was sitting upright searching the road ahead.

"Pull the choke full out. When I say so, stop the car, leave the engine on, get out and stand as if you were looking at the view in front. Don't look back in the direction we've come from—"

She shrugged but didn't speak and the roar of the engine increased as the choke came out.

"There—"

Owen pointed. It was a narrow grass verge on the right with a low safety wall beyond and the river below. She pulled in, they both got out and stood gazing down the valley. Behind them the motor throbbed noisily.

"What are you doing?"

Owen had put his arm around her shoulder. She stiffened instantly and tried to pull away.

"Stay where you are and watch the water—"

The pool was twenty feet beneath them, broad and flat and gleaming in the sunlight. For a moment there was nothing except the reflection of the mountain pass at the upper end of the valley. Then it came, a tiny blue dazzle in the distant trees like the tip of a jay's wing. The dazzle went, hidden by some bend in the road, flickered over the water again and disappeared once more.

Owen waited but it didn't return. They must have seen

that the Citroën had stopped and were probably watching the two of them through binoculars, having parked the car somewhere in the trees high above. He stayed there for a further few minutes, his arm still draped across her shoulder. Then he straightened up.

"It's like yesterday—"

They were back in the Citroën and Owen was explaining.

"They've been tracking us by sound. Only, today they've been more careful—they've stayed further back and they've been coasting. That's why I didn't hear them—"

He gestured at his window which he'd kept half-open ever since they'd left Varençon.

"I couldn't see them either because of the distance and the way the road winds. Stopping with the choke out and the engine running confused them just enough—enough to think we were still traveling and show themselves before they realized we weren't. They probably don't know that but at least we do."

"Fire buckets, choked engines, reflections in water," she smiled. "What else did they teach you, Mr. Owen?"

"Enough to stay alive."

"And you still really believe while I'm with you any of it's going to be necessary."

"It may be."

"When do we find out?"

"Somewhere after Orange, I'd guess."

She shook her head and went on smiling. The unshake-able confidence in her own invulnerability was still there, but the scorn of the night before had gone.

They reached Orange at six, drove through the town

and took the right-hand fork towards Perpignan outside. It happened half an hour later.

By then they were down in the foothills of the *Massif Central,* with the coastal plain ahead. The road was as winding as the highway through the mountains and even narrower. There'd been no traffic for twenty kilometers, but as they reached a side turning, a truck suddenly pulled out in front of them—a heavy old general-purpose vehicle with a massive iron towing bar at the back.

Hélène de Sourraines braked and hooted angrily. A few moments later she pulled out to overtake it. Veering into the middle of the road the driver blocked her. Hooting again she tried once more and then a third time. Each time, the truck drifted across in front and forced her to drop back.

She swore with her hand jammed down on the horn. "He's either drunk, deaf or some bloody-minded peasant. Ah—"

The driver had suddenly switched on his nearside indicator and pulled in towards the verge to let her by. She changed down, swung out and began to accelerate.

"No—!"

Owen's warning shout came as the hood of the Citroën drew level with the truck's rear bumper. As she hesitated the truck started to swing out again.

"For Christ's sake, brake and drop back—!"

This time she understood. The towing bar was already touching the Citroën's right fender. She stamped on the foot brake, the engine howled as she jabbed the gearshift into second to control the skid, the bar ripped through the fender like paper and the truck swerved viciously to the left—inches in front of them.

It was the speed of her reflexes that had saved them. An instant later they'd have been alongside the truck's rear axle. The force of the impact would have hurled the Citroën across the road, through a light wooden fence studded with cat's-eyes and down into a rocky hundred-foot ravine on the far side.

"Hell—!"

Owen was swearing now. He'd turned in his seat, looked back and seen what he'd expected—a second truck, identical to the first, just behind them.

"Listen." He turned around again. "They've got us sandwiched, there's another one behind—"

She glanced at the mirror, saw the second truck and nodded.

"What do you want me to do?"

Her face was white and the tendons of her wrists were trembling. For a moment Owen thought it was a combination of fear and shock after the collision that could have thrown them into the ravine. Then he realized it was something quite different.

She wasn't afraid—she was angry. Furiously, implacably angry. The inconceivable had happened. She, Hélène de Sourraines, had been almost killed, deliberately, by a peasant in an ancient farm truck. Her only response was rage.

"Don't go above third, and stay back," he said. "They want an 'accident' and they'll try to jostle us into one. Keep your hand on the horn as if you still think the one in front's just some maniac—"

She pushed the button again and the horn wailed incessantly over the engine.

"Right." Owen was shouting over the sound. "If there's a side road, even a track, take it. I'll check the map—"

He reached out, fumbled in the shelf under the dash-board and suddenly jolted forward. Behind there was the sound of splintering glass and crumpling metal.

"Don't stop! Keep going—!"

He shouted again and pushed himself up. The truck in front was still fifteen yards ahead and there was blood trickling into his eye. He'd cut his forehead when he'd lurched against the shelf.

The driver of the second truck hadn't been taken in by the echoing horn. He'd realized they knew what was happening and he'd decided to take the initiative—by ramming the Citroën from the back. He came at them again as Owen sat upright, wiping the blood from his face. There was another shuddering jolt, the same crunch of metal and shattering glass—the lid of the trunk had burst open, snapped back and broken the rear windshield.

The car slued around, she turned into the drift, corrected it and accelerated until they were nosing the front truck's bumper again.

"Second gear and just do what I say—"

Owen scanned the countryside on either side of the road.

There was only one chance now—and it depended on her and the car. If they stopped they were finished. Whoever was directing the men in the trucks—two in the one behind and probably as many in front—wanted an "accident." If he didn't get it while they were moving, he'd arrange it as soon as they pulled up—sending the men in, beating them unconscious and then wheeling the Citroën to a point in the road where it could be pushed down into the ravine.

Three men separated in darkness were possible. Four

together in daylight would overwhelm him instantly. Yet if they went on, sooner or later one of the smashing blows from the back would wreck the Citroën's suspension, force them to stop—and the "accident" would happen anyway.

The sole possibility was to get off the road.

"Leave the horn—"

She took her hand off the button and the wail died away. There were less than fifty yards between the three vehicles now and the truck behind was already moving up for another assault on the Citroën's mangled rear.

"The moment I tell you, turn right, go straight down and keep listening—"

She glanced quickly to the right, realized what he meant to do and nodded.

"I'm ready—"

The ravine was still on their left, but on the other side the landscape had changed. Before, when the truck ahead had first waved them by, there'd been a low hill rising upwards. The hill was behind them now and the road was running along a steep raised embankment between the ravine and a series of lavender fields. Not the neat, trimmed bushes which encircled the chateau at Este, but acre on acre of deep chest-high violet—the flowers which supplied the scent factories at Grasse.

The fields started at the edge of the road and fell sharply for a hundred yards to a stream. Beyond the stream was an occasional farm—and tracks leading away into the distance.

"Now—!"

He'd picked a point where the stream had widened into a shallow pool with what looked like pebbles below the surface.

Hélène swung the wheel, the car swerved at right angles, bumped over the verge and plunged down. An instant later lavender surged over them like surf, blinding the windshield and side windows with a rustling violet haze.

"Doesn't matter. Just keep going down—"

As he shouted there was a crash and an explosion behind. Owen jerked around in his seat and looked back up the lane they'd flattened through the bushes.

The rear truck had been on their bumper when they left the road. Its driver had either deliberately tried to follow them or, taken by surprise, had skidded off accidentally. Whatever the reason the turn had been too fast and the incline of the field too steep for its center of gravity. It had toppled over, the gas tank had ignited and it was tumbling downwards in a cloud of flame and smoke.

Owen wiped some more blood off his face, grinned and turned back.

The violet haze was still billowing around the car but they could only be yards from the end of the field now—and the stream.

"Right, listen again—"

He was directing her like ground control talking down the pilot of a Boeing through thick fog.

"Any moment we'll come out of the bushes. There's a space of sand, then the stream. Swing around immediately you see the sand so we're facing back up the hill. Get into reverse and take the stream backwards. Give it everything. Whatever you hit keep your foot hard down on the pedal—"

She nodded, the bushes parted and they were on the sand.

Hélène circled almost in the car's length, pushed the

shift into reverse, gunned the motor until it throbbed, let out the clutch and they roared backwards. Traction was everything now, to keep the wheels moving through the water—and to pray it was as shallow as it looked from above.

For a moment Owen thought they wouldn't make it. Spray sheeted up on either side, a rock thumped savagely somewhere against the undercarriage, the engine howled and they seemed to hang spinning in midstream. Then the wheels bit against the pebbles, they moved backwards again and suddenly they were up on the far bank—another slope of sand that shelved up into a field of grass.

"I want to have a look at the damage—"

They'd stopped a few yards from the bank on the grass. She nodded again as Owen got out. He walked first around to the fender which had been ripped by the towing bar, leaned on it and forced it down into an approximation of the shape it had had before. Then he went to the back and knelt down. The bumper had been sliced off entirely, both the rear fenders were crumpled and the trunk lid was open, with its lock smashed.

Yet none of the twisted metal was touching the wheels and, although the crankcase was badly dented by the rock in the stream, no oil was leaking out. He lashed the lid to the trunk with a piece of wire he found inside. Then he stood up: the car was unrecognizable as the elegant black Citroën in which they'd set out, but it was still serviceable.

"Let me see your head—"

While he'd been examining the back Hélène had gone down to the stream and soaked a handkerchief in the water. She wiped off the drying blood and looked at the cut.

"You'll live." She smiled. "I don't think we even need the vet this time."

"What about you?"

"The odd bruise." She touched a swelling lump above her eye. "Otherwise nothing. I'm fine."

"The car's much the same—battered but it works."

"So we can go on?"

"Yes, except I'll drive now—"

"No." She cut him off, shaking her head adamantly. "If you think something like that can stop me, you're making the same mistake they did."

Owen hesitated. Her face was still white and the bruise was darkening as he looked at her. Then he grinned. As before, it wasn't either fear or shock—it was just anger.

"All right," he said. "For a chauffeur it wasn't such a bad piece of driving. I'll go on as a passenger."

She smiled back, they got into the car, bumped over the field until they found a track and followed it to the main road. Then they turned west again.

She drove for three hours. When they stopped it was almost eleven and the Spanish border was only a hundred kilometers away. They came into a village, saw the lights burning in a hotel on the main square and she drew up in front of it.

This time there was no argument about rooms. Hélène walked into the hall and rapped on the counter for the desk clerk, who came sleepily out of the office behind.

"A room, please," she said. "Your best double room— and collect our cases from the car, would you?"

17

"What are you doing?"

"Waiting."

Midnight. The room in total darkness except for one pin-prick of light—a star's reflection on the brass bedpost. Owen at the window, Hélène de Sourraines lying in bed.

He'd thought she was asleep. The clerk had taken them upstairs, Owen waited until he went down again, then he'd stood outside in the corridor while she undressed. Afterwards he'd gone back in. That had been an hour ago.

"In case they come?"

Owen nodded. "It's possible. They know where we're going and the route we've got to take to get there. The blue Simca might have picked us up again after we rejoined the road."

"And you'll stay there all night?"

"Yes."

The rustle of bedclothes as she sat up; the lighter flaring, then the glow of a cigarette.

"Why don't you put the chair there and sit down?"

"I like standing."

"Because of your hip?"

"Yes."

Another rustle, the ancient bedsprings creaking and the patter of bare feet on the floorboards. Owen glanced down.

There was a porcelain stove by the window which had caught the glow of a street lamp and made a dim pool of light. She was kneeling there in her nightdress—lace at the wrists and neck and the rest sheer, transparent. Beneath it he could see her body, lean and firm and strongly muscled like a swimmer's.

"And tomorrow?"

"We'll go on to Bac—"

Bac-sur-Challey. The last safe-house before the Spanish border.

"They seem to be hell-bent on seeing we don't get there. So if there is a final answer, I guess that's where we'll find it."

Silence. Smoke coiled up from her cigarette and drifted out through the window.

"When you told me about your hip, about what happened in Algiers, you said it was five years ago—"

"That's right."

"What have you been doing since?"

Owen shrugged. "They gave me a desk job in London. I've been there."

"Then why this?" She was frowning now. "Why leave that and come out and get yourself hurt again?"

"Because someone had to do it. I look after what we call the French desk, so I was the logical person to choose—"

Owen stopped. It was plausible and true—but only partly true. There was another reason, the reason Mathieson knew, the reason which had made it inevitable he'd accept the assignment and return to the field.

"I grew up in a small valley in Wales. My family were miners like almost everyone else in the village. I was lucky, I was different—"

He spoke slowly and simply. It was the first time he'd told anyone, the first time he'd even fully acknowledged it himself. As before he didn't know why. But he told her now —told her the truth.

"I went to school, to university, then, well, let's call it the Foreign Office. That hadn't happened to anyone from Nantynth, my village, before. They're very proud of me. In Algiers that night I made a mistake, a bad mistake. Through stupidity, carelessness, not thinking, I nearly died. That would have been bad enough; I'd have wasted years of training and money and work. Worse, I blew our best source in the country, got him killed, wrecked the network we were building around him—"

Owen stopped and she said, "And this is to make up for that?"

"Maybe."

"But you're married, aren't you?"

"Yes—how did you know?"

"When they brought you into Este, your wallet fell out of your jacket. It landed open on the floor. There was a photograph of two children."

Owen said nothing. A couple appeared in the square

below the window, a young man and a girl. They walked over to the fountain and sat with their arms around each other, gazing into the water. He watched them for a while. Then he looked back at the stove.

She was still kneeling beside it but she seemed to be trembling. At first he thought it was the cold. Then he realized she was crying silently, her body shaking as the tears streamed down her face.

"Are you all right, then?"

Owen stood above her awkwardly, embarrassed, not knowing what to do. In seven days he'd learned to expect anything from this stiff iron-willed woman—anything except tears.

"It's nothing—"

She shook her head and the weeping stopped. Then she glanced up, pale-faced and with the tears still glistening on her cheeks, but calmer now.

"Could you get my cigarettes, please?"

He went over to the bedside table and came back with a packet of Gitanes and the gold Cartier lighter. She pulled out a cigarette and tried to light it, her hands unsteady and fumbling. Owen took back the lighter and struck it for her.

"Thank you." She blew out the smoke. "I'm sorry, it was stupid of me. I suppose what you said just reminded me of—I don't know, the past perhaps. I was married once too. Did my grandfather tell you that?"

"No."

"Well, I was. Oh, I wasn't crying for him, for my 'husband.' He just happened to be there at the time. He also happened to be a bastard. It lasted three months. Then it took me two years and a million francs to get rid of him."

"That was in Paris?"

"So my grandfather told you that?" She nodded. "Yes,

that was in Paris. A lot of bad things happened there—and it certainly wasn't the worst. But no, not for that."

"For what then?"

"Does it matter?"

Her face lifting again and her voice partly cynical, partly vulnerable. Owen shifted by the windowsill.

"Sometimes it can help to say."

"Perhaps." She hesitated. "Well, I suppose it was for all the things that might have been and weren't. Once—"

She paused and shook her head violently, dismissively.

"The hell with it! Regret, self-pity, that's all it is. Except there was a time, even in Paris, even with all the bad parts, when I wasn't afraid to make mistakes. Then I decided not to anymore, not even to take the chance of making them, let alone repairing the ones I'd done. Maybe it was the wrong way—"

She stood up suddenly, ground out the cigarette on the tiles around the stove and went back to the bed.

Below there were the sounds of shutters being barred and doors locked. Ancient medieval France, where each house, each inn was still treated like a fortress. Even if they'd been tracked to the little hotel, no one would gain entry now before daylight.

Owen moved again and settled himself against the sill to wait.

"What happens if you lie down?"

She'd returned to the stove—he remembered he hadn't heard the bedsprings creak—and was standing beside him.

"It's fine then."

"Well, go and use the bed."

"No, I'll be all right here, I'm used to it. You get back into bed, you'll get cold outside—"

"I wasn't thinking of staying up. I was going to lie down too—"

The reflected starlight on the stove had gone, but he saw a glimmer of white in the darkness as she smiled.

"You may be surprised, Mr. Owen, but apart from my husband it won't be the first time I've had a man beside me in bed."

Owen rubbed his chin, pushing his palm against the bristles that had grown since he'd shaved that morning. Then he checked the square again. The courting couple had gone from the fountain and there was no one else there. Afterwards he walked over to the bed and rolled in between the rough calico sheets.

"Tell me about her, your wife."

Lying on his back with his arms crossed behind his head, he could see a mirror above a cheap pine bureau against the far wall. Occasionally a pair of truck lights splintered over it—long-distance freight trucks heading north towards the Rhône with a cargo of fruit or meat—and the room throbbed with the noise of their engines.

Otherwise there was nothing—apart from her breathing beside him.

"Meg? She's like me, she comes from the valley—"

Owen described her, talking more easily now. The girl he'd met as a child and grown up with in the village. Their courtship and marriage after he'd been offered the job at Baker Street. The years in London, the children, the long periods abroad, the way they'd drifted apart, her return to the valley and his weekend visits ever since.

When he finished he realized it was another part of his life he hadn't spoken to anyone about before.

"So that's the only time you see her now, Saturdays?"

"Yes."

"It's strange—"

She moved on the pillow and he sensed she was smiling.

"We've gone in directly opposite ways, haven't we, the two of us? You out from where you came, me right back in—"

She paused. Owen didn't answer, but she was right—not just about herself but about him too. Unconsciously, believing it was required of him, that he was moving forward, he'd tried to separate himself from Nantynth just as finally as she'd tried to wall herself up in the chateau at Este. The paths were different—but the end was the same.

"Hold me, please—"

Owen turned, put his arms around her, felt the strength he'd seen in her body as she'd knelt by the stove, but softness now too.

"Harder—"

He pulled her to him, touched her breasts, her flat stomach, the long straight legs. Then they were making love—urgently, passionately, hungrily.

"What is it?"

Later. Owen was on his back again and she was curled against him, her head on his shoulder and her hair—the thick chestnut hair he remembered haloed by sunlight in the hall at Este—spread out on the pillow. He'd smiled and she'd felt the movement of his cheek against her own.

"There's a saying in Welsh about women. If they're good they're 'shrewd in the marketplace, pious in chapel—and frantic in bed—' "

Owen grinned.

"I'll take the marketplace and chapel on trust. But for the rest you'd have made a fine Welshwoman."

She laughed back. "I don't know about the Welsh, but as *barbouzes* go you've just been moved from the middle category to the good."

Afterwards she slept peacefully. Owen dozed from time to time but mostly he lay awake—waiting for the morning and the end of the line.

18

Bac-sur-Challey. A tiny village, white-walled, ochre-roofed, perched on a hilltop, with the valleys sweeping green below and a river winding at its foot.

It took them an hour to get there. Owen rose early, went out, found the local Avis agency and rented another car, a gray Renault, as soon as the office opened at eight. By the time he returned to the hotel Hélène had dressed and was having breakfast. He joined her for a coffee, paid the bill, then they set off—leaving the battered Citroën in the hotel garage.

She only referred once to the night before, when she

reached out—Owen was at the wheel now—put her hand on his and smiled.

"You said you'd only ever made one mistake. Well, I'm an expert—I had three years nonstop experience. Last night wasn't one."

Owen smiled back. "No."

She didn't speak again and the rest of the drive was like the first two days: Owen constantly watching the mirror—there was no sign of the blue Simca or any other car following them—and Hélène sitting in silence beside him. Yet there was a difference, an immeasurable difference. They'd left Este in mutually suspicious and resentful tandem, she the autocratic employer saddled with a distasteful, truculent but necessary servant.

Now, running in the morning sunlight through the western Languedoc countryside, everything had changed. Her anger, her hostility, the impatience and the casual arrogance, all had gone. Instead she might have been a companion Owen had known all his life—known so well they didn't even need to talk. What had happened to her, coming out again after the ten years of total self-imposed isolation in the chateau, he could partly understand.

Yet for himself—Owen shook his head and looked at the village drawing closer in the haze above the Perpignan plain.

"I'll go in first—"

They'd climbed the hill, asked directions of a boy on a bicycle and stopped where he'd told them. It was a bakery attached to a farm by the village wall. White like the rest of the houses, with a large door and a sign above it, chipped and warped, showing a slender young girl in a nineteenth-century smock and the legend below—Veuve Lachasse et Frère.

Owen nodded and waited by the car on the cobbled street while she went in.

The air was already warm with the heat that would come later. Butterflies, great yellow and black swallowtails, clustered around the flowers of a gnarled magnolia, and the scent drifted across to him. Beyond, cows were lowing in the pastures that ran down to the river. Buckets clattered, the church bell rang the hour, a horse-drawn cart rumbled across a wooden bridge.

Even with the Spanish border so close, this was still heartland France. Rich-earthed, slow-moving, tranquil, changeless.

"Come in—"

Hélène's voice calling from the doorway. Owen walked over and went inside.

A great raftered room with a scoured red brick floor and the ovens at either end, one with its door half-open and the coals glowing inside. Down the center a long table, inches thick and patinated with flour. Behind that, a rack of baking ladles shaped like canoe paddles. The strong, fresh smell of new-baked bread and everywhere wide, flat baskets brimming with loaves—round, crusty, golden brown as the sunlight caught them through the window bars.

Like the village, it might have been there for centuries. So might the woman.

"This is Madame Lachasse," Hélène said.

"Monsieur—"

She wiped the flour from her hand onto a striped apron and reached forward.

A massive woman, almost six feet tall and weighing maybe two hundred pounds. About sixty, with gray hair knotted above a face that Breughel might have painted and arms like sides of beef—her grip was crushing as she shook Owen's hand.

"You can see the family likeness!"

It was obviously her favorite joke for greeting visitors, and laughter rumbled as she gestured towards the fragile young girl on the sign outside.

Owen smiled. "Madame, if I'd come alone I wouldn't even have needed to ask your name."

She roared with laughter again.

"So you've come with Marie's daughter? Ah, when they made that one they broke the *tasse*—"

She picked up a pottery mold, tapped it on the table and shook her head.

"And you want to know about the *groupe* here in Bac, about the line?"

"Yes—"

Owen stopped. His back was to the doorway but as he spoke he saw something flash across the surface of a brass pan hanging on the rear wall—a metallic ice-blue flicker.

He turned, walked quickly to the window and looked out. The car had already gone; it had probably stopped somewhere out of sight further around the village wall. He waited for a moment but there was nothing else. Then he came back and glanced at Hélène.

She'd seen it too. She nodded and turned towards the woman to explain.

"Madame, there've been people following us who don't seem to want the line talked about. We wouldn't want you to say anything which might cause problems for you afterwards."

The woman looked at her expressionlessly. Then she lifted her head and shouted.

"Max! Jean-Paul!"

They came through from the back, two young men, her sons obviously—the same powerful jaw, the same steady eyes. And both of them built not just on the same massive scale, but towering even over her.

She reached under the table, pulled out a kindling ax, its chopping blade honed razor sharp, and balanced it lightly in her hands like a toy, although it must have weighed ten pounds.

"You'd want to cause me problems, m'sieu?"

Owen looked at the three of them standing shoulder to shoulder. Huge, implacable, remorseless. If he'd come out onto a rugby field and seen they were the front row of the opposing team, for the only time in his life he'd have gone straight back to the dressing room.

He grinned and shook his head. She heaved with laughter again.

"Don't worry about us, m'sieu—save your worries for your companions outside. Max." She tugged the younger one by the elbow. "Wine for our visitors."

The wine came, they sat down on stools around the table, then, with the glasses filled, she started.

"I was twenty when I met your mother first. In Belain, it was, about fifteen kilometers from here—"

The Lachasse bakery hadn't only supplied bread to the village. Like a small country version of the Cochon Rouge in Paris, it had also delivered *tartes* and cakes to the houses of the local gentry. Among them had been a family who owned an estate at Belain.

Marie de Sourraines, searching for someone to run the final sector of the line, had driven to the estate, which then belonged to a cousin of hers by marriage. She reached the house in the early hours of a Saturday morning and she was still up—drinking coffee in the hall—when the Lachasse van arrived.

"It was like everywhere." The woman shrugged. "We supplied the Vichy command post, so we had a permit and gas. The gas you could stretch out—coasting down the hills, giving *tartes* to a soldier ,and getting extra liters in return—many ways. Anyway, there was enough to go on delivering to the families—"

She'd been driving the van that morning, she'd met Marie in the hall—and they'd taken to each other instantly. The fervent young aristocrat and the big rawboned baker's daughter, both with the same toughness, the same energy, the same hatred of the Germans and Vichy France.

"Thought I was a maid at first, Marie did," she chuckled. "Told me to get her more toast and another cup of coffee. 'We're all maids now, madame,' I said, 'I'll make the toast and you heat the coffee.' And she laughed, she just laughed—"

On the point of going to bed, Marie had changed her mind. She'd gotten into the van and the two of them returned to Bac. There they'd worked out a plan.

"You can still see—"

The woman stood up and Owen and Hélène followed her to the oven on the left, closed and dark instead of bright and hot like the other. She jerked open the door and Owen peered in. Dimly he could see the baking space and a long-dead pile of ashes.

"Looks just the same, doesn't it? Only, try with this—'

She handed Owen one of the long wooden ladles. Both ovens, built like conical brick huts, were set twelve feet into the room from the side walls. He thrust the ladle forward and three feet from the door it thudded against something solid.

Then he realized what they'd done. The rear part of the oven had been sealed off with a false partition. The area behind must have measured nine feet by six and as much again high—enough to hide at least two men indefinitely in cramped but tolerable safety.

At the vineyard staging area at the mouth of the Rhône valley, the pilots would have been switched from the empty barrels to a grain-delivery truck heading southwest. Buried in the unground wheat, they reached Bac at dusk. During the night they were transferred to the rear of the oven, crawling into it up the ashes flue.

"We kept them there until Friday, market day. Then I'd go into Vézey and bargain for a guide. Those guides—!"

She shook her head scornfully. They were back at the table and she was pouring more wine.

"Tinkers, gypsies, smugglers, thieves, that's what they were—what they still are. But they're the only ones who know the routes across the border and up into the mountains on the other side. And the better they know them, the greater the villains. *Mon dieu!* I remember one called Antoine—"

She broke off speechless for a moment at the memory of Antoine's villainy.

"How did you get them from here to the border?" Owen asked.

"Moved them the same day, soon as I'd got a guide. Apart from the van, we used donkeys then, everyone did around here. We'd load up half a dozen with loaves, dress the boys up, give them a halter to hold and set off for Vézey. Market days there'd be farmers and donkeys like that coming in from every side—"

The donkey train would wind through the woods towards the little town that almost straddled the border. Half a mile outside it the pilots would be dropped off in a clump of trees, where they'd wait until nightfall for the guide to collect them.

"We had something for that too. Look—"

She scooped a loaf from a basket behind her and pushed it across the table. Owen picked it up.

As in every country bakery throughout Europe, each lump of dough was pricked with a tiny brand before it went into the oven. When the baked loaves came out they all bore the symbol of the bakery. In this case it was three letters—VLF.

"For Veuve Lachasse et Frére," she said. "My grand-mother, the widow, started this place. Then, when the business grew, she took in her brother. But wait—"

Chuckling again, she stood up and went to the back of the room where she sorted through a rack of branding irons. She found the one she wanted, wiped off the dust that covered it and took it over to the oven. There she kneaded two tiny lumps of dough, pricked them with the brand and let them bake on the red-hote plate.

"Now look—"

She gave one each to Owen and Hélène, small hot rolls with the brand on top. At first glance they looked the same as the others. Then Owen saw there were four letters now instead of three—and extra "L" had been added at the end.

"See?"

Owen shook his head puzzled but Hélène spotted it immediately.

"VLFL—*Vive La France Libre*," she said.

The woman nodded, laughing. "We put that on the loaves we gave the boys to eat on the journey through the mountains. When the guide came to collect them, they'd show it to prove who they were—that they'd come from here. That was something else Marie and I thought up—"

She paused, gazed at Hélène and shook her head.

"You have her eyes, her face, her hair, everything, child. It's extraordinary. It could be her sitting where you are now, like the last time I saw her before those bastards picked her up in Larras."

"Tell us about that." Hélène leaned forward.

"The last time? It was a few months before the end—" She wrinkled her face remembering.

"Marie came down here. There'd been big raids up in the north, many pilots shot down and she was worried about whether we could cope with them. Normally they came in pairs. Now she said there might be five or six at a time. I said we'd hide them with friends if we couldn't fit them in here—"

She gestured at the disused oven with its walled-in space at the back.

"Marie wouldn't have it. Too dangerous for the line and the village, she said. She wanted a reserve safe-house, a proper one with someone she knew and could trust to run it. She went away that night and when she came back next evening she'd fix it up—"

"Another house?" Owen frowned. "I thought this was the last point on the line."

"So it was. In the end we never had to use that other one. The pilots came in pairs after all like before. But it was there in case. I even christened it—"

The deep-throated chuckle once more. As with the blind old man in Paris and the little mechanic Faure, there was nothing in the past for her to be fearful or evasive about.

Owen had said he'd settle for finding a third just man

on the line. Whatever else, they'd found him now—except "he" turned out to be a woman.

"Marie called all the houses after the stars, well, you know that. But she'd run out of names. I can see her sitting there now, scratching her head. 'Us country girls, Marie,' I said, "We may not have much book learning but there's things we've forgotten as you city ladies never even knew —and we've got names for them too." It was September and I took her over to the window and there was a great big moon rising. "Do you know what that's called?" I asked her. She didn't and I'll wager you don't either, child—"

She glanced at Hélène, who shook her head.

"*Le gros renard,* that's what. The 'fat fox,' for the harvest moon. I never knew where the house was, except close, but then we never did. We worked the cut-out system and I'd have been sent a contact if we needed to use it. Like I said, it didn't happen. But that's what the house was called, *le gros renard.*"

She repeated the name and smiled, thinking back to the evening thirty years before when she'd told Marie de Sourraines the country name for the harvest moon.

"Madame—"

Owen leaned forward now too, his elbow on the table and his arm touching Hélène's.

"This contact you'd have been sent if the reserve house was needed, presumably it was the person Marie knew and trusted to run the place—?"

She nodded. "That's right."

"Tell me something—"

Owen was sitting very still. Madame Lachasse might not have known the site of the safe-house she'd code named the "fat fox"—but Owen did. He'd recognized the phrase instantly. It was one of the entries written in the margin of the leather-bound road atlas he'd found in the attic of the chateau at Este, an entry he'd thought had referred to some motoring trip before the war.

The atlas was in the Renault outside. He could see the page clearly. A large-scale map of the area around Perpignan, the words *le gros renard* penciled in across the bottom—and an arrow to its precise location.

"How would this contact, this person, identified himself to you?"

"The same way we ran the rest of the operation," she shrugged. "A code name. He'd give me his, I'd give him mine, then we'd arrange what to do."

"So until he came you wouldn't know who he was?"

"Of course not. And as he never came, I never did."

"But Marie gave you his code name?"

"Obviously."

"Can you remember it?"

She finished her glass, heaved herself back on her stool and laughed.

"Remember it? Listen, m'sieu, I'm reminded every Saturday. The children's program, but I like it too—"

She waved over her shoulder. There was a door half-open into a kitchen behind the bakery. Through it Owen saw a television set on a shelf above the stove.

"The little man with the flapping *pantalons* and the feet turned out like a duck. Charlot, that's what he was called. Charlot—after the clown."

She went on laughing. At his side Owen felt Hélène stiffen. He said nothing.

"Max—!"

She was shouting again for her son.

"The carafe's empty! More wine, so we can drink to Marie, her daughter, the line and Charlot!"

"Where now?"

Owen smiled. "We're going to spend a day by the sea."

"By the sea?"

Hélène looked at him, startled. They'd drunk a last toast with Madame Lachasse, felt the same bone-crushing hand-shake as they said good-bye, now they were back in the car heading for the Mediterranean.

"That's right—"

He glanced in the mirror. The Simca, the ice-blue shape that had hovered behind them for three days, was barely a hundred meters back, not even bothering to conceal itself in the morning traffic streaming down towards the coastal highway.

"And we're going to have company all day—or at least until we leave for *le gros renard.*"

As Owen told her about the entry in her mother's writing, she pulled out the atlas and found the page.

The pencil line led from the words to an arrowhead in a green-shaded area of forest ten kilometers north of Bac but slightly closer to the Spanish frontier—so that it was almost equidistant from the border village of Vézey, where the guides had been hired. The map's scale wasn't large enough to record individual houses, but it showed a track through the forest to a small hamlet. Anyone in the hamlet, Owen guessed, would be able to tell them what buildings there were in the surrounding woods.

"What do you think it is?"

Hélène closed the atlas and sat back in her seat.

Owen shrugged. "A cave, a charcoal-burner's cottage, a farm, it doesn't matter. What matters is what he does later—"

He. Charlot. The man who'd used the name of the little tramp with the baggy trousers. The man Marie had known and trusted to run the last reserve safe-house on the Orion line. The man, Owen was certain now, who'd set up the collaboration ring, betrayed the network—and was still killing to protect what he'd done.

"We'll find that out tonight. Until then you can forget there ever was a line at all."

Owen smiled again and turned right onto Route Nationale 9, the broad highway that followed the sea to the border.

He found what he was looking for ten minutes afterwards. A hotel-restaurant on the left of the road with a parking lot in front, a pine grove behind and flat yellow-gray sand beyond.

"The lock's gone and our *valises* are in the back—"

Owen had parked the Renault and was talking through the open window to the attendant, a copper-faced old man in a dirty yachting cap who'd shuffled forward when they stopped.

"We've got a train to catch from Narbonne at five, so we'll be back here by four, latest. Meantime, don't take your eyes off the car, understand?"

He handed over a ten-franc note.

"Oui, m'sieu."

The old man nodded happily. It was five times his usual tip and there were only two cars in the park anyway.

Owen got out and walked into the entrance hall of the hotel. He could see the restaurant through glass doors on the far side. Oak tables under the pines, red-and-white checked tableclothes fluttering in the breeze, a Danish tourist and his wife, both fleshy and blue-veined, reading a copy of Die Blaagsat which they carefully divided between them —their Saab with its DK plates had been parked next to the Renault.

"Please—"

Owen stopped by the reception desk and beckoned to the clerk. He turned around from the message board, assessed Owen, then Hélène in her pale tweed suit, silk blouse and Gucci bag that could only mean Paris—and money.

"M'sieu?"

He came up to the counter. Young, bland, smiling, helpful.

"We'd like a swim first, then lunch," Owen said. "But

we must be away by 4:00—we're meeting friends off a yacht at St. Laurent. As my watch has stopped, can you send someone out at 3:45 to tell me?"

"Of course, m'sieu."

He noted Owen's instruction. Then he showed them through to the changing rooms, gave them towels and offered them the selection of bathing costumes the hotel kept for guests who arrived without their own.

By the time Owen had put on a pair of dark-blue shorts, Hélène was already waiting for him on the sand. She'd picked a simple brown bikini that probably came from St. Tropez and was almost the same color as her skin. Looking at her, Owen suddenly remembered a day as a child when he'd gone to the pithead and watched his father with the other miners in the colliery showers after they'd come up the shaft, their bodies chalk-white under the coal dust.

Against her deep suntan his must have looked the same now.

"A train from Narbonne? A yacht at St. Laurent—?"

She was frowning. It was the first chance they'd had to talk since the clerk left them.

"And that's not all." Owen grinned. "There's our Costa Brava trip too. You'll see soon."

He didn't explain further, she shrugged, laughing, and they walked down to the beach.

There were a series of small coves, screened by dunes and all of them deserted—it was too early in the season for the summer visitors who would throng them later. They picked one, then quickly and quite unselfconsciously Hélène took off her bikini, walked to the water and plunged in. Owen sat watching her; the wounds from the attack in St. Julien still weren't fully healed and he didn't want to risk opening them again in the sea.

She swam as she did everything else—strongly, effort-
lessly, gracefully. Afterwards she came back and lay down
on the sand beside him, still naked, with her hair wet
against her head and the salt drying on her skin. They
stayed there for an hour. Once, as in the car, she stretched
out her hand and held his wrist, smiling.

"How's my *barbouze*?"

"*Barbouzes* get trained to stay alive, but I'm not sure
they had this way in mind when they trained me."

"It could become a habit."

"It could be." He smiled back. "And what's it like outside
Este?"

"That could become a habit too."

She laughed and rolled onto her back. It was the only
time they spoke.

At two they returned to the hotel, changed and sat
down at one of the tables under the shadow of the pines.
The Danish couple had gone and there was no one else
there.

"No—"

She'd reached instinctively for the menu to order for
them both as she'd done before. Owen took the card from
her hands.

"This time I'll do it. And as it's going to be on the house,
for a while at least, we'll have the best."

She hesitated. Then she laughed again happily.

"I'm sorry."

The habits of a lifetime were still there, the automatic
assumption that in everything, even in choosing a meal, she,
Hélène de Sourraines, gave the orders. Only now, as with
everything else, her response to being contradicted had
changed. Instead of anger there was acceptance—and con-
tentment.

Owen asked for a bouillabaisse and a bottle of Moët et Chandon, the oldest and most expensive on the list. The fish and the champagne came and they ate slowly in silence. Beyond the trees the sun was hot on the shore, the small waves curled and broke in dazzling white spray, a schooner, full-sailed and leaning into the wind, crossed the horizon.

Stillness, ease, peace, quietness. He'd never felt them so powerfully, so tangibly, before. Once, as she'd done, he reached over the table and touched her, pushing his fingers through her hair, thick, salt-crusted, gleaming chestnut in the broken light. She'd caught his hand, held it, laughed, then they both laughed.

"Garçon—!"

Five minutes later. Owen called for the waiter—and it was finished instantly, abruptly. Somewhere outside was the blue Simca, beyond, in the woods, a house that had been coded the "fat fox," and somewhere a man who'd called himself Charlot.

"M'sieu?"

He appeared by the table. Behind him, through the glass doors, Owen could see the silhouette of the clerk by the desk.

"What's the time, please?"

The waiter glanced at his watch.

"3:30, m'sieu."

"Fine. That gives us half an hour. We're spending the night across the border in the Costa Brava, so I want to be away by four sharp. We'll have another stroll along the beach. Then I'd like two coffees and my bill here in fifteen minutes."

"Yes, m'sieu."

As he started collecting the empty plates Owen stood up and they walked down towards the sea.

"Where are we going?"

They'd reached the shore, Owen had taken Hélène's arm and they were moving, much more quickly now, west along the beach hidden from the hotel by the dunes.

"Up to the road," he said. "But further along. The Renault's being watched from the front. While it's there they know where we are. Only, in thirty minutes all hell's going to break loose. I told the desk clerk to send out a message at 3:45. He'll give us maybe fifteen minutes grace. Then he'll start asking. The parking lot attendant's going to say we've got a train to catch, the waiter that we're heading for the Costa Brava, while he's been told we're meeting some yacht. They'll be running around in all directions—not least because there's an unpaid bill for their bouillabaisse and their best Moët et Chandon."

"And the men in the Simca?"

"With any luck they'll see it all—even the police. Because if I were a hotel clerk faced with an abandoned car, a dud account and three wildly different stories, the first thing I'd do would be to call the gendarmes."

They were a kilometer along the shore from the hotel and Owen turned inland towards the road.

"But those people watching, they'll know where we've gone—"

Owen shook his head. "They're just hired thugs. They'll learn we've disappeared and telephone in for instructions. Then it'll be up to Charlot—and Charlot will have a problem. By now he'll have been told we were in Bac this morning with his maquis contact. She doesn't know where *le gros renard* was but there must be a possibility we do. And if we do it's equally possible we could find a record some-where of who Charlot really is. A lease, a deed, an entry in the *mairie* register, something—"

A bank of sand sloped up in front of them, they climbed it, walked down the other side through a thicket of low sweet-scented rosemary and came out onto the highway.

"There's only one way for him to check whether we know about the house—to see if we go there. He could tell his men in the Simca to stake the place out. But that way he exposes his own connection with it. I don't think he wants to do that even to his own people. I think he'll go there himself."

The highway curved sharply left at the point where they'd reached it. They walked around the corner and Owen saw another seaside hotel-restaurant in front of them. It was much the same as the one they'd just left except there were more cars in the park and two yellow taxis waiting outside the entrance.

"Where do you want to go, m'sieu?"

The driver looked around as Owen opened the door of the first cab for Hélène to get in.

"It's a little village a few kilometers the other side of Bac." Owen settled himself beside Helene on the rear seat. "I'll give you the directions when we get there."

The driver thought for a moment. Then he shrugged.

"I can take you but I'll have to charge for the run back—I just work the coast."

"That's fine. We'll pay both ways and there'll be a bonus if you do something for us when you return here."

The man took in Hélène and her bag as the clerk had done, nodded, turned around again and swung out onto the road.

The journey took an hour and a half. They bypassed Bac,

continued north for a while, then Owen made the driver slow down until they found the track leading south again through the woods. They turned left, bumped down it and reached the hamlet ten minutes later. There was only a cluster of cottages, a bar and a small shop, but Owen had guessed correctly—the first person he asked knew what they were looking for.

"You must mean Le Sarne, m'sieu—"

It was the woman in the shop. Owen had left Hélène in the taxi outside and gone in alone.

"Le Sarne?"

"It's an old hunting lodge in the trees maybe two kilometers along the way you've come. Here I'll show you—"

She went with him to the door and pointed back down the track.

"If you turn around and go back you'll see a white pillar on the right. The lodge is about five hundred meters into the woods there."

"Do you know who owns it?"

She shook her head. "They say it's some gentleman on the coast. But he never comes here, it's years since anyone's been."

Owen thanked her, returned to the taxi and they drove back along the track.

The pillar was just where the woman had said, a chipped white post two kilometers from the hamlet, with another even more rutted track leading beyond it into the trees. Owen told the driver to stop and asked how much they owed him. The man loked at the meter, calculated the charge for the return trip and said one hundred francs.

"Right." Owen pulled out his wallet. "There's fifty more if you do this—"

He explained what he wanted. The driver was to go to

the hotel where they'd had lunch, find the clerk and say they'd decided on the spur of the moment to make a detour inland. Would the clerk please see their car and luggage was looked after until they returned? Meantime here was the money for their bill—Owen handed over more notes with the fifty-franc tip.

"Un plaisir, m'sieu."

The driver took the notes and smiled.

To him, as to the parking lot atttendant, the tip was handsome by any standards. For the clerk in the hotel the story would be plausible—and acceptable. There'd been no need for the police after all. The bill had been paid. Parisiennes with expensive Gucci handbags were liable to be eccentric: if the car was taken care of, he could count on a discreet but substantial expression of gratitude when they came back to collect it.

Owen and Hélène got out, the taxi disappeared, then they set off along the grassy lane between the trees.

"No—"

Owen caught her arm and pulled her back. They'd come to the end of the track, the trees had opened out and the lodge was in front of them in a clearing.

"Wait here a moment—"

He left her on the track and walked slowly around the clearing through the bushes that encircled it.

The lodge was at its center. Low, wood-framed, walled in birch planks that had weathered to a smokey gray, with a flight of steps leading up to a railed porch running around all four sides. Once huntsmen had sat there on rocking chairs at evening, glasses of wine in their hands as they discussed the day's shooting. Now the balcony was deserted, the boards rotting, the doors padlocked and the windows shuttered.

"You're about to lose an arm—"

Owen had completed the circle, returned to the track and was looking at the tweed jacket draped over Hélène's shoulder.

"That's just of the jacket." He grinned. "The real one goes later if we need it."

He removed the jacket, spread it out on the turf, knelt on the back and ripped off one of the sleeves. Then he started unraveling the yarn from which it had been woven.

"We're assuming Charlot's coming and he'll come on his own," Owen explained as he worked. "All he needs to find out at this stage is whether we even know about the lodge. If he sees fresh footprints that'll be enough—"

Owen pointed over his shoulder. Between the edge of the grass and the walls of the building was a two-meter band of flat, dusty earth. Anyone stepping onto it, as Hélène had been about to do, would leave unmistakeable traces behind her.

"He won't risk going inside, he'll just leave instantly. But if we're going to talk to him, we've got to have him in there. That means getting in ourselves without any sign— and hoping to hell he comes in, too, to be absolutely sure."

The tweed thread unraveled easily and he had about ten meters of it now, coiled at his feet on the ground. Owen stood up, walked off the track into the wood and uprooted a dozen bushes of wild broom, short and dense and springy. He carried the bushes over to a point opposite one of the shutters and linked the thread around their roots. Then he pushed them onto the band of bare earth, unrolling them like a carpet in front of him and walking carefully across the branches until he reached the wall of the lodge.

The base of the shuttered window was at eye level, its sill covered with a layer of the same thick dust on the earth beneath. The shutter clasp looked easy enough, a single metal arm on the inside which he could lever up with a sliver of wood pushed through the central crack. But at either end of the sill was a small loop of wire—curling out below the shutter, around the old-fashioned vertical hinge and then in again on the other side.

Owen examined one of them closely. The woman in the shop had said it was years since anyone had visited the lodge. She was wrong. Someone quite recently had installed a simple but effective alarm system; if the shutters were opened, the hinges would revolve, the circuit would be broken and somewhere a bell would ring. The wires weren't even tarnished, which meant they'd been replaced in the past few months, after the end of the winter rains.

"I need your cigarette case—"

He'd walked back across the carpet of broom to the grass. Hélène normally smoked from the blue-and-white cardboard packs of Gitanes, but she also carried in her bag a large gold case that matched her Cartier lighter—Owen had noticed it the night before in the hotel bedroom.

"And something else—"

She'd handed him the gold case and he was standing in front of her frowning.

"Is this important?"

Owen touched a bracelet around her wrist, a rope of fine plaited silver strands buckled with an emerald-mounted clasp.

"That?" Hélène looked down and smiled. "I've never worn it before. It was my mother's. I put it on when we left Este. Why?"

Owen explained and she nodded immediately, unclipping the bracelet and handing it to him.

"Whatever you want."

She smiled again, they both sat down on the grass and started.

It took them an hour. First Owen wrenched off the emerald clasp, hammered the bracelet flat on a stone and split the silver rope down the center into two sections. Then they unplaited the tiny strands, separating and straightening each one until they had two glittering piles of wire fragments. Finally Owen strung them together again—this time into a single delicate chain.

He walked back to the lodge along the broom and clipped one end of the chain to each of the loops on the shutter hinges. Now, even if the shutters were pulled back, the circuit—and the alarm it controlled—would remain unbroken. With the alarm neutralized he opened Hélène's cigarette case and using his handkerchief swept all the dust on the sill inside. Then he lifted the shutter bar with a twig, parted the two wooden panels, raised the sash behind and climbed in.

There were two floors, one on the porch level, the other up a shallow flight of stairs above. Owen explored them both quickly. The ground floor consisted of a hall with windows on either side of the front door, a gun room, a large salon —presumably used for meals after the day's hunting—and a kitchen beyond. The upper level had a wide landing, a windowless game larder with vents in the roof, and twin passages leading to a number of small bedrooms.

Apart from a few chairs and a pine table in the salon, there was no furniture. The shuttered air smelled stale, plumes of powdered wood coiled in the dim light as Owen walked through, mice rustled behind the wainscot, gray gypsy moths fluttered against the walls. The alarm system might be new but *le gros renard* itself hadn't been used for at least a generation.

"Take your shoes off and walk slowly with your feet as flat as possible—"

Owen had returned to the window and called to Hélène, waiting for him outside on the grass. She did as she was told and he helped her over the sill.

"Now let's see if we can find a bulb that works. With that alarm in place the electricity must have been left on."

They tried all the switches on the ground floor without success, but upstairs two bulbs still glowed—one in the game larder, the other in a bedroom. Owen left the one in the larder but took the second one, screwed it into the socket on the landing and switched it on; with all the doors open it faintly illuminated most of the lodge.

Then he went back to the side window and pulled in the carpet of broom with the tweed thread; there were some ripples on the earth beneath but no trace of a human footprint. He tied a length of the thread to the silver chain, spread the dust in the cigarette case evenly back over the sill, closed the shutters so the circuit was re-established and, jerking lightly at the thread, drew the chain in through the crack.

No one checking the outside of the building now would have any idea it had even been approached, let alone broken into.

"Right, we're almost ready—"

Owen dusted off his hands on his trousers and walked through to the gun room.

He'd noticed the locker when he'd explored it first, a heavy wooden box by the door. Kneeling down, he lifted the lid, rummaged inside—and found exactly what he was looking for. Whoever had installed the alarm had done it himself and left his tools behind. There were hammers, screwdrivers, junction points, coils of wire, a bundle of cord and, most important of all, a big flashlight.

Owen tested the batteries and found they were almost new—a solid beam of light leaped across the floor as he touched the trigger switch at its base. He removed the flashlight and the cord and closed the lid. Then as he stood up he noticed something else lying on the boards by the locker.

"Do you know what this is?"

He handed it to Hélène, who took one glance at it and nodded.

"Of course—it's a priest."

Inevitably, with her countrywoman's knowledge she'd recognized it instantly. A "priest"—the angler's name for a club used to administer the *coup de grâce*, the final bene- diction, to a landed fish. This one was much larger and heavier than normal, a length of antler with a chased bronze rim around the head. The legacy of some long de- parted visitor to the lodge, it had probably been used to kill animals too.

"Maybe we can use it to introduce ourselves to Charlot."

Owen grinned and went back to the hall.

Almost opposite the front door, on the wall by the stairs leading to the upper floor, was a row of iron brackets—sup- ports for tackle, game bags and hunting coats. Owen lashed the flashlight between two of them, tied one end of the cord to the trigger switch, passed the rest of the cord over the next bracket and then around behind the stairs to the door.

Through the crack in the shutters of the window to the left of the door he could see the track between the trees;

through the crack on the other side a flat space of grass below the porch—the logical place for anyone arriving in a car to park. Owen moved from one to the other, turned to face the stairs and tried the cord, tugging it hard towards him. The beam cut across the floor again, this time angled directly at the door.

Someone coming in would be immediately bathed in light —and Owen would be unseen, in the dark.

"That's all."

Owen turned off both the flashlight and the bulb on the landing.

"What do we do now?"

Hélène was standing by the stairs, her torn jacket slung back over her shoulders and one arm shining white in the dusky late-afternoon glow that filtered in from outside.

"We wait."

The moon was already rising over the trees, owls were calling in the wood, a fox barked in the distance and a light wind stirred the grass.

Owen settled himself down by the window, with the cord between his fingers.

20

He came an hour after dark.

Headlamps first, a flicker on the silver underside of the leaves at the bend in the track. Next the sound of an engine carried to the lodge on the evening wind. Then a pale shape in the distance between the trees. Finally all three together: the beams wavering over the ruts, the throb of a motor in low gear, the silhouette of the car itself—a new white Citroën DS.

"Get back against the wall."

Owen had stationed her around the corner of the stair-well on the upper floor.

"I'm already there."

Both their voices were echoing whispers in the silence of the wooden frame. Owen paid out the cord to the flashlight and moved to the left-hand window. He couldn't see the track or the car now, but he was looking directly down at the space where he guessed the man would stop and get out. If he stopped. If he got out. If he was alone. So many guesses and each one had to be right.

Each one was right.

The Citroën drew up below him, the man got out and he was alone. Clouds covered the moon as the car door opened and Owen only saw him for an instant. Tall, a black pinstriped suit, gray hair, a fleshy protruding nose. Then darkness, the glimmer of the parked car and, when the moon came out again, he'd gone.

Owen waited immobile by the window frame and began to count. Five. Five, walking slowly, because he'd be looking at the earth too, to the first of the windows on the north side. Ten more while he checked the shutter latch, the dust on the sill, the alarm wire. Then another five and another ten for the second window. Afterwards the same along the back and then again as he came up the southern wall.

Ninety in all and he should be standing before the front porch. Fifteen to check the dust there. Now a last fifteen to think, to collect himself, to decide whether that was enough and he could leave satisfied no one had been there. Or whether he wanted to be absolutely certain, to climb the steps, open the door and come inside.

He wanted to be certain. His feet rang on the boards and Owen stiffened, the bronze-tipped priest in one hand, the cord taut in the other. Silence again on the porch as he examined the lock. Then the rattle of a key, a click as it slotted home, the rasp of rusting hinges and a square of moonlight on the floor.

Now.

Owen jerked the cord and the beam blazed out. There was a hiss, a scuffle as the man whirled towards the light, then the roar of a gun. He fired three times in succession. The noise was deafening in the shuttered hall, the woodwork behind the torch splintered and the air filled with smoke and the stench of cordite.

Owen waited a moment longer. Then he stepped forward and lashed down from behind. The club caught the man's wrist at the function with his hand and the gun clattered to the floor. He moaned and lurched forward, buckling at the waist. Owen kicked the gun towards the door.

"Kneel down—"

The man knelt, cradling his wrist to his stomach with his other arm.

Hélène—"

He tugged the cord again, the torch went out and she came downstairs.

"Get the gun and come here—"

She crossed the moon-bright space of the open doorway and stooped. Then she was beside him, the gun in her hand. Owen took it, snapped open the breech with his thumb and probed inside. It was a heavy Swiss-made Berchers revolver with one unfired bullet in the chamber and two more in the magazine. He closed the breech and gave the gun back to her.

"Put it against the base of his spine. If he does anything, if he even breathes, just pull the trigger."

The instruction was for the man's benefit, not hers, but it was unnecessary. The club had shattered his wrist and he was incapable of anything.

As she leaned over with the barrel jabbing into his back, Owen knelt down too, pushed him onto his side and began to search him. Quickly, methodically, brutally. Pulling off his shoes and socks. Feeling up his legs to his groin. Unzipping his trousers and dragging off his belt. Going through his pockets, around his rib cage, under his shoulders.

Apart from some loose change, a pair of spectacles and a wallet, there was nothing.

"Get up—"

The man moaned again as he stood, one hand holding up his trousers, the other, the broken one, dangling limply at his side.

"Now upstairs—"

Owen took the gun from Hélène and prodded him towards the staircase. They climbed slowly in procession, illuminated only by the glow of moonlight through the door below.

"In here—"

They'd reached the upper floor and the game larder was in front of them, windowless and impenetrably black. Owen pushed the man inside and heard him stumble blindly in the darkness.

"Are you all right?"

He glanced around at Hélène behind him on the landing, looking at her for the first time since the shots were fired.

She nodded calmly. "I'm fine."

"Good. Get the flashlight, lock the door, then come back up here and watch the track. We'll decide what we're going to do later. First I want to talk to our friend."

Owen walked into the game larder, felt for the light-switch, found it, slammed the door shut and turned the switch on. The man was standing at the center of the room, swaying and groping out with his one good hand. As he blinked in the sudden light Owen knocked him onto the chair and dragged his jacket over its back, imprisoning him.

Then Owen reached into the man's pocket and pulled out the wallet he'd felt when he was searching him. Expensive black crocodile with a thousand frances in new notes, some credit cards and a sheaf of business cards. The name on the cards was Jacques D. Villemorin. It matched the gold-blocked initials on the leather.

"Monsieur Villemorin, is that right?"

"That's my name."

Owen tapped one of the cards against the wallet. Then he crumpled it in his hand.

"That—and Charlot."

For a moment he didn't deny or acknowledge it. He simply sat there, half slumped, half trapped. Tall, elegant, gray hair brushed flat, face tanned, eyes dark and set in wrinkles. In his early sixties but still handsome, a ladies' man, Owen thought, with the sexual symbol of the big red-veined nose jutting aggressively forward. A ladies' man—and a successful one.

The superbly cut black suit came from Saville Row, the shoes were Italian, the pin on his Cardin tie had a diamond head. Whatever else, Villemorin was rich, very rich—even pinioned on the chair he had the presence of an affluent banker.

"Who the hell are you?"

He propped himself upright against the chair back. The blow on his wrist had torn the skin and a trickle of blood was staining his thigh, but maybe because the pain was starting to dull some threads of defiance were coming back.

"You know who I am," Owen said flatly. "Just as you

knew who Walpole and Baring were—didn't you, Charlot?"

Silence. There were hooks around the walls where the game had been hung—pheasants, partridges, quail, deer. Now they were blackened and rusting away.

"I was known as Charlot in the war." Villemorin managed to shrug. "But what's that got to do with you—?"

"This came from the war, did it?"

Owen cut him off and pointed at the small scarlet button of the Légion d'Honneur in his lapel.

"Yes."

"Lovely then, isn't it—?"

Owen leaned forward and fingered the button smiling. Then he suddenly chopped his hand across Villemorin's nose. Not hard enough to break the bone but enough to jolt his head back, make him wince, bring tears to his eyes.

"Tell me about the war, Charlot."

"Salaud!"

He'd put his hand to his face and was shuddering from the new pain.

"Aren't I, just?" Owen stepped back. "Only I can do better than that, a lot better. I will, too, all night until I get what I want. And I want everything, Charlot. The Orion line, the ring you set up with the Germans, Walpole, Baring, those thugs you sent after me, everything."

"I don't know what you're talking about."

There was blood running from his nose as well as his wrist, but his face was expressionless.

"You don't? Then why did you fire that gun at me in the hall?"

"I didn't know who I was firing at. It's my property. I have a police license to carry a revolver. When the light went on, I thought it was an intruder. I was right."

"So right you already had the gun out and you didn't even have to check to make sure?"

"The police will accept that—"

"Oh, they will, will they? The police will *accept* that?"

Owen moved behind the chair and leaned against the wall.

Villemorin had made a mistake, they both knew it and instantly it had changed everything. Until then, denying knowledge of anything Owen put to him, he'd been an innocent property owner, licensed to carry a gun and firing on what he thought was an intruder. Now, with a single ill-chosen word, he'd tacitly admitted that he was expecting them to be there, that he'd arrived ready to kill, that he'd prepared a story for the police to explain what had happened afterwards.

Owen broke off one of the game hooks, shredded the rusty metal in his fingers and waited.

"What's the time?"

Villemorin had twisted himself around to look over the chair. Owen glanced at his watch.

"A quarter past ten."

Villemorin calculated silently. When he spoke again there was a viciousness in his voice that hadn't been there before.

"You've got forty-five minutes, maybe an hour, at most."

Owen nodded. He'd guessed that too. Someone of Villemorin's experience, with his maquis training, with the legacy of the thirty years when he'd killed mercilessly and efficiently as the occasion required, wouldn't have left himself without a fall-back—without cover.

"How did you do it?"

Villemorin turned and shrugged again with his back to Owen.

"That's my concern."

"Well, let's make it mine too—"

Owen pushed himself away from the wall, gripped the broken wrist and started to bend it back.

"Because if not you're going to be surprised to learn how much a *salaud* can fit into forty-five minutes."

Villemorin tensed, half-screamed and shook his head, sweat spraying his jacket.

"They're at Bac—"

Owen dropped the wrist and listened.

"In a telephone kiosk outside the town. I left a sealed envelope with them. If I don't call by 10:45, they'll open the envelope. Inside there are directions on how to get here and what to do when they arrive. It won't take them more than half an hour. That's the truth."

"I believe you."

Owen stepped back once more. It was the truth, he was sure of that. All pretense had gone now and they were talking equally on common ground.

"But I'll still have you, then, won't I?" Owen said. "However many arrive, there'll still be me and this—"

He balanced the revolver on his palm.

"What are they going to do when they see it stuck into the back of your neck?"

"They'll call the police, wait until they come, then leave it to them."

Owen looked down at him. His face was white under the tan and sheeted with sweat, there was a runnel of blood on his chin, a spreading stain on his trousers, and his arms were still caught in his jacket sleeves. But even as Owen watched he could see his confidence returning.

"You think of everything, Charlot, don't you? But then you always did."

Villemorin thought he'd won. All he had to do was hold out for less than an hour. Owen could hurt him badly in the time but not enough to make him tell the truth about the line. For Villemorin there was still too much at stake, as there had been for thirty years—he'd hold out.

When the hour was up his men would arrive. They'd call the police and vanish as soon as the gendarmes got there. Then the positions would be reversed. There was nothing to connect Villemorin with the attacks on the road. Instead Owen would have to explain why he'd broken into the lodge and assaulted an innocent man—and not even Hélène de Sourraines could save him from charges on that.

"Listen—"

Villemorin gazed up. There was cunning in his voice now, the plausible cunning of a man who made shred bargains and kept safe secrets.

"It'll serve neither of us if the police come in. Trouble for you, embarrassment, publicity, talk for me. You don't know now and you'll never prove anything whatever you do. Leave it, go away, go back to wherever you came from and I'll forget it ever happened."

Owen said nothing for a moment. Then he bent over the chair and started to unknot Villemorin's tie.

"What are you doing?" Villemorin's chin jerked up. "Doesn't that make sense for both of us?"

"It makes perfect sense to me—"

Owen went around to the back of the chair and lashed around Villemorin's good hand to it, so that he was help-less.

"The trouble is we've both forgotten one thing." He stood up. "There aren't just two of us—there's a third. And she's got rather a special interest, hasn't she?"

Owen opened the door, switched off the light, closed the door behind him and walked down the passage.

Hélène was waiting silhouetted against the side window above the track. She turned around as Owen came up and listened in silence while he told her what had happened in the game larder. Then she lit a cigarette.

"He's telling the truth?"

Owen nodded. "I think so. It's what I'd have done in the same situation. He may have juggled the time a bit to pressure me, but not by much. An hour and a half at most and they'll be here."

"So we know everything—and nothing."

"Yes."

Everything. The penetration of the line, the network of collaborators along its length, the reason for Walpole's and Baring's deaths, the location of the last safe-house, even the identity of Charlot. Yet in the end it was all worthless, it was nothing. The explanation for the original betrayal and the killings that had punctuated the thirty years which followed, only Villemorin knew that—and in sixty minutes their final chance of learning, too, would be gone.

"I want to know—"

Hélène ground out her cigarette and paused.

The moon was higher and the light stronger now. Looking at her, Owen remembered the two photographs in the Count's drawing room. Mother and daughter. Both with the same thick chestnut hair, strong jaws, wide, direct eyes. But where in Marie the strength had been passionate and engaged, in Hélène it had been distant and withdrawn.

Now that had changed too. The energy, the power, the candor were still there—but the commitment in the face against the glass was Marie's.

"If there's anything we can do, anything at all, and whatever it means, then we should do it."

Owen shifted his weight to his left leg and rubbed his thigh, aching after the long hours of waiting.

"There's one possibility, an outside possibility," he said. "It's a guess, it'll be difficult, dangerous and expensive. But it may be the answer—"

He explained carefully, feeling for the words, trying to work it out for himself, reaching back into the past, into his memory, into what he'd read and been told and taught. Gathering together the elements of greed and law and probability that might hold it all together—and break Charlot in the crucible where they met.

"We'll go."

Hélène interrupted him before he'd finished. He followed her down the passage to the larder, opened the door and turned on the light.

Villemorin screwed up his eyes at the brightness. He was still sitting in the center of the floor, but he'd slipped his good arm out of the jacket sleeve and was gnawing at the knot in the tie Owen had wrapped around his hand. As they came in he lowered the hand to his lap and looked up at them.

"This is Madame de Sourraines," Owen said. "I think you knew her mother, didn't you, Charlot—?"

Villemorin didn't answer. He glanced at Hélène impassively, then back at Owen.

"Are you going?"

"Yes, we're going—"

Owen went over to the chair, forced Villemorin's arm back into the sleeve and lifted his jacket up onto his shoulders so he could move again.

"We're all going. We're going into Vézey, we're going to find a guide and we're going to cross the border. Get up—!"

He grasped Villemorin's elbow and tugged him to his feet.

"*Le gros renard* wasn't used in the war, but it's being used now. Because that's what it was for, Charlot, wasn't it? To get people out of France and into Spain—where you're going."

Owen pushed him towards the door. As he lurched forward Owen saw the Frenchman's face was white and the tendons in his neck were trembling.

21

"Something else too, something unmistakable—"

Owen paused. Behind him, on the rear seat, Hélène frowned and thought.

They were in the white Citroën in a copse off the road half a kilometer above Vézey, with the lights of the border village glimmering through the trees below. Owen had driven there straight from the lodge in Villemorin's car. Villemorin hadn't spoken during the drive. He was still lying where Owen had put him when they left—face down on the floor with Hélène above him holding the gun.

"This?"

She'd already given Owen her identity card and checkbook with the de Sourraines name stamped below a Roth-schild's private account number. Now she opened her bag and handed over another object—the little bun Madame Lachasse had pricked in the bakery with the letters VLFL, the wartime maquis code for the passengers traveling down the last stage of the line.

"That's perfect—"

Owen put the gun in his pocket and opened his door.

"Change places with me. I don't know how long I'll need, maybe a couple of hours, but watch him all the time. It's like before. If he even stirs, don't ask why—just fire."

As she got out Owen went around to the back, squatted down, reached into the car and lifted Villemorin's head off the floor by his hair.

"Did you hear that, Charlot?"

"You're mad!"

Villemorin's face was still white and blood-caked, but for some reason the hoarse voice was defiant and confident again.

"We'll see. Meantime just remember while I'm finding out that you've got Marie's daughter looking after you."

Owen slammed Villemorin's head down and heard him moan. Then he stood up, checked that Hélène was behind the wheel with the revolver and set off down the slope through the wood.

He'd told Hélène it might take him two hours—and that was even if the man was there at all. Owen was wrong. He needed only forty-five minutes.

"It'll cost you a bit—"

"How much?" Owen asked.

The man spat out a damp Gauloise butt, scratched his chin, then drank slowly from the pottery mug of wine—

taking his time before he answered. Owen watched him in silence.

Antoine. The best—and in Madame Lachasse's view the most villainous—of the guides who'd handled the border crossings. Owen had been lucky. He'd found him in the first bar in Vézey he'd entered, asking the patron for the Antoine who'd worked with the resistance and being pointed to a table at the back. Antoine was sitting there alone.

He could have been anything from fifty to seventy, a rawboned, taciturn man with an ageless peasant's face, seamed and sun darkened, small blank eyes and grizzled hair under a faded beret. Owen had bought two drinks at the bar, asked if he could join him and sat down at the table. He showed him Hélène's checkbook, her identity card and the little branded bun to establish his credentials. Then he told Antoine the story.

He was traveling with Marie de Sourraines' daughter and someone else, someone who'd been a wartime collaborator with the Germans. He and Hélène wanted to take the man over the border into Spain. They had to cross that night and they were prepared to pay well for an escort. That was all.

Antoine had listened impassively while the other drinkers talked and laughed at the counter. Now he was considering the price.

"Five thousand francs," he said finally. "In cash before we leave."

Owen whistled. "That isn't a price—that's a ransom."

"It's not so easy recently. All the *bagarre* with the Catalan nationalists and they've doubled the patrols on both sides." He shrugged. "If I get caught the fine's twice that You won't find anyone who'll do it for less."

Owen hesitated for a moment, but he knew Antoine was right. With the Basques and Catalans using France as a base for their raids in northern Spain, the border tensions—and the dangers in crossing it illegally—had increased dramatically over the past few years. Also Antoine was the only chance they had.

It was 10:45. Any minute Villemorin's men would reach the lodge, find it deserted and contact the police. Within an hour a general alert would be out for the white Citroën and its three passengers. There'd be other guides in Vézey but Owen wouldn't be able to find one and agree a better price in the time. And by midnight, when news of the police search reached the village, no one would be prepared to take them over.

"All right," Owen said. "But only two thousand in cash, it's all we've got with us. The other three on a bearer check—"

They argued for another five minutes before Owen convinced him that a combination of the de Sourraines name and a Rothschild account guaranteed the check would be cashed. Then Antoine nodded.

"There's a bridge on the Ste. Denise road a kilometer up the valley. Wait for me below the arch by the stream. I'll meet you there in half an hour—"

Owen listened while Antoine told him how to find it. Then he stood up, shook hands as if he were saying goodbye and walked to the door—thanking the patron on the way out.

Hélène and Villemorin were still in the car as he'd left them—Villemorin lying on the floor at the back, Hélène in the front seat with his gun. Owen beckoned her outside and told her quietly what he'd arranged. Then he opened the rear door.

"Get out, Charlot. We're on our way."

Villemorin pushed himself up and stumbled out, standing swaying on the grass in the darkness of the copse. His broken wrist had caught the car door—his other hand was still trussed by the tie—and his face was rigid with pain.

"You'll never make it, you're crazy!"

As his voice rose Owen slapped him hard against the cheek with the palm of his hand.

"If you speak again before I tell you to, you won't even be here to discover—I'll just break your neck too."

Owen swiveled him around and pushed him forward onto a path that ran parallel to the road down into the valley. Then they set off, Owen in front, Villemorin behind him, Hélène at the rear still carrying the gun.

Twenty minutes later, following Antoine's directions, they reached the bridge on the Ste. Denise road. Owen clambered down into the bed of the stream. There was a bank of sand on either side, a stone arch black against the sky, and the water—rock-stewn and stippled with stars—foaming through the center. Villemorin and Hélène joined him on the sand. Then they waited.

Occasionally, through the wavering grass above, Owen saw the lights of Vézey, their reflections cupped and held for an instant in the leaves of the roadside trees. Beyond them to the south a glow like a coronet marked Bac-sur-Challey. And dominating the entire horizon in an immense sweep from right to left were the foothills of the Pyrenees. Dark, rounded, wind swept, rising to the snow flanks on the mountain slopes—and the Spanish border.

"You're ready—"

Owen swung around. He hadn't heard him arrive, but it was Antoine's voice, coming from the deepest shadow under the arch.

"Yes."

"And the money?"

"Here."

Owen gave him the two thousand francs in notes and the check Hélène had written out by the car. Antoine took them, stepped back into the moonlight, counted the money and examined the check.

"Madame's with you?"

"Yes, she's here."

"Can she come forward a moment?"

Owen turned. Hélène was behind his shoulder under the other side of the arch. As Antoine spoke she moved out and stood in front of him on the bank. Antoine gazed at her face in the reflected light from the stream. Then he nodded, satisfied.

"I knew your mother, madame. She was a fine lady."

It was all he said and he didn't even glance at Villemorin. He put the check in his pocket, came back into the shadow of the arch and stood there, listening and smelling the air. Then he touched Owen's elbow and climbed up to the road. Owen waved Hélène forward to follow him, prodded Villemorin behind her and took the rear position himself. They crossed the road in file and set off through the fields beyond.

The first hour was easy. They were crossing the belt of farmland that ran in from the sea along the coastal plain. The fields were flat and cultivated, wide spaces of young vines or firm, scented grass, and they moved quickly in the shelter of the hedgerows that bordered them. Later it became more difficult. The fields ended, the land sloped upwards in planes of scrub and rock, and after a while Owen heard Villemorin laboring and panting in front of him.

They went on for another half hour. Then, with Villemorin lurching from side to side, Owen walked forward to join Antoine at the head of the column.

"Is there somewhere we can take a rest?"

He spoke in a whisper although they hadn't seen any lights since the last of the farms below. Antoine pointed ahead.

"In half a kilometer."

It turned out to be a gully with oleanders overhanging the sandy-walled sides. The slid down through the bushes and Villemorin promptly slumped to the ground. Owen left him there and rejoined Antoine, who was sitting on a rock, smoking.

"How far have we come?"

"About six kilometers."

"And to the border?"

"Maybe another three."

"That's all?"

"The distance isn't the problem—"

Antoine drew on his cigarette, holding it cradled inside his fingers so the glowing tip made a small pink lantern of his hand.

"Where we are now, it's the start of what we call *le chemin du tire-bouchon*. The next kilometer's not too bad. The path winds up, but gently and with big open sections between the rocks—"

He revolved his other hand imitating the corkscrew that had given the gully its name. Then he spread out his fingers and inclined them sharply upwards.

"After that it splits. Twenty, fifty, perhaps even a hundred other gullies. All of them narrow and steep and hard right up to the border and across the other side. With the patrols, the Spanish *guardias,* we have to go four kilometers beyond before it's safe. For madame it won't be difficult—"

He nodded towards Hélène, who was kneeling on the sand listening.

"She moves like her mother, like a hill farmer." He smiled. "Nor for you, m'sieu. But that one—"

Antoine gestured in the direction of Villemorin.

"I don't know. He's your responsibility, not mine. If he breaks down, then we either leave him and continue, just the three of us, or, if you wish to stay with him, I go back on my own. I tell you that in fairness. At night, even with the Catalan troubles, they leave *le tire-bouchon* alone. But by morning there'll be gendarmes all over."

"He won't break down," Owen said, "but if he does I'll carry him."

Owen turned and touched Hélène's hair.

"How's the hill farmer?"

"Learning what it's like to live like a *barbouze,* but I'll survive."

She smiled, and he walked down the gulley to where Villemorin was lying propped against the sandy wall with the oleanders cascading over his shoulders.

"We're going on, Charlot."

"I can't—"

It was after midnight and the air had cooled sharply with the height and the darkness, but his face was covered with sweat again. The drops had run down his nose and streaked the dried blood on his chin.

"Listen." He pushed himself away from the sand. "I had a coronary two years ago, a bad one. If it happens again, it's over, *fini!* And it will up here, I know the *tire-bouchon.* How's that going to help you?"

"Then talk now and we won't have to go any further."

Villemorin looked at him, taut, murderous, silent, his broken wrist tucked under his jacket, the other hand—the tie around it tattered and sweat-stained too now—resting on his knee. Then he spat.

"You bastard!"

Owen hit him twice lightly, sharply, taunting—going for, and getting, the response he wanted. Anger. Anger that would override Villemorin's fatigue, trigger an adrenalin flow, goad him into a mindless reaction of hate—a reaction that would carry him up the hill slopes ahead to the border.

"*Espèce de cen!*"

Villemorin's crippled hand flailed out wildly towards Owen's head. Owen leaned back, chopped the hand down as it swung past him and caught Villemorin's arm, clenching his fingers tight around the muscle.

"Get up—"

Owen dragged him to his feet, and pushed him towards Antoine and Hélène.

"Let's go."

He tapped his knuckles against Villemorin's spine, Antoine nodded and they set off along the gully.

A hundred yards further on Antoine raised his arm and the other three paused while he disappeared around a boulder. An instant later he came into sight again, beckoning urgently for Owen. Owen told Villemorin in a whisper to lie down and went up to the boulder with Hélène.

"Did anyone else know you wanted to cross tonight?" Antoine asked.

Owen shook his head. "We only decided a few hours ago. Apart from you we haven't seen or spoken to anyone else since then. Why?"

"Look—"

On the far side of the boulder there was a well of shadow

cast by the rising moon. Antoine stepped back into it, Owen and Hélène followed him and stood gazing in the direction in which the guide was pointing.

To their left the wall of the gully continued upwards, steep and thick with bushes. But on the right the sandy bank had abruptly flattened out and for fifty yards the ground was clear. Below it the hillside fell in a barren slope that opened like a widening funnel onto the plain. Antoine's arm was angled down over the slope.

It took Owen a few seconds to trace what he was pointing at. Then he saw them. Four figures, black silhouettes against the moonlit earth, climbing quickly and purposefully up a narrow track towards them. They were still almost a kilometer away but at the speed they were moving, they'd reach the gully in little more than ten minutes.

"Are they gendarmes?" Owen said.

"No. The police patrols are uniformed and they have dogs."

"Then maybe another group crossing? Basques or smugglers?"

"Using that route in the open?" Antoine shrugged dismissively. "Not a chance; they'd take the *tire-bouchon* like us. You know what I think? I'll tell you. Look over there—"

He swung his arm west towards a craggy spur that towered high above the gully just in front of them.

"From the top you can watch all of the gulley until it splits. The police sometimes put patrols up there, that's why I checked. If anyone uses the *tire-bouchon*, they see them crossing the open sections. There aren't any gendarmes on the hill tonight, but those people, that's where I guess they're heading."

Owen waited an instant longer. Then he swung round, went back to Villemorin and bent down.

"There are some men out on the hillside, Charlot. Are they yours?"

Villemorin lifted his head and started to laugh, a vengeful triumphant laugh that creased his skin and sent the dried blood flaking onto the ground.

"I told you you'd never make it, you little bastard—"

Owen crouched lower, swiveled slightly and hit him again, much harder than before, jolting his knuckles into the Frenchman's mouth so that he was slammed back against the sand.

"Just answer, Charlot, and if they are, tell me how. Because if you don't there'll be nothing for them to collect when they get here."

"Someone in Vézey—"

Shuddering, gasping, blood running from his mouth again, Villemorin levered himself upright and started.

By then Owen had almost worked it out for himself, and it explained the Frenchman's periodic flashes of confidence ever since they'd left the lodge. When they'd vanished from the beach that afternoon Villemorin had posted a man at the border village in case they reappeared there and tried to make a crossing. If they did the man was to telephone the others in Bac and go with them to the spur that commanded the *tire-bouchon*—the logical route they'd take if they followed the course of the line to its end.

The man must have seen Owen when he entered the village to find Antoine and carried out his instructions. He'd contacted the rest of the group, they'd driven up the valley from Bac, and now they were within minutes of reaching the spur.

"And if they spot us from the top," Owen said, "you've told them to shoot?"

"Listen, that's not necessary now—"

The confidence was still there, the certainty he was safe, but pain had blunted the triumph and Villemorin's voice was wheedling.

"I'm no use to you as a hostage. They could walk right up and take me away and you couldn't do anything. Because if you kill me you'll learn nothing. And either way you'll still have them to deal with. But if you let me go I'll stop them and you can go too—"

"Shut up!"

Owen jabbed him savagely in the chest so that he rolled back against the gully wall. Then he got to his feet and returned to the boulder. Antoine and Hélène were still standing in the shadow watching the shelving hillside. It was three or four minutes since he'd left them and although the black silhouettes had momentarily disappeared, hidden by a fold in the ground, they could only be a bare five hundred yards below.

"Is there any way we can track back and make a detour?"

"Without being seen?" Antoine shook his head. "We'd have to go down to the plain again and start from somewhere else. They'd pick us up the moment we left the *tirebouchon*."

Under his breath Owen began to swear. Slowly, deliberately, viciously. Repeating in Welsh the words and phrases he'd learned as a boy from the miners at the pithead. It was the first time in years he'd used them and as he did so he incongruously remembered the ancient dictum that however many languages a man speaks, at the end he'll always count, pray or curse in his native tongue.

It was the end—the end of the one fragile chance of uncovering the truth behind the Orion line. If they'd been

254

able to cross the border with Villemorin, he'd gambled on the Frenchman being forced to take the other side. Now he'd never even know if the gamble would have worked. Whether they went on or turned back they'd be seen from the vantage point of the spur as they crossed one of the open sections of the *tire-bouchon*.

As soon as that happened they were finished. Slowed by the speed at which Villemorin could move, they'd be over-taken in minutes by his four thugs. Then they'd have no choice but to hand him over. Until he'd talked, as he said himself, he was worthless as a hostage. All he had to do was keep his nerve and any threat to kill him would be meaningless.

With the same furious intensity Owen swore again, quietly but this time out loud. The two weeks since he'd walked out of Mathieson's office, the thousand-mile journey across Europe, the unraveling of a thirty-year-old past woven from courage, greed, deceit and treachery, the attack in St. Julien, the days at the chateau, the inexorably emerging pattern of violence and betrayal, the discovery of the lodge and Charlot's identity—all of it reduced now, with the final questions still unanswered, to a hollow impasse on a border hill flank.

Then he heard something. Hélène's voice low in the shadow behind him. He turned and saw she'd been speaking to Antoine. As he watched Antoine pulled her check out of his pocket. She took it, altered it quickly with her pen and gave it back.

"All right?" she said.

Antoine nodded. "I'll get him and we'll go."

He stepped around the boulder and disappeared into the mouth of the gully.

"Listen to me—"

Owen had been about to ask her what was happening but she caught his arm and spoke before he could.

"It's a kilometer from here to where the gully splits. Fifteen, maybe twenty minutes, Antoine says, even with Villemorin. After that it's safe. There are pine woods, rocks, ravines, a hundred different tracks. They'd need an army just to cover half of them."

"But they'll see us on the first open stretch—"

"Not if they don't reach the spur."

Owen looked at her, bewildered for a moment. She was still holding Villemorin's revolver and she worked the breech quickly, expertly, checking that there was a bullet in the chamber and the safety catch was off before she put the gun down on a ledge in the boulder.

"Give me the box—"

As she held out her hand Owen realized what she intended to do. He stiffened and opened his mouth but again she went on before he could say anything.

"I've used guns all my life, I'm probably a better shot than any of them. And I've got everything on my side, cover, surprise, the *tire-bouchon* to hide in, while they'll be exposed, out in the open. All I'm doing is buying fifteen minutes."

"Hélène, for Christ's sake—"

Owen burst out now, shaking his head, suddenly cold and confused and disbelieving.

"There are four of them, armed thugs. You've seen what they've tried to do already. You think I'm going to leave you here alone—"

"You came out here to learn what happened on the line." She cut him off. "The one way you'll find out now is with Charlot across the border. But you aren't the only one who wants to know. There's me too. For my mother, for the others who got killed, for everything since. I said I wanted to lay a ghost—"

She smiled, calm, confident, utterly sure of herself with the night wind tugging at her hair and the collar of her blouse fluttering against the blackness of the rock.

"The ghost I've lived with all my life, being Marie de Sourraines' daughter and hating it, hating her even, because all I saw was the exploitation of what she'd done. The lies, the greed, the phoney romanticism, the people grubbing for money out of their cheap new Jeanne d'Arc. That's what I knew, what I grew up with, and because of it I thought she was the same. Well, I was wrong, totally wrong, and this week with you I laid that ghost to rest. The Orion line was valuable and right. Only it's not finished, is it? And unless it is, unless it's cleaned, unless we know the truth, then there'll just be another ghost to live with—"

She broke off as Antoine reappeared with Villemorin. The guide was half-supporting him with one arm tucked under his shoulder and resting across his neck. If Villemorin tried to shout Antoine could chop backwards and silence him instantly.

They paused in the shadow, Hélène waved them forward, Antoine pushed Villemorin out onto the turf, then she looked back at Owen.

"Give me the box, Gareth, and go on with them."

Owen hesitated, glanced over the open grass, then down the funnel of the hillside. The four silhouettes were still hidden in the folding ground, but it could only be seconds now before they came into sight again.

He turned back, gazed at her, tried to speak and shook his head helplessly.

"Just that box—"

Her hand was outstretched again and she was still smiling and Owen knew there was nothing he could do to stop her. The chilling logic of the old Count, the implacable courage of her mother, both of them had fused in her. Except that she was now neither prisoner nor rebel to either. She was her own person.

"I'll need an hour at least after we cross—"

Owen fumbled in his pocket, found the heavy cardboard box of ammunition and gave it to her.

"Then maybe another two hours to get back. Say six hours in all. It'll be dawn by then."

"I'll meet you by the bridge on the Ste. Denise road where we started—"

She put the box down by the gun, paused, laughed quickly, leaned forward and touched his face.

"Don't worry, I'll be there. Just make sure you come back with the truth. Go on now!"

Owen waited a moment longer. Then he turned and raced across the turf. He caught up with the other two as they reached the point where the gully started again, settled himself on the opposite side of Villemorin to Antoine, and the three of them plunged into the bushes.

They heard the first shot a minute later, a thin distant crack muffled by the winding walls of sand. Owen checked, jerked his head up and listened. There were two more close together, a pause, a fourth and silence. Then Antoine pulled Villemorin forward again and they went on. Twice in the next ten minutes the sound of firing drifted up to them on the wind, but each time the shots were fainter and when they reached the end of the *tire-bouchon* the noise stopped.

Afterwards there were two chilling, muscle-aching hours

of unremitting effort. The ground grew constantly steeper. They wound through snaking corries, climbed great banks of loose shale, glistening blue-gray in the moonlight, trudged up long slopes of moorland, clambered over heaps of rocks hanging above the little streams that tumbled down from the mountains.

Once Antoine froze and beckoned urgently towards the ground. They lay face down, Owen with his hands around Villemorin's throat. Somewhere above them he could hear voices and the clatter of falling stones—a border patrol, he guessed, although he couldn't tell what language they were talking. The voices faded, they waited another fifteen minutes, then, stiff and shivering in the raw air, they climbed on. Villemorin had long since virtually collapsed and they were dragging him between them—a shambling groaning figure with his pin-striped jacket flapping and his Italian shoes slashed to ribbons by the rocks.

Owen never knew when they actually crossed the border or how far they'd gone on the other side, but at 1:30—with the snow flanks gleaming above them—Antoine stopped.

"We're there?"

Owen was rubbing his face, running with sweat in spite of the cold. They'd let go of Villemorin and the Frenchman was lying heaving at his feet.

Antoine nodded. "There's a shepherd's hut—"

He pointed downwards. They were on a hogbacked ridge with a little plateau just below them to their left. Owen looked down and saw it—a shack framed by a clump of pines.

"It's only used in winter. We'll be safe there for as long as you want."

They heaved Villemorin up, manhandled him down the

slope and across the plateau to the door. Antoine hammered off the padlock, kicked open the door and they went inside. As the guide hunted for a candle Owen stood in the darkness with Villemorin gasping on the floor. He was gazing back down the hill flanks and for an instant he'd forgotten about everything except Hélène laughing by the boulder, the shots echoing over the gully and the bridge on the Ste. Denise road. Then a match flared and he turned around.

First there was Charlot and the answer to the guess he'd made as he stood with Hélène by the window in the lodge.

22

"Tell me—"

Owen leaned against the wall and shifted his weight onto his right leg.

"Tell me everything."

Twenty minutes later. Antoine had found two candles and they were burning at either end of the hut—a small sturdy box built against the mountain winds and rain, with a pine table, a couple of chairs and an iron stove. He'd also kindled a fire in the stove and brewed coffee, producing an oilskin sack from his jacket and using an ancient kettle.

Villemorin lifted his head slowly, wearily, hopelessly.

He'd partially recovered from the climb but all the defiance had gone now, crumbling like the façade of a ruined house. Instead there was just an exhausted and frightened old man with a heart condition.

"What happens if I do?"

"Let's start with what happens if you don't. We're ten kilometers from the nearest village. From there it'll take us five hours by taxi to Barcelona. Say eight hours in total from here to the *guardia* headquarters—and that's all you'll have left. That and maybe as many months again before the trial."

"You won't be able to prove it to them."

"You think so—?"

Owen stepped forward. Villemorin's head had dropped back onto his chest and the words had been a mumble, a final desperate attempt to avoid what was coming, but Owen knew he'd won. He jabbed his palm under Villemorin's chin and lifted his face.

"Fine, if you want to gamble on that, you just say so and let's save time. But I'll tell you something. I think I can prove it—and I'll go to the bloody ends of the earth to see I do."

He stood there tense, furious, his hip aching and throbbing from the strain of the climb. Then he removed his hand abruptly, turned away and propped himself against the wall again. Antoine was squatting, uninterested, over his mug of coffee by the door.

"And if I tell you?"

"You can go back to France."

Villemorin's head jerked up once more, startled and incredulous this time.

"I can go back?"

Owen nodded. "Use your head. You know where I come from, what my business is. Not revenge, not even justice—simply intelligence. Once I know I don't care a damn about you. You can return the way you came, go on doing whatever it is you do—"

Villemorin was still peering at him disbelievingly.

"Listen," Owen went on, "if I hand you over to the Spanish authorities, first of all I've got to prove it, like you said. Then I'll have to stay here for the trial. Finally, I'll have some problems of my own—like explaining why I came over the border that way. You really think I'm going to waste a year and look for that sort of trouble if I can avoid it?"

It was close enough to the truth and it worked. Villemorin said nothing for several minutes. Then he slumped forward over the table.

"Is there some more coffee?"

Owen got the kettle from the stove, filled his mug and went back to the wall. Villemorin collected himself and drank. Then, with the candles guttering, he began.

Narcotics. A recurring image in Owen's mind had triggered the guess—the Marseilles registration number on the plates of all the vehicles that had followed them. The ice-blue Simca, the two trucks, Villemorin's own white Citroën. Marseilles, the hired thugs with the thick southern accents, the ring of collaborators all those years ago, the gold, the crossings of the Spanish border—once Owen had made the connection the rest of the chain unraveled inexorably.

It meant that for Villemorin Spain represented an infinitely greater threat than anything he could encounter in France. After the civil war ended Franco had progressively declared amnesties for all crimes against the state—all except one. Autocratic, puritanical and unyielding, the Generalissimo had repeatedly said that for narcotics smuggling there would never be a statute of limitations. Even now, more than thirty years later, Villemorin could still face trial, imprisonment, conceivably execution.

Owen knew it as well as the Frenchman and the issue had hung unspoken between them from the moment he'd said he was taking Villemorin over the border. Finally, despairingly, Villemorin had challenged him to prove it. Owen had accepted the challenge and hurled it back. Now, gray-faced and exhausted, Villemorin had conceded defeat. He started to talk and it should have been the end, the explanation for everything connected with the Orion line.

It wasn't the end. What had happened afterwards was different, totally different, from anything Owen had imagined, and as he listened his mind numbed with bewilderment. The story didn't even begin with narcotics.

"The company I worked for had the concession for selling American cash registers in all the departments of the littoral—"

He was speaking about the years before the war began. His voice was dull and tired but in its very flatness the truth came through. Villemorin had been the company's best salesman. A few months before the German invasion he set up on his own—still as a concessionaire but now with a small group of subagents working directly for him.

"The Germans gave me a license and let me go on. We had a big stock of machines, we were selling to bars and cafés, it made sense to them—to help keep business going, the wine flowing, the people happy. Then one day they came to see me, the Gestapo—"

It was the same story the blind old man in Paris had told

Owen about the traitor Soldat. And, as Soldat had claimed, it might have been true.

Villemorin was married with one daughter. His license allowed him to travel at will throughout southern France. The Gestapo told him to report any approach he received from the maquis. If he didn't—and they discovered it—his wife and daughter would be transported to a concentration camp in the fatherland. Villemorin agreed.

"What else could I do?" He shrugged. "What would anyone have done? I said, yes, then I just prayed the maquis would leave me alone. For two years they did. But one morning I was in Claville, near Lyon, in a bar where I'd sold a register and the patron had complained it had a fault. I went there to check, I was having a coffee afterwards, then a lady came in—"

Not a woman but a "lady"—and Villemorin carefully looked away as he used the word. The lady was Marie de Sourraines.

By then the Orion line had been operating for six months and Marie had just linked up with SOE, the British support arm to European resistance. SOE had offered her everything she needed to keep the line open: weapons, radio communication, forged papers, clothing—and gold. Marie, of necessity, was constantly on the move: the SOE drop zone was on the plain around the northern border of the *Massif Central*: she had to have someone to coordinate, collect and distribute the supplies that were being flown in.

The person she chose was Villemorin.

"How she found me, I never knew. And until then I'd done nothing with the Germans—*nothing!*"

He swung around and looked at Owen, haggard, shadow

eyed, pleading for understanding. Owen's eyes never flickered.

"All right." He looked away again. Yes, I told the Gestapo. The Orion line was too big. They'd have found out anyway and once they knew I hadn't told them, they'd have done what they said at the start. My wife and daughter to Dachau, Belsen, Buchenwald—"

Villemorin shivered at the memory. Owen didn't know if the response was real or a theatrical attempt to win sympathy. It didn't matter. Voluntarily or under pressure Villemorin became Charlot—paymaster to and original betrayer of the Orion line.

Original—but not the only traitor. The line spanned most of Belgium and the entire length of France. For the Gestapo it was essential to know how it operated not just in the southern sector, but right back to its start. They instructed Villemorin to acquire a chain of informants throughout the network. He didn't even have to use threats to get what they wanted: now he had something just as good—gold.

Traveling up the line in his role as paymaster Villemorin had systematically chosen the right men—the weak, the vulnerable, the greedy—bought them with the pouches of sovereigns and turned them. Bienaimé, 'Guette, maybe Soldat in spite of all his protestations, certainly others. Collaborators purchased with British gold to betray British pilots and agents.

Owen remembered the photographs hanging in the bar at Baker Street and shook his head grimly.

"Only they weren't the only ones to get a payoff, were they—?"

Villemorin had paused and Owen prompted him.

"What was your cut?"

He didn't answer for a moment. Then he burst out suddenly, angrily, wildly trying to defend himself.

"You wouldn't understand, but I started with nothing, nothing at all. I grew up and I worked eighteen, twenty hours a day until I had my own company. Then the war came and by 1943 the business was collapsing. The stock had gone, I couldn't get any more machines, there was no one to buy them if I had. You know what I'd have been when the war ended? Over thirty, broke, back to where I came from and with nothing to begin again—"

Villemorin said he wouldn't understand but Owen understood—he understood all too well.

The others like Bienaimé and 'Guette had been greedy, but none of them as greedy as Villemorin. And in Villemorin's case the greed had been harnessed to ambition, energy, cunning and a passionate resentment about what he'd made and lost. He'd broken out of the Marseilles slums. Now, with the end of the war in sight, he saw himself back there, penniless in a ruined economy. The prospect was intolerable, but then he saw a way not just to avoid it—but to create a richer future than he'd ever dreamed of.

Villemorin realized that in the chaos of the postwar world there'd be one commodity in shorter supply and even more valuable than gold. Heroin.

Keeping five, ten, fifteen of the Judas sovereigns for every one he handed out, Villemorin changed them for heroin in the underworld markets of Marseilles he knew so well. The powder was sealed in flat packets labeled "Documentary Evidence of German Atrocities," passed to a contact in Vézey and given to the pilots when they arrived there for the last stage of their journey. The pilots would transport the packets across the border and leave them as instructed in deposit boxes in Bilbao or Santander.

By 1944 Villemorin had accumulated a quarter of a million dollars' worth in the two Spanish ports. He flew to Spain a year later, identified himself at the banks where the heroin was stored, collected it and went on to New York. There he sold it in bulk and returned to France with the proceeds.

"And you've been doing it ever since?" Owen said.

"Dealing?" Villemorin shook his head. "I never touched it again. I formed a new company with the capital and I started again."

"What sort of company?"

"Insurance, life insurance mainly."

"Life insurance!"

Owen laughed bitterly. The man who'd ended so many lives had finished by insuring them. The irony was a perfect complement to the pin-striped suit, the Cardin tie and the Italian shoes.

He could check on that and the rest of the story—there'd be records, for instance, in the Spanish banks—but in essence Owen had little doubt it was the truth. It fitted in with everything he'd learned as he retraced the line south to the border. The old man in Paris, the little mechanic Faure, Varençon's sly, plausible "official" guide, the indomitable belly-laughing Madame Lachasse—all of their separate accounts slotted together now.

Yet the central question was still unanswered. *Why had the killings gone on and on?* Sir Roger Walpole in 1958, yes, that could have been an understandable mistake. The war was a recent memory, feelings about collaboration—legal and visceral—still ran high, Villemorin might have thought he was threatened and arranged the murders blindly, in panic.

But Baring's death in 1971, and now the attacks on Owen himself? They were inexplicable. Even if Villemorin had been exposed, the most he'd have faced was public disgrace and possibly a brief prison sentence—nothing compared to the appalling risks he'd taken and penalties he'd have paid for murder.

"So what happened afterwards?"

For the first time Villemorin didn't answer. Owen waited a moment. Then he stepped in front of him, swept the empty mug to the floor and smashed his hand down on the table. The mug shattered and Villemorin's head jerked up.

"They found out and they said they'd kill me."

"They? Who were they?"

"The maquis."

"What do you mean—the maquis?"

Villemorin's skin had been white during the climb, gray with fatigue after they'd entered the hut. Now it was red again, flushed with fear, and his mouth was twitching.

"The communists. They found out and they came to see me. Only I'd learned something too and I'd written it down, I'd left it with my lawyer, and I told them—"

He stuttered, broke off, then started again—pouring everything out now in a tangled flow of blurred words and broken sentences as Owen stood above him, utterly still, listening.

The reserve safe-house of *le gros renard*, the lodge in the woods, *had* been used once. Six months before the Normandy landings a message came down the line for Villemorin to open the house and prepare to receive a single pilot. The message didn't reach him through his usual contact, but he recognized the code name of the source and he followed the instructions.

"It was early January. I drove to the lodge from Marseilles and waited in the hall. They arrived in the evening—"

There were three of them. The pilot was unmistakeable: young, small, fair-haired, pale and tired from the strain of his journey across Europe. His two companions were older, maquis veterans in peasant jackets who'd escorted him there. Villemorin didn't know either or them, but given the cell structure of the resistance he wasn't surprised. What did surprise him was what happened after they walked in.

Before they'd even identified themselves, one of the escorts asked Villemorin if the "other" one had arrived yet. Puzzled, Villemorin said no. In the past, escaping pilots had invariably been accompanied by a single guide. There might have been some special reason for the two who'd come with this young man, but Villemorin's contact hadn't mentioned a third traveling separately.

"I took the pilot into the kitchen and gave him some soup. Afterwards, while he was drinking it, I went back to the hall. The other two were talking together—"

Villemorin's voice had slurred to a whisper.

"One of them was watching through the window. As I came in he lifted his hand and pulled out a gun. I didn't know what was happening; I just waited in the doorway. Then he put away the gun and said: 'It's all right, it's him.' It was dusk then, dark inside but with a half-moon rising over the wood. The front door opened, the new man walked through and I saw him—"

Villemorin's wrist trembled. This time, Owen knew, it

wasn't theatrical. It was something else—an uncontrollable tremor of terror from the thirty-year-old memory of a face he'd seen once in the dim light of the lodge.

"He was maybe twenty-seven. Medium height, blond haired, blue eyed, very stiff and formal; he almost might have been a German officer. Only I'd seen many of them and even in the worst there was something you could understand: something sadistic or proud or vicious or coarse. This man was different. There was nothing in him at all. He was just empty, empty with that white face and a coldness coming out of it you could almost touch—"

He stopped again and again Owen prompted him.

"And then?"

"One of the maquis people spoke to him and when he answered I realized he wasn't French. That was all. They just exchanged a few words. Afterwards the other maquis man told me I could go, they'd handle everything else, like getting the pilot over the border. I said fine. It was unusual but I didn't really think, I just wanted to get out of the place. So I left them there and went back to Marseilles. Then a year later I saw the photograph—"

The war was over and Allied military intelligence units were deployed throughout France gathering information about German activities during the occupation. Their prime source was former members of the resistance. As far as anyone knew Villemorin, with his newly awarded Légion d'Honneur, had fought underground as a heroic patriot ever since he was recruited by Marie de Sourraines.

He was asked to go to the intelligence liaison center in Lyon for a debriefing. Villemorin went there and told what he knew, the "public" account of his role in the Orion line. Then, as he was about to leave, the Allied interrogation officer—a bilingual American major—asked him to look at some photographs. With one exception, the faces were unfamiliar.

The exception was the man Villemorin had seen that night in the lodge.

"I don't know how they got hold of it. He was younger then and in uniform, but the face was unmistakable—I could never forget it. Of course I said no, I didn't recognize him. The American thanked me and I went out. But I realized then and when the maquis came for me I told them I knew."

"How did they discover about you?"

Owen struck the table again as Villemorin's chin sunk back onto his bloodstained shirt.

They. The true maquis. Men like Faure who'd fought not just against the German invaders, against fascism, but *for* something—a philosophy, an ideal, a vision of society that would change their country and the world. Merciless, dedicated, unforgiving men who'd learned of Villemorin's treachery and come to extract their own vengeance—only to find he held an equal weapon against them.

"One of the people I hired in the line—"

Villemorin's whisper was almost inaudible.

"He thought I'd cheated him over the money. It wasn't true but we had a quarrel and he said he'd expose me. He couldn't, of course, because he'd have exposed himself too. But later he found out he had cancer, he was dying. So he wrote a letter confessing and implicating me."

"Which he sent to your comrades in the resistance?"

Villemorin nodded. Yes, Owen thought, it was exactly what an embittered dying man would do. By exposing his fellow traitor to the French authorities he'd only have gotten Villemorin imprisoned for collaboration. But in telling the maquis he believed he was guaranteeing Villemorin's death. Except he'd been wrong.

"So what did you agree with the maquis when they came to see you?" Owen said. "What devil's bargain did you make?"

"That they wouldn't touch me if I kept silent and if I dealt with anyone else who might discover too."

"And you accepted that, you accepted to kill for *them* to keep *their* secret?"

"I had no choice." The weak fatalistic shrug again. "They said they'd risk what I knew and kill me if I didn't."

"Jesus Christ!"

Owen shook his head. Suddenly everything had fallen into place but the explanation was so extraordinary that he stood there for a moment, dazed, as he tried to take it in.

For thirty years Villemorin had been a man under sentence of death. Not for his wartime activities as a collaborator with the Germans or because of the fortune he'd made from his traffic in narcotics. Instead, for a piece of information he'd acquired in the Orion line—the same information he'd used to barter for his life when the maquis came to execute him. Villemorin knew the identity of the third man who came to the lodge that night; he'd also guessed correctly why he was there.

Right from the start the French resistance movement had been led and controlled by the communists; it was why the party became and remained so strong after the war. Originally their sole source of outside support was the Western Allies, but by 1943 the Russians had joined in too. Well before D-Day there were as many Soviet agents as British SOE officers working with the underground—funneling in supplies, providing weapons, training sabotage units, mounting counterpropaganda.

Yet the Russians were concerned with far more than immediate victory over Nazi Germany. They were preparing for the future, for what would happen after the war ended —setting up networks, recruiting sources of information, creating an intelligence structure for the years ahead. Fully aware of what the Russians were doing, the Allies had built up files on as many Soviet agents working with the maquis as they could trace. The man who came to the lodge—and whose photograph Villemorin was shown later by the American major—had been one of them.

Villemorin had denied that he'd ever seen the man. But later, when the maquis, the communists, came for him after he'd been exposed by his dying colleague in the ring, Villemorin told the truth—and gambled. The truth was he'd learned that the man with the pale, empty face which had haunted him ever since had been a Soviet intelligence agent. The gamble was on what the Russians had been doing in the company of the small, tired young pilot in the last hours before he crossed the border to freedom.

The price Villemorin had paid for being right—the killings he'd been forced to arrange as part of the bargain— was small, almost irrelevant. All that mattered was that the gamble had paid off—and it had saved his life.

"The young man—"

Owen's own voice was hoarse now, his hip was throbbing steadily and his eyes ached from the guttering candlelight, but he gathered himself together and bent over the table again.

"That little pilot you've been protecting all these years, tell me about him."

274

"How can I tell you—?"

The same whisper between the same struggling breaths, except the words were even fainter.

"I saw him just those few minutes when I gave him soup in the kitchen. He was like all the others who came down the line, as I've told you—"

Villemorin paused. Then he frowned and wiped his lips with a shaking hand.

"Only one thing was different. The others, they couldn't speak French apart from maybe a few words. But he could, he spoke perfectly. Except for a slight accent I couldn't place it might have been his own language. I remember him smiling at the soup and saying it was the same he used to have on holiday as a child—"

Villemorin checked again, the memory of the pilot's smile triggering something else.

"Yes, that was when I noticed his eyes. There was a candle on the table and he looked up at me and I saw they were different. One gray, the other brownish. But nothing more. He drank the soup, I went through to the hall, then I left."

"And later," Owen said, "how did you know whom to deal with? How did you know about Walpole and Baring?"

"Someone telephoned me. Then it was my responsibility, it was up to my judgment—"

"Whether they came close enough to be a threat?"

"Yes."

"Who telephoned you?"

"I don't know—"

He was mumbling almost to himself and Owen had to bend lower still to hear.

"Just a voice. I didn't even know any of the men who came to see me first."

"And someone telephoned you about me?"

"Yes."

"So he's still there, isn't he?"

He waited a few moments but Villemorin didn't answer. Then Owen straightened up stiffly, turned away and walked to the door. As he reached it Antoine got to his feet.

"Are you finished with him?" The guide asked.

Owen glanced back. Villemorin had slumped down onto the table, either asleep or semiconscious. His head was lying on one side and the veins in his great bulbous nose glistened red in the dim light.

Charlot. The avaricious youth from the Marseilles slums who'd cheated, lied and betrayed his way to a fortune only to find himself living for thirty years with a vicious double-blackmail, to which his contribution was to kill and kill again for a man he'd met once over a bowl of soup in the safe-house called *le gros renard*.

Yes, Owen had finished with him. For Villemorin, the broken bloodstained wreck at the table instead of the elegant businessman who'd stepped out of the white Citroën eight hours earlier, the deceit had ended now and the blackmail was over. Yet the man he'd murdered for, to protect, the last traveler down the Orion line, was still alive and functioning. So too was the line's other legacy —Hélène.

Owen nodded and added quickly, "I want to get back."

Antoine glanced at the sky. The moon had disappeared behind a mountain peak but the stars were thick and bright.

"They change the patrols now," he said, "so with luck we won't cross any of them. Also, going down it's much faster. I'll take you over the border to a cut above the *tire-bouchon*. From there you can do it easily on your own. It's the way we came up."

"And him?"

Owen gestured towards Villemorin.

"I'll come back after I've left you," Antoine said.

"To bring him down later?"

"M'sieu, I know they say many things of us, the guides who worked the border in the war—"

Antoine's face was expressionless and his little eyes were still blank.

"Some of them are true; we had a living to earn. But I knew the lady's mother and I was listening when he talked to you now. Maybe he and I have things to talk about too. We can discuss them out on the ridge when I return."

Owen thought of the sheer thousand-foot falls to the twisting valleys along the route they'd followed and said nothing. Antoine went back to the table, shook Villemorin awake and told him he'd return in a couple of hours. Then he stepped outside and Owen walked with him across the plateau.

As the guide had said, the return journey was much easier and faster than the climb up. Little more than an hour after they left the hut, they'd recrossed the border and reached the cut above the *tire-bouchon*. Antoine stopped in a small ravine that led to the mouth of the gully and told Owen how to retrace it down to the point where they'd first entered it. From there Owen would only have two kilometers of open country to the Ste. Denise road. Then Antoine shook hands and without another word vanished back up the hillside.

Owen looked at his watch: it was 4:45 A.M. Already a cone of gray light was widening on the eastern horizon, birds were stirring in the trees and he could just make out the contours of the land below. Another hour and it would be full dawn—the time for his rendezvous at the bridge. He crossed the ravine, slid down a shelf of rock and stepped into the gully.

The early light hadn't penetrated the overhanging bushes and with the moon down it was impenetrably dark in the tunnel. Owen moved slowly, warily, using his hands to guide himself around the rocks and pausing every few steps to listen. Then when he came to the start of the first open stretch he stopped again, waiting immobile in the shadow as he searched the graying empty space of grass ahead. There was no sign of anyone and after a few minutes he went on, his confidence growing with every yard he covered.

In the turmoil of the last five hours—the urgent straining effort to haul Villemorin up the hill flanks, the interrogation in the hut, the rapid descent with Antoine—he hadn't had time to wonder about Hélène. Now he could think of nothing else. She'd said she'd hold off Villemorin's men for fifteen minutes and then hide herself in the gully until they'd gone—as they were bound to do once they realized they'd lost the person who was firing at them. With patrols on every side, no one, least of all four illegally armed men who almost certainly had criminal records, would stay out in the border area for longer than absolutely necessary.

At the end of the fifteen minutes, when Owen, Antoine

and Villemorin reached the gully's head, the sound of firing was still echoing up on the wind. If Hélène had done what she'd intended she'd have withdrawn then, backed into the thickets below and waited until she could make her way safely down across the farmland to the road. Remembering her—the laughter, the confidence, the casual ease with which she'd handled the gun, the implacable determination—it was inconceivable she hadn't achieved it.

Owen came to the last of the open stretches, paused, checked the spur that commanded the gully, then walked forward onto the turf. An instant later, out in the open, he stopped again. The boulder was forty yards in front, with the well of shadow still circling its base. Before the shadow's rim had been cut sharp on the grass and the space inside black and empty. Now the rim was blurred with the dawning light and something fluttered beyond it—something white and fragile and torn.

Owen started to run, hurling himself across the grass with a blind, desperate intensity. He reached the boulder, dropped to his knees, looked down and stretched out his hand. Then he lifted his head and closed his eyes.

Hélène was lying huddled on the ground with one arm across her head and her hair, thick and windswept, tangled between her fingers. Somehow they'd gotten behind her, doubling back along the fold in the hill, crossing the gully below and firing down from the rim on the other side. There were two bullet holes in her spine. The shots, angled flatly downwards, had ripped away her blouse— Owen had seen the tattered silk fluttering against the rock —and blood had pooled on her back from her neck to her waist.

She must have died instantly, yet one of them had come

up afterwards and kicked her savagely, viciously, mean-inglessly in the face. Her cheek was bruised, her mouth was cut and more blood had flowed out between her teeth. Opening his eyes again Owen was vaguely aware of what might have caused that mindless gesture of hate. There was another crumpled bundle out on the slope and beyond it a second. In the fight before she'd been killed she'd dropped two of the four who'd climbed up the hill to cut them off.

Owen didn't even bother to see if either of them were still alive. He reached down and touched her cheek as she'd touched his when he left her there. Then he stood up and turned into the gully again. The dawn was coming fast now, gray light changing to gold, pigeons rising over the pink oleander blossoms, dogs barking in the distant farms, delicate, dewed shadows tracing the footprints in the sand. He walked steadily downwards. Tired, cold, aching at hip and knee as he headed towards the road.

There'd be no rendezvous by the bridge where they'd watched the constellations between the bending stems of grass. But Owen was thinking of something else: the pale young pilot with the different-colored eyes who'd smiled as he tasted Charlot's soup on the last stage of the Orion line.

23

Sun on the grass. Not the lavender-scented bee-humming sunlight of southern France, but sun all the same—the pale, fugitive sun of a late London spring.

Owen moved out from under the tree to look at the clock in the Admiralty Arch at the other end of St. James's Park. A child ran past bowling a hoop and in the distance a band was playing on the wrought-iron stand, the first concert of the year. It was almost five. Another few minutes. He stepped back under the branches and waited.

Friday afternoon, still less than thirty hours since he'd returned to London but already the second afternoon he'd spent waiting there. The morning before, he'd walked back from the border into Vézey, rented a taxi to Marseilles and taken the midday flight to Heathrow. Four hours later he turned off Baker Street into the side street behind. He saw the paneled door, the elegant rose-brick façade, the old wind- and rain-polished panes in the graceful white frames—and suddenly he stopped.

He paused an instant, motionless on the pavement. Then he swung around and walked quickly away. Half an hour afterwards he was standing where he was now—at the center of the park, looking across the grass towards Horse Guard's Parade and the massive gray block of the Ministry of Defence.

Owen shook his head wearily; in spite of his exhaustion, he'd only slept fitfully during the night and by dawn he'd been restlessly pacing the floor of his apartment. Then he heard the Admiralty clock chime five. He pushed himself away from the trunk, gazed over the sun- and shadow-checkered turf, waited another five minutes and finally saw him, just as he'd seen him the previous afternoon. Trim, punctual, meticulous. A neat little figure pacing resolutely between the trees, not in tunic and boots this time, but wearing the quiet tweed suit of an officer and gentleman leaving for his weekend holiday.

Air Marshal Bouverie. Anglo-Belgian pilot, escapee from Nazi-occupied Europe, decorated war hero, distinguished public servant—and agent of the Soviet intelligence service.

Why? Owen had speculated endlessly; on the flight back, turning in bed at night, looking out over Bayswater as the morning came, all through this long, warm day. Yet he was still no closer to understanding than when he'd first connected him with Villemorin's pale young pilot who spoke perfect French with a slight accent, a Belgian accent, and had different-colored eyes. Perhaps there'd been something in Bouverie's childhood which had made him rebel against the hermetic and privileged world in which he'd grown up. Perhaps the conversion had come suddenly and traumatically as a student, when foreign fascism swamped his country, and he saw that only the communists were challenging it and fighting back. Perhaps there were other factors—solitary, particular, uncommunicable —which only Bouverie would ever know.

Whatever the explanation the record was clear now, and there'd be evidence to support it in a thousand archives. At some stage in Brussels in the early years of the war Bouverie had been recruited by Russian intelligence. Later, as the Allies grouped for the invasion of France, he'd been fed into the Orion line. He'd been escorted down to *le gros renard,* met his KGB control for a final briefing, crossed the Spanish border and traveled to England.

Afterwards, austere, efficient, loyal and ambitious, he'd worked his way up the hierarchy of the Air Force until he reached the position he held when Mathieson had introduced Owen to him. And all the while, throughout all those years, he'd been relaying information to his masters in Moscow. If Villemorin hadn't cracked, next year there'd have been a command with the nuclear strike wing of NATO, and later maybe an appointment to the joint chiefs of staff.

If Villemorin hadn't cracked—but Villemorin had cracked and thirty years of deceit were over.

Bouverie came closer, Owen moved further back into the shadow, then after he'd passed the tree and was heading right towards the Mall, Owen set off behind. He'd followed him the afternoon before and he knew exactly where they were going. They crossed the Mall, walked past St. James's Palace—Owen thirty yards back, with a crowd of homegoing pedestrians between them—and turned into St. James's Street.

They were in Mathieson's country now, his entire world symbolized by this single quarter mile of bow-fronted clubs, wine merchants who'd held the royal warrant for two hundred years, hatters who'd supplied the shakos for the cornets at Waterloo, cobblers with lasts that had been used for the hunting boots of eighteenth-century squires. Then, half-way up the street, Bouverie did something which for an instant seemed so totally unexpected that Owen, watching him in amazement, collided with a man in front and knocked him into the street.

Bouverie stopped at the entrance to Mathieson's own club, nodded familiarly as the porter on the steps raised his hat, and went inside.

He was only there a minute—he was probably checking to see if there was any mail for him—and moments later they were swinging left into Piccadilly. But in that minute, as Owen stood waiting for him to reappear, everything suddenly snapped into focus. It wasn't incongruous that Bouverie and Mathieson were members of the same club. It was natural, almost inevitable, because the world they shared was the same too, and in that realization Owen knew instantly why he'd turned away from Baker Street the day before. He also knew with a chilling, implacable certainty what he was going to do.

The small erect silhouette appeared again, threaded his way among the throngs under the arches of the Ritz, then they came out into the sunlight of Piccadilly. Fifty yards ahead was the Green Park tube station. Bouverie trotted down the stairs, bought a ticket from an automatic vending machine and walked along the tunneled corridor to the platform. Then he stood behind the jostling lines of passengers waiting for the next train.

"Excuse me—"

Owen had also bought a ticket and followed him down. As he touched his elbow Bouverie turned around.

"I'd like to speak to you for a moment, sir."

Owen used the form of address instinctively. Bouverie looked at him for an instant, his face impassive.

Then he said, "What can I—?"

The roar of an approaching train drowned the rest of the question. The train pulled in, the doors jolted open, a guard bellowed through a loudspeaker, the passengers surged forward, then the coaches disappeared in a shower of sparks and rocking lights.

"Maybe it would be easier there—"

Owen gestured along the platform towards an alcove at the far end. Bouverie hesitated, shrugged almost imperceptibly, then followed him to the mouth of the tunnel. Behind them a new wave of passengers was pouring in from the corridor to the street.

"You remember me?" Owen asked.

They were standing facing each other in the alcove. A wind was blowing past them, grimy and smelling of oil, and other trains rumbled distantly through the tiled wall that separated them from the northbound line.

"Yes, of course." Bouverie nodded. "We met first with Colonel Mathieson. Then you came to see me a few weeks ago. You were making inquiries about the Orion line—"

His voice was as Owen remembered it from their last meeting, dry, clipped, without color or tone or emotion.

"I imagine you've finished them now. How did they go?"

"I found a man called Charlot and I talked to him yesterday morning. Since then he may have died. It doesn't matter. Before I left him he told me everything."

The force of the wind increased as another train clattered out of the darkness into the station. The air brakes whistled, the doors slid back, the crowd heaved forward as the loudspeaker blared again, then it too was gone.

"I see—"

Bouverie fastidiously touched his head, his hair ruffled by the turbulence of the train's passage.

"And you've discussed all this with Colonel Mathieson?"

"I've discussed it with no one."

"With no one? Then why have you come to see me?"

Even as Owen's control started to dissolve then—boiling away in rage and fatigue—he was still awed by the man's composure.

Bouveire must have believed him dead, killed at his own instruction like everyone else who'd touched on the vulnerable sectors of the line and threatened to trace the maze of treachery back through Villemorin to the lodge in the woods. Then without warning Owen had appeared at his shoulder—alive, knowing everything, equipped with information that after thirty years would finally expose him as his career reached its climax—and still his only reaction was a polite, disinterested question.

"Why? Because although I came back, there were others who didn't. And it's been like that ever since the line was rolled up, hasn't it? Innocent ones like Walpole, muddled alcoholics like Baring, more I'm bloody sure I'll never know about—"

Owen spoke with a cold, furious intensity, driving the words out between his teeth as he tried to smash through the iron barrier of reserve and indifference.

"All of them dying to protect you while you sat here safe and remote and isolated. Well, yesterday someone else was murdered. Not Charlot—a woman. A woman who was brave enough to want the truth known, even if she had to be killed to prove it—"

He shook his head for an instant as the image of Hélène came back—lying crumpled in the shadow of the boulder with her fingers laced through her thick chestnut hair.

"Marie saved your life and died. Yesterday you killed her daughter."

Owen broke off, sweating in spite of the wind that was moaning through the tunnel and whirling scraps of dirty paper around their feet. Bouverie gazed at him steadily. Then he frowned, tilting his head and looking briefly at the glistening rails below before he spoke.

"You came to tell me that, Mr. Owen?"

Owen said nothing and Bouverie went on.

"Then let me tell you something," he said. "On a personal level I regret what's happened, that Hélène has died. Yet measured against the work we do, both of us, it isn't important. We're intelligence officers, you and I. We share the same trade and we operate by its conventions. We both accept that in our world people get killed. The guilty, the innocent and, well, those who are either not so guilty or not so innocent—"

He smiled, tugged lightly at his tie, gold wings on a deep-blue background and glanced away.

For a moment Owen thought he might be about to run and he tensed, rocking forward on the balls of his feet. Then he realized it was impossible. For Bouverie there was nowhere to run to now, no point in attempting anything. He hadn't even challenged Owen to explain, but again there was no need. The one name, Charlot, and it was all over—his life and world destroyed. And yet still he went on, calm, imperturbable, as if they were discussing some academic issue in a Ministerial minute.

"Those deaths?" Bouverie looked back. "They're like all the others, an unfortunate hazard of becoming involved in what we do. But if we let any one of them affect us, cloud our judgment, then we diminish ourselves professionally and we damage whatever ideology we're dedicated to and paid to protect and advance—"

Bouverie paused, but even before he finished Owen knew what was coming.

"It doesn't matter what ideology it is; we can leave that to our respective superiors and the future. Meantime, we're the same, Mr. Owen. Make your report to Colonel Mathieson, as I would do if I were in your position. No doubt he and I will discuss it shortly; these matters can be agreed and arranged. But whatever you have to say, say it objectively. Don't let any personal factors intervene—"

He smiled again, the rare smile of extraordinary charm that Owen remembered from the conference room in Whitehall and later in Bouverie's office.

"As a much older member of the profession, may I give you some advice, Mr. Owen? You've broken the rules once. Make sure you don't break them again."

Then he tapped Owen gently, almost protectively on the arm and turned towards the platform.

Owen watched him standing above the track. He'd known it when Bouverie walked into Mathieson's club. Now it had been stated aloud in that quiet, deliberate voice.

The same world, the world they both shared—they and Mathieson and Bouverie's control and all the others on either side. A world with its own considerations and procedures and conventions. Bouverie hadn't said how those conventions would affect him, but once more there was no necessity. He knew as well as Owen the bland sequence of events that would unravel once Owen stepped into Baker Street and made his report.

The discreet background inquiries. The delicate confrontation. The futile questioning—futile, because there was no chance of Bouverie talking, of learning his recruitment, his contacts, his control, the systems of instruction and delivery and cut-out he'd followed throughout those thirty years. The questions would simply be a ritual required by the occasion. Bouverie was strong and a professional and alone. He'd never speak. Then the elaborately arranged early "retirement" on grounds of health, with medical reports to justify it. And afterwards the sighs of relief, the closed files, the silence.

They were the "rules"—the rules Owen had accepted and lived by ever since he'd joined the department. Only now, inexplicably, they were no longer adequate. There'd been too much waste, too much deceit, too many lives callously, cynically squandered. There were also the recurring memories of Héléne, laughing as she pushed him forward along the gully, and then her body on the grass.

Owen stepped forward. It was five-thirty, the peak of the Friday evening rush hour, and another train was approaching. The wind gusted fiercely, the tunnel vibrated and pulsed with the roar of the incoming engine, lights dazzled across the tiles and the rainbow-colored posters on the arched walls, the dense column of passengers, three- and four-deep, pressed forward to the lip of the concrete shelf above the shining rails. The platform vibrated, the loudspeaker crackled, the engine exploded out of the dark—and Owen gripped Bouverie's elbow.

Owen never knew if Bouverie realized what was happening. One moment the figure of the little Air Marshal was beside him, stiff, taut, upright, his face jerking around puzzled at the pressure on his arm. The next, as Owen lifted and hurled him forward, a shape like a tiny rag doll haloed in the brilliance of the headlamps was cartwheeling slowly down onto the track. A woman screamed, then another, faces swiveled around, a battery of white ovals below the still-dark roof, the brakes shuddered and whined, the loudspeaker choked and broke off, then groups of people began to ripple sideways towards the alcove.

Owen had dropped to his knees. The train had stopped, the wheels, bright and clean before, were bleared with something that was trickling down onto the gravel, and shreds of cloth—ragged gray-brown tweed—were waving like miniature pennants in the breeze that kept blowing through the tunnel. The knots of appalled, gesticulating, whispering passengers enveloped him, he stood up, backed his way unnoticed through the crowd, and headed for the street.

The sun had lowered now and most of Piccadilly was in shadow, only the roofs of Mayfair still warm with the golden, slanting light. Owen hesitated at the tube entrance, then turned and walked down the pavement towards Hyde Park Corner. Five minutes later he heard the wail of an ambulance siren. The vehicle passed him, weaving through the evening traffic, and the siren faded into silence by the Ritz.

290

Owen didn't even look back. The tiredness had gone, so for the moment had the fury and bitterness, and for the first time in years he felt utterly at peace. Mathieson, without once hinting at it, had blackmailed him into accepting the Orion assignment because of that night in the hotel outside Algiers. He'd broken the rules then and he'd lived with the knowledge of that mistake, that failure ever since. The night in Algiers no longer mattered; he'd made restitution for that over the past weeks as he tracked the line back to the end.

What mattered was that he'd broken the rules again—not once but twice. Only now he'd done it of his own deliberate choice, shattering every convention of the shared world in which Bouverie had such confidence that he could casually regret Hélène's murder, tap Owen on the arm and turn to wait for the next train. The Orion line had finally been closed down, but Owen had closed it in his own way and on his own terms, and he'd say as much when he made his report to Mathieson on Monday morning.

Yet Owen wasn't thinking of Baker Street then, he was thinking of Wales—and something Hélène had said to him Wales with the pithead against the stars, the cramped stone cottages of the village, the summer-dry grass on the hills where he'd chased the hunting foxes as a boy, the voices and the laughter in the pub at night. And then what Hélène had said—that they'd both gone in opposite directions. She right back inside, into the chateau at Este. Owen the other way, away from the valley totally. She was right—and they'd both gone too far.

Hélène had made her peace and come out into the world she'd walled herself against. Now he'd do the same. Return to Nantynth, talk to Meg as he hadn't done in years, see together what they could make again. There was a night train from Charing Cross which reached the village at dawn. Owen would be on it.

Only first there were the promises he'd made, the promises to keep. The burly chief inspector Miles, the chain-smoking journalist Blair, he could deal with them on Monday too. But not the third—the Count who wanted to know the truth about his daughter and the betrayal of the line. Well, Owen could tell him the truth about Marie now. He also had a separate, private truth to tell him about Hélène.

Owen crossed Hobart Place and turned into Eaton Square. Then he walked slowly under the trees towards the building where he knew the old man would be sitting framed in the wings of the armchair.